K. El

Fantasy

Butch,
Thanks for the Support!
[illegible]

URBAN LIFE STYLE PRESS

Published by Urban Lifestyle Press
P.O. Box 12714
Charlotte, NC 28220

www.ulppublishing.com

Editor: James Sims and K. Elliott

Cover Design: Marion Designs
www.mariondesigns.com

Book Layout: Shawna A. Grundy
www.shawnagrundy.com

First printing May 2007

ISBN: 09717697-5-3

Oral Pleasure

There ain't no shame when I say that I aim to please
As I pull my hair into a bun and drop down on my knees.

I gently caress his manhood and admire the shape, the size, and the pleasure that it brings.
It hardens into position and stands erect as I tease.
Like a soldier ready for action.
He smiles and tilts his head back
Because he knows there's no limit to the satisfaction that he's about to receive.

The softness of my kisses,
the warmth of my breath,
the gentle stroke of my hand,
and the smoothness of his skin
makes me cream with excitement as I passionately pull him in.

My hands begin to sweat
and I feel his body start to tremble.
I think to myself, "Damn, what a high!"
As I feel the wetness of my sweet temple slowly dripping down my inner thigh.

He penetrates me deeper
and my kisses become more intensified.
He knows that I aim to please
and make sure he's satisfied.

He lets out a soft moan as he releases his precious treasure.
He relishes with delight
and was fulfilled by my oral pleasure.

Rikki Morgan

Fantasy

Chocolate Stick

Allison Hobbs

Outside her apartment, Marissa heard the trill of the telephone as she slipped her key into the lock. The persistent sound of the ring informed her that the call was from one of the two men whom she was sleeping with. Marissa gave a sly smile and deliberately took her time unlocking the door.

Both men knew exactly what time she arrived home from work, thus she was always greeted by the sound of the ringing telephone the moment she approached her apartment door.

Inside her apartment, she took unhurried steps toward the kitchen. She poured herself a glass of water before she bothered to even glance at the caller ID. The caller ID spelled out Isaac's name. Marissa leisurely reached for the phone, but suddenly changed her mind. She withdrew her hand and allowed the call to transfer to her answering machine.

She wasn't ready to talk to Isaac; she'd give him a call later. Perhaps.

It depended on her mood. She was a chocoholic and chocolate definitely hit her spot, but the type of chocolate she craved changed from day to day.

Isaac was milk chocolate—creamy and smooth. And her other man, Basille, was dark chocolate—sweet with a bitter aftertaste. Both flavors awakened her taste buds and satisfied her yearning.

A few moments after she'd listened to Isaac's message, Basille began to blow up her cell phone. The phone vibrated inside her purse with such intensity, she could practically hear Basille shouting, *Yo, pick up the damn phone!* It was as if Basille was on high alert and intuitively sensed that his position in her bed was threatened by another man.

Marissa let the call roll over to voice mail. *I'll get in touch with Basille later. If not tonight, I'll talk to him tomorrow night.* She pulled open the refrigerator and took out a chilled bottle of sparkling wine.

At the moment, she was in need of a relaxing, long, hot bath and the blissful buzz of sparkling wine. There was plenty of time to decide which chocolate flavor she'd indulge in tonight.

Marissa hadn't always been so blasé about matters of the heart, but after a dozen or more love disasters, she had no choice but to presume that men were incapable of fidelity. So why waste another second of her precious life waiting for *happily ever after* if the notion of true love and monogamy did not exist and was nothing more than a farfetched dream?

For Marissa, it was now all about sex—getting her spot hit on the regular. She had no patience for ordinary lovemaking. No, her man had to satisfy all her senses; he had to be uninhibited—a ferocious, fuck-until-dawn lover.

Never again would she fake an orgasm to appease a man's ego. Nor would she overly exert herself to bring a limp dick back to life. She would not endure an inexperienced premature ejaculator. Quick shooters had no business being in her bed. She would not tolerate an unimaginative lover.

She knew how to take care of a man in bed and keep him coming back for more; however, her own sexual pleasure was at the top of her list and her carnal needs could not be fulfilled by just one man.

After taking the word *love* out of her vocabulary and changing it to *lust*, Marissa discovered she was in a much better position. She liked being the one who called the shots. The one who set the tone of the relationship—the one who was in control.

Sexing Isaac one night and then getting it on with Basille the next was indeed a juggling act. But Marissa was a skillful performer and had yet to drop the ball.

There'd been several close calls, like the time Isaac searched under her bed, looking for his boxers, which had gotten misplaced during the heat of passion. When Isaac lifted up the satin dust ruffles, he not only retrieved his boxers but rose from the floor holding a man's belt. A belt that did not belong to him.

It was Basille's belt, black leather with an oversized square silver-plated buckle, inscribed with an ostentatious gold-colored letter **B.**

Isaac dressed somewhat conservatively while Basille dressed and accessorized with the style and flamboyance of a thug.

"What's this?" Isaac had asked, holding the incriminating evidence, his eyes narrowing suspiciously.

For an instant, Marissa held her breath, speechless, but she recovered quickly. "Oh! I was looking for that," she exclaimed, reaching for the belt. "My cousin Craig's been buggin' me all week about this belt. He said he left it here, but I couldn't find it."

"Why would your cousin leave his belt *here*?" Isaac lifted his brow doubtfully.

"I let him use my place last week remember? It was . . . " Marissa paused and looked up in thought. "Last Wednesday…the day I went out of town on that business trip. You remember, don't you?"

Isaac shook his head and continued to look at her skeptically. "But your cousin Craig's first initial is *C*."

"Yeah, I know. He said his girlfriend bought the belt for him; she calls him, *Boo*." Marissa's mouth curved into a triumphant smile. Her eyes sparkled, holding Isaac in a challenging gaze. Although he was not thoroughly convinced, Isaac conceded and lowered his eyelids.

Marissa had to give credit where it was due. She was good at her game, even if she said so herself. She'd learned the rules of deception the hard way; but as they say, experience is the best teacher, and she was a quick study.

She recalled the morning she and Basille had torn the bedroom apart searching for the belt. His favorite, Basille had told her. Disappointment turned down the corners of his mouth when Marissa informed him that they had to stop the belt search; she had to get dressed for work. "I'll look for it later, Boo," she'd told him and gave him a quick kiss.

Marissa stifled a snicker as she envisioned Basille leaving her apartment, using his hands to hold up his baggy jeans, which threatened to fall off his ass.

Neither Isaac nor Basille had tangible evidence that Marissa was an unfaithful woman. But her numerous disappearing acts, her frequent excuses for unanswered calls—*I hit the silent button by mistake; I didn't hear my cell ring*—her constant lies and cool detachment kept both men on their toes and made them subconsciously compete for her time, affection, and her good sex. And more than likely, they both wanted her love. She laughed to herself because she knew that, in their hearts, both men wanted to wife her.

Isaac and Basille were as different as night and day. Besides their obsession with her, they didn't have much in common. *No, that's not true*, she chided herself. She almost forgot. They both had big feet and large hands, which meant they both were amply endowed with big chocolate sticks.

Giving the subject more thought, she realized that the two men had something else in common. They both went the extra mile in bed. Both served up good dick, giving it to her hard and long—the way she liked it—trying their damnedest to fuck her until she was whipped.

But Marissa realized the perils of being dick-whipped, so she kept her pussy muscles in good shape. Her inner muscles were taut but also flexible enough to snatch, grab, clutch, and tightly squeeze a dick. She had that snapping pussy that made a man curl his toes and grit his teeth to keep from screaming out her name.

Her pussy was so extraordinary, it could endure marathon fucking without trying to siphon off a little love along the way. Marissa didn't have a hidden agenda. Her cards were on the table: *Fuck that emotionally needy stuff; I don't need to know if you love me; all I want to know is . . . nigga can you make me cum?*

After her bath, as Marissa towel-dried in her bedroom, she considered her two options. It was a difficult decision to make since she enjoyed Basille and Isaac equally. One was as good as the other. They were interchangeable lovers. Therefore, when her phone rang again, she decided she'd accept her bedmate on a first call, first *cum* basis. Revved up and horny, she was ready for an all-night joyride with whoever was on the other end of the phone.

Wanting to enjoy the element of surprise, she picked up the receiver without looking at the caller ID.

"Hello?"

"You get my messages?" It was Basille. "Man, I been blowing up your phone for hours and left a million messages. Why didn't you call me back?"

"I'm sorry, boo," Marissa said. "I've been so busy; I haven't had a chance to check my messages yet. Is something wrong? Whassup?"

"I was just tryin' to find out if you wanted to go out and chill with my man and his girl tonight. We were thinking about going to the Caribbean Reef. You know, kick back, have a few drinks, and listen to some sounds . . ."

"That's sweet, Basille. But you know I have liquor and music right here. I'm not in the mood for a big crowd; I want to be alone—just you and me," she said breathily. "Is that all right with you?"

Basille gave a low chuckle. "Yo, you the only Shorty I know who don't wanna be wined and dined."

"Some females need all that romantic fluff to feel like a woman, but I'm cool. I like to cut to the chase. The only thing I need..." Her voice trailed off as she released a sultry sigh. "The only thing I need is hanging against your thigh. So do me a favor and tell your friends to hollah back; we'll get with them some other time."

"So whatchu sayin' . . . You just want me to come over and hit it?"

"That's exactly what I'm saying."

"Oh, ai'ight; you just wanna get your freak on. I can dig it but, damn, Marissa, why you gotta treat me like I'm a piece of meat?" Basille asked, pretending to be offended.

"Well how about if I kiss that piece of meat and make it feel all better? You want me to do you like that?"

"Mmm," he uttered; the sound was a low growl that vibrated through the phone. "Yeah, ai'ight, baby girl. That'll work."

"You sure you just want me to kiss it? Because I can skip that part and get right on that chocolate stick and give it some serious suction."

"Umph," Basille grunted lustfully. "Yo, stop that. You making my dick rise."

Marissa could imagine Basille pushing down his stiffening bulge that popped up inside his jeans.

"I'll see you in a short; I'm on my way," Basille told Marissa.

Marissa had been caressing her clitoris during her conversation with Basille. Stroking it, fondling it as his voice caressed her ears. There was moisture between her legs and on her fingers. She put her fingers up to her nose and sniffed. Her nipples stood up as she became aroused by her own scent. As she replaced the receiver of the phone inside the base, she considered masturbating. With her kitty cat acting up, being demanding, and purring so loudly, she figured she might have to calm it down with a two-finger appetizer before her scrumptious chocolate desert arrived.

Marissa squeezed her breasts and pinched her nipples. Then her middle finger traveled down her abdomen and glided past her navel. When her finger journeyed through her thick forest of pubic hair, the phone jangled again. Her finger halted; her eyes flitted to the caller ID. It was Isaac—again.

She sucked her teeth; Isaac was too late. She'd have to avoid him tonight and make it up to him tomorrow. Hell, she owned that dick; Isaac really didn't have any choice other than to hope she could fit him into her schedule.

The phone rang again and Marissa felt conflicted. Her vagina was hungry; it tensed with anticipation. But she'd already made her choice. And her choice was dark chocolate. Her choice was Basille.

She ignored the ringing telephone, but could practically feel Isaac's disappointment. But there was nothing she could do. Juggling two men wasn't easy. Someone always had to lose.

With all her bravado and sexual liberation, Marissa still wasn't bold enough to live it up and fulfill her most cherished fantasy. Night and day, she dreamed of having Isaac and Basille together with her—in her bed, lying across her pink satin sheets. She yearned for two pairs of hands caressing her body. Two sets of lips sucking her breasts. And two exquisite dicks alternately thrusting inside her vagina.

The mere thought of her fantasy coming true caused her inner muscles to clinch up. Thus, she squeezed her legs together as she tried to placate and soothe her throbbing pussy.

If only she had the nerve to reveal her secret fantasy—if only she'd take a chance and dare to play it out, her world would become even more enlivened and vibrant—her sexuality would be at its peak. However, as bold as she was, she didn't know how to present her grand scheme to two men who each thought himself the center of her universe.

Marissa emitted a long sigh as she realized she had a hidden agenda after all. She wanted to get with two men at the same time. But she didn't have the guts to express that desire. Well, one thing was for sure. She'd never get what she wanted if she continued to keep the fantasy in her mind. Shit, men lived out their fantasies all the time, so why shouldn't she?

She sucked her teeth in disgust as she contemplated the double standards by which most men lived. The average man wouldn't hesitate at the opportunity to have two women in bed, but he'd balk and recoil at the suggestion of sharing his proclaimed pussy with another man.

Then she brightened suddenly. She had pussy power and feminine wiles as backup. And dammit it was time to take her relationships to another level; it was time to start plotting on getting Isaac and Basille to submit to some three-way action. She had skills and she'd formulate a plan—she'd have to figure out a way to gently persuade Basille and Isaac to give her what she needed—to make her fantasy come true.

Marissa's wheels started spinning and she mentally put a plan in motion. She decided to invite both Isaac and Basille over and tell them that they all needed to have a sit down. Suddenly amused, Marissa imagined the confusion and then the anger that would flash on her two lovers' faces when she admitted that she was a cheat—that they'd been chumped.

To dissolve their fury, she'd hold her head in her hands and take a deep, anguished sigh. At that point, both men would feel sympathetic and soften toward her.

Tears of regret would begin to well in her eyes and, by then, Isaac and Basille would be putty in her hands. Giving an academy award performance, she'd dab at her teary eyes and tell them: *I really care for you both, but I know what I've done is wrong* . . . Wracking sobs would halt her words and then she'd straighten her shoulders and compose herself. *Unfortunately, I have to tell you both goodbye.* Those final words would come out in a choked voice with tears streaming down her face.

Now if the situation went as planned, Basille and Isaac would be unable to walk away in anger. Neither man would be willing or able to let go of the best pussy he'd ever had.

Isaac and Basille would have to work out a compromise and agree to a ménage-á-trois. A three-way with her as the star attraction.

It'll be our secret, she'd tell them. We'll be discreet. *No one ever has to know.*

Feeling much better, feeling more empowered, Marissa picked up the phone and returned Isaac's call.

"Hi, sweetie," she purred. "I just got in; I had to do a little overtime."

"Oh yeah?"

"Uh huh. You know how crazy my job can get."

Isaac grunted a response and then spoke clearly. "Do you have some time for me tonight?"

"Aw, sweetie, I'm so tired. I wish I could see you, but I can barely muster the strength to take a shower. And after I shower, I'm planning to fall right into bed."

"Can I fall in bed with you?" Isaac's voice was low and sexy but held a subtle pleading quality.

"Not tonight. I'm so beat; I know I won't be an exciting lover. And you know how I do . . . I like to put my back all in it; I give as well as I get."

"But you don't have to do anything," Isaac said beseechingly. "Let me come over; let me do you," he cajoled. "I'll give you a massage from your head down to your toes, and when my fingers get tired, I'll massage your body with my lips."

Isaac's sexual innuendoes were starting to stir her desire, making her wet. She was tempted to tell him to come over, but she knew Basille was already en route.

"Isaac," Marissa interjected.

"What?"

"Are you dressed?"

"Yes," Isaac said excitedly. "I can be there in twenty minutes or less. Unlock the door, lay down and wait for me."

"No, no. Listen. Do you have on a belt?"

"A belt? Yeah, why?"

"Unbuckle your belt and unzip your pants," she said using a sultry tone.

"Oh!" Isaac said. His breathing quickened as he began to comprehend the meaning behind Marissa's words.

"What color are your boxers?"

"Blue," he told her. His voice was strained.

"I want you to run your hand over that blue cotton until you feel your dick swelling and getting hard." She paused. "Do you feel it? Is it getting big for me?"

"Yeah, baby. I feel it; it's real hard. It wants you." Isaac's words rushed out in a shuddering whisper.

"Now I want you to imagine my lipstick stain where the fabric splits on your boxers. Can you see my lips?"

Isaac moaned.

"Slip your hand inside, sweetie," Marissa continued. "Pretend that it's my hand touching you, squeezing that big dick." She felt extremely powerful and sexy. It was a good feeling knowing her voice had the effect of an aphrodisiac. She knew her soft purr had Isaac feeling as sensitive as if he'd just popped some E. "Touch it, sweetie. Rub it for me," she implored.

"I got it," he moaned. "It's in my hand."

"Is it hard?"

"Real hard," he groaned. "Damn, I wish you were here; I want you so bad."

Marissa could hear Isaac's labored breathing; she could hear the sound of rustling and friction as his hand brushed against fabric and stroked his rigid flesh.

"Slow down. I don't want you to cum yet. I want to take your thumb and rub it up against the head of your dick. Mmm. It feels all slippery and moist. Now, hold onto it and rub it against my pussy. Don't put it in," Marissa cautioned. "I just want feel that good feeling of the head of your dick pressing up against my clit."

"Ugh," he uttered. "I wanna put it in; I wanna fuck you so bad; I wanna give you all this dick."

"Okay, you can fuck me in a minute. But not now. Right now, I want you to get me real hot, make my pussy so juicy, that my sticky stuff is covering your dick like a second skin."

"Okay," Isaac agreed, panting. "Just the head," he said.

"Wait a minute, Isaac. I have to take off my panties. Can you wait for me?"

"Yeah, but you have to hurry up, Marissa," he urgently whispered as he stroked himself.

Marissa flung off her silk robe. She reclined on her bed and settled against three plumped-up pillows and then she opened her legs. She parted her inner lips with an index finger and circled her clit until it became firm and sensitive to her touch. Next, she inserted two fingers into her slippery hole. Her flowing juices, thick and syrupy, made a sensual slurping sound.

"Listen," she told Isaac. "I want you to hear something." She placed the phone between her legs so he could hear her pussy talk. Then she brought the phone back to her ear. "Did you hear my pussy; did you hear it talkin' to you, sweetie?"

"Oh damn, girl. You're really fuckin' with me. I'm about to bust!"

"No, not yet. Wait!" she whimpered. She wanted to cum with him, with their toes curled as they harmonized their plaintive wails. But she was too late; she knew that her pussy talk was too much for Isaac. It was more than Isaac could bear. There was no way he could have possibly held back much longer. As she'd feared, Isaac gave an impassioned cry and ejaculated into his own hand. Marissa gave a heavy sigh.

Damn, her pussy was on fire, but she'd have to wait for Basille if she expected to get the release she needed.

Isaac continued to groan and mutter incoherently. Finally, he found his voice. "What the fuck! I felt like I was really inside you. I don't know what you're doing to me but, damn, girl, I love the shit out of you."

"Yeah, sweetie, I dig you too," Marissa said, deliberately leaving out the word *love*.

And then the doorbell rang. "Look, Isaac. I have to go. I'll talk to you tomorrow," she said hastily. There was no time to murmur softly and pretend to cuddle after having phone sex.

Not tonight. Basille, slinging good-ass dick, was standing outside her door.

"Was that the doorbell? Were you expecting someone?" Isaac demanded.

"Pizza delivery," she said. "I have to eat something before I go to sleep."

"Oh, okay," he said, sounding unsure. "Well, okay. Pleasant dreams; have a good night."

"Oh, I will," she said, quickly. Too quickly. But what the fuck. She was excited about Basille and no longer cared about making Isaac suspicious.

She hung up the phone and trotted to the door. Grinning from the knowledge that Basille's joint was already rigid, knowing her man was packing a rock-hard, dark chocolate dick, sent Marissa's sex drive into second gear.

She flung open her apartment door. "Hey boo," she said to Basille. She was butt-ass naked. Her nipples were hardened, and a creamy dew was gathering between her legs. Her eyes devoured him; she licked her lips in anticipation of tasting the bittersweet nectar that would be intermingled with hard dark chocolate. The combined tastes were simply delectable.

One look at Marissa's naked body and Basille groaned and grabbed his crotch. Wordlessly, he swooped her up in his arms and kicked the door shut. Using his lips to brush aside her red tinted locks, Basille kissed and nibbled on her neck as he made long, urgent strides toward Marissa's bedroom.

Sitting on the edge of the bed, holding Marissa as if she were a newborn, Basille used his chin to brush her locks from her face. He kissed her eyelids then quickly sought her lips while gently rotating her nipple between his index finger and thumb. With his free hand, he rubbed her belly and smoothed her tangled pubic hairs before slipping a long, thick middle finger into her silken wetness.

There was such an assortment of stimuli; Marissa lifted her butt from Basille's lap and jutted her pelvis as she eagerly parted her legs. Accepting her unspoken invitation to probe deeper, Basille explored her inner lips and walls. Then, using his finger as if it were a hard penis, he drove in and out causing her pussy juices to splash and trickle down her thighs. Unable to endure much more of this sustained torture, Marissa expelled an endless gasp. "Oh God! Basille! Baby, stop…" she said in a faltering whisper. Then building up to a crescendo, she screamed, "Baby, please. Put it in. Give it to me. Now."

Basille withdrew his finger and eased Marissa from his lap. He laid her down on her back; her legs dangled off the side of the bed. Then Basille stood and positioned her with her legs spread, knees bent. The heels of her feet dug into the mattress as Basille dropped to his knees and licked the juice that poured down her thighs and then drank from her shimmering pool.

Anyone listening would have sworn that Marissa had found religion as she chanted and called on Jesus, speaking fervently in what sounded like a foreign tongue.

She felt that familiar buildup to a climax and urgently pressed herself hard against his mouth. But Basille removed his beautiful full lips, rose and reached for her hand and gently pulled her upright. He guided her mouth to his stiffened dark penis.

Marissa shuddered as she opened her mouth wide. She had to brace herself for the massive size that always overwhelmed her initially and which often felt like an oral invasion. On numerous occasions, when she wasn't prepared, she'd choked on Basille's big dick.

He eased himself inside her warm and willing mouth. Her tongue flicked against his shaft. "Mmm," she murmured. She liked the flavor and after a few moments of generous licking, his dick became slick and smooth.

She sucked Basille's dick, applying pressure with her lips, careful not to scratch him with her teeth. Then, enjoying the feeling as the head of his dick brushed against the soft and warm part of her cheek, Marissa threw her head back and allowed the chocolate stick to slip and slide against her tongue, her gums, and the roof of her mouth, giving her a delicious oral massage. Pre-ejaculation oozed from the head of his penis; it tasted bittersweet.

The moment his dick began to expand and pulsate, Basille withdrew. Marissa crawled into the middle of her king-sized bed and bent down into a crouch. Basille steadied himself by gripping her butt cheeks, but his hands were so sweaty from excitement, they slipped from her smooth skin. He grabbed her again, held on, and this time he plunged inside. Working his back, he rotated in slow motion. It felt so good, Marissa cried out softly. Her sensitive insides craved this personalized attention.

The wonderful sensation of his hard flesh, embedded inside her softness, made her buck and thrash until she became downright unruly.

Marissa was so aroused, she felt crazy—insatiable—as if possessed by a sex demon. She couldn't control the profanity that escaped her lips: "Oh goddamn!" Marissa screamed. "Fuck me harder . . . Oh shit!" she shouted.

The profanity began to run its course, but when Basille sought and located her hidden place—her G-spot, Marissa cussed like a sailor until the words transformed to a prolonged orgasmic scream.

Burying her face in a pillow, she attempted to smother her cries. Her pussy muscles tightened and clenched uncontrollably. She could feel Basille trembling violently before he discharged a booming roar. Marissa's vagina seized Basille's quivering appendage and held it in place, throbbed against it, and sucked its semen until it went limp and became dry.

Exhausted and sweaty, Marissa and Basille clung to together. Her head was nestled against his chest. The feeling of his well-muscled arm wrapped around her and the sound of his strong and steady heartbeat provided a comfort that she hadn't realized her heart still yearned for.

Luckily, Marissa would not be fooled again; she realized that the peaceful allure of the feeling that came in the guise of sexual satisfaction was nothing more than a set-up—a dangerous trap that would lead to pain and heartache.

"So, where we headed, baby girl?" Basille wanted to know. His words were a gentle whisper inside the dimly lit bedroom. Words that enticed, tugged on her womanly nature, softened her. Made her weak.

Briefly warmed by his words, Marissa's eyes darted about wistfully. Then, she came to her senses. Weakness was doom and damnation. An arrow in the heart. She cleared her throat and shifted her position. She sat up straight. "What do you mean?" She asked, buying time.

"You ready to take this to the next level or what?" Now his voice sounded rough and demanding.

"What's the next level?" She suspected Basille was trying to take her to a place she refused to revisit.

"Live together. Get engaged. You know . . . commitment. Fuck it, I'm ready to wife you." Basille laughed, but the sound was without mirth. "Man, I can't even believe I'm talkin' this shit. You got me acting like a bitch."

Better you than me, Marissa thought cynically. She already knew that the next level would not be to her benefit. After buying into the hype that their relationship was solid and would last forever, Basille would gradually begin to change. And she'd be caught up—trapped in a place where she was emotionally neglected and made to feel insecure. Forced to tolerate blatant disrespect. *Where you going? How long will you be gone?* She'd whine at first. Then, as time passed and his lack of sensitivity became more pronounced, the whining would escalate to a hysterical shriek.

You're cheating. I know it; so stop lying and tell me that bitch's name. Marissa shook her head. *Thanks but no, thanks, Basille. Been there, done that.*

"Basille, that's sweet. I'm flattered. But I'd like to keep things the way they are." Marissa wrinkled her face. "You know… Uncomplicated."

Basille didn't speak a word. He responded by leaning down and kissing her forehead, a sweet gesture. A loving surrender.

* * *

"What do you feel like watching? Drama, Comedy, or an action flick?" Isaac asked.

"Whatever you like is fine with me."

"Are you hungry, baby? Want me to bring you something to eat? What are you in the mood for? Pizza? No, you had that last night. How about Chinese?"

The hell with Chinese food; tonight she'd have some yummy milk chocolate. But she didn't share that with Isaac. "I'm not hard to please, I'll eat whatever you're eating," Marissa said, sounding as demure and low-maintenance as a Stepford wife.

She gave a soft chuckle. Once Isaac caught a glimpse of the black cherry candy panties she wore beneath a black lace negligee, he'd forget all about his silly movie and Chinese food.

The aroma of Szechuan Chicken wafted into her apartment when Isaac arrived. Marissa took the bag from him, opened it, and felt around inside. She pulled out a single packet of duck sauce. "This is perfect for my appetizer. It's all we'll need for the moment." With her teeth, she ripped open the packet. "You know I love duck sauce on my egg roll."

The glimmer in Isaac's eyes told her that he was bracing himself for a sensual surprise.

Marissa backed Isaac into a wall. Her gaze wandered to his groin, and then she began to unzip his pants. She quickly found what she was looking for—a penis that instantly sprang to life. She fondled it until he moaned with desire. Next, Marissa squeezed the orange-colored sauce onto Isaac's fully erect penis and watched it pulse with excitement.

She lowered herself down to her knees. Murmuring sounds of pleasure, she licked the thick, tangy sauce from his dick. After licking it clean, she stood, reversed their positions, and leaned against the wall. "Want some candy, baby?" She asked as she seductively raised her black negligee, exposing black cherry candy panties.

Isaac dropped to his knees and hungrily bit the sides of the candy waistband, but he didn't bother to eat the hard candy. The real sweetness, he knew, was between Marissa's legs. What she had for him was thick and rich—sweet and syrupy.

Marissa placed one foot on Isaac's shoulder to allow his tongue better penetration. His experienced tongue drove inside her slit, lapping up the rich honey, slurping and lapping hungrily until Marissa removed her foot from his shoulders and nudged his head away.

Isaac looked disappointed, but she smiled and led him into the kitchen where she gracefully eased up on the kitchen table. With her rear-end practically hanging off the edge, a smile flickered across her face and she crooked a finger, beckoning Isaac to oblige.

He didn't need much coaxing. He instantly inserted his well-hung milk cholcolate into her dripping vagina. "Hit that pussy. You know it belongs to you, don't you, baby?"

"Yeah, it's my pussy," Isaac murmured huskily. He released a groan as he drove inside; Marissa wrapped her legs around his waist, her hot pussy convulsed and tightened around his thick rod. Isaac's breathing increased; his thrusts intensified; and within seconds he exploded, involuntarily ejaculating a hot gusher.

"I'm sorry, baby," Isaac said, sounding embarrassed. He pulled his glistening dick out of her pussy; he sat down on a kitchen chair, his pants gathered around his ankles. "I don't know what happened, babe. I just couldn't hold it," he explained with an apologetic expression, his tone solemn.

It was not the norm for Isaac to perform so poorly. He was usually a long-lasting lover. However, the sensation of his dick being slathered with duck sauce, as if it were an egg roll, had caused Isaac to lose his ability to maintain control.

"It's okay, sweetie." Marissa smoothed the hair on the side of his face. Actually, Isaac's blunder provided her with the leverage she needed to execute her plan. "I know you couldn't help it. Let's just eat and watch the DVD you wanted to see." Her tone was deliberately self-sacrificing. But her face was set in a scowl.

"No, I don't want to eat yet. I can get it up again. I can't leave you hanging like this," he said, shaking his head adamantly.

"No, really. It's okay, sweetie," she said softly. "I'm really not in the mood anymore. Go ahead and eat. I'm going to take a shower and just go to bed." She had the resigned look of an unsatisfied woman, a woman whose man was unable to make her reach her peak. And her expression was fashioned to give the impression that she may have to look elsewhere.

Isaac stroked himself; he was frantic as he tried to bring his sex organ back to life. But without Marissa's assistance, his self-manipulation was useless. His dick was hopelessly shriveled and limp.

Marissa was glad that he couldn't get it up. Pleased that he felt guilty and ashamed. Isaac's sense of sexual inadequacy, his inability to perform, would ensure his willingness to satisfy her and fulfill her fantasy.

She suppressed a giggle. It wouldn't be long now. Soon, she'd invite both Isaac and Basille to her pussy party where she'd be served up some milk chocolate and dark chocolate. Mmm. It would be thugaliscious—a double chocolate treat.

Having enjoyed multiple orgasms from Basille the night before, Marissa didn't mind the sacrifice of being sexually unfulfilled. In bed, she turned her back to Isaac, curled into a ball, and soon drifted to sleep.

The next morning, she awakened to the feeling of Isaac's face between her legs. He had spread her legs and lay beneath the covers inside the large V created by her opened legs.

Marissa threw off the covers. "Sweetie. Stop! I have to get ready for work. I don't have time."

"Just a quickie, baby. Please. I don't like it when you don't cum. It's not right."

She eased off the bed, threw on a silk robe, and headed for the bathroom. "We'll have to finish tomorrow. I really don't have time."

Isaac sat on the side of her bed, looking pitiful.

Better he than me, she thought to herself and trotted off to take a shower.

Later that evening, she licked melted chocolate from Basille's scrotum while giving him a handjob with a palm covered with motion lotion. Basille also succumbed swiftly, busting a nut before he'd even touched Marissa.

And once again, she pretended everything was just fine, but sulked and was ominously pensive, giving the impression that Basille's days in her bed were numbered.

Marissa refused to answer her phone for two days. Between Basille and Isaac, there were dozens of pleading messages on both her home phone and her cell.

Finally, she decided to show a little mercy. She called Basille first. "Hey boo."

"Marissa!" he shouted. "Where the hell have you been?"

"I've had a lot on my mind and we need to talk." She became quiet, allowing the meaning behind her words to sink in.

"Is something wrong?" Basille asked nervously.

"I'd rather talk about it in person. Can you come over tonight at eight?"

"Yeah, I can come through tonight, but I wish you'd tell me whassup. You got me feeling real fucked up. Why you being so secretive? Talk to me. Whassup?"

"We'll talk tonight," Marissa said firmly. "I'll see you tonight, boo."

She hung up and her lips spread into a big cheesy grin. One down, one to go.

She called Isaac next. When he answered, she took on a somber tone. "Can I see you tonight, sweetie? It's really important."

"Of course. Are you all right? I can come over right now," he said sounding panicked.

"No, I'm fine. But what I have to say, I prefer to tell you face-to-face."

She could hear Isaac swallow. In fact, it sounded like a frightened gulp. Then, he cleared his throat. "Are you dumping me, Marissa?" He asked in a tone that was clearly distraught.

"No," she protested and then deliberately sighed and paused.

"Are you there?" Isaac asked.

"Yes, I'm here. What I'm saying is . . . I don't want to break up. But maybe you'll want to see other people after we have our talk."

"Are you crazy! I'm in love with you; why would I want another woman? No one can compete with you."

"Thanks for the compliment," she said solemnly.

"It's not empty flattery, Marissa. I love you. You know that."

"I dig you too. I'll see you tonight at eight." She hung up and began to pace, cradling her chin thoughtfully. Should she write a script or just wing it? She flopped down on her cushy sofa and allowed her mind to marinate on the subject. Finally, she decided to wing it; she'd let the men set the tone.

After Isaac and Basille realize that neither had been her only lover, she'd let the scene play itself out. If things went according to her design, she'd be a very happy woman tonight.

* * *

Marissa mixed together banana liquor and equal portions of light and dark spiced rum. A dash of grenadine sweetened the taste; a cherry and an orange slice made the drink appear harmless. But Marissa knew her Rumrunner was potent, a surefire way to loosen up her male guests—make them feel uninhibited. Make them willing to submit.

Basille arrived first. He was nervously puffing on a blunt. "Here you go, boo," Marissa said, handing Basille a tall glass of her special tonic.

"What's this shit? You know I don't fuck with this girly stuff," he said gruffly.

Marissa realized Basille's agitation was actually a case of nervous jitters; he was more annoyed with himself than with her. He hated the position he was in—he despised being at her beck and call. She knew he'd prefer a more equitable relationship. It irked him to jump whenever she snapped her fingers; it was not a manly thing to do. But did he have a choice. Hell no! Not if he wanted to stay in her good graces.

"It's rum, boo. I just sweetened it a little," she said cajolingly.

"Rum?"

"Uh huh."

"Bacardi 151? 'Cause that's what I need right now; I don't need nothing diluted and sweet. I need a strong drink, something that's beyond 100 proof."

"Try it," Marissa said with a knowing smile.

Basille placed the blunt in the ashtray and took a big gulp. "Oh ai'ight. I can fuck with this."

He took a seat on the couch, relit the tobacco-leaf-covered weed, and alternated between deep puffs and taking giant swigs of the Rumrunner Marissa had mixed.

Marissa walked over to her sound system, clicked a button, and paused as soft music filled the room.

"So, whassup?" The muscles in Basille's face had relaxed; his tone sounded more agreeable—more open for suggestions.

"Well, I was thinking . . . " The buzz of the doorbell interrupted Marissa.

"Who's that?" Basille inquired, his face scrunched up in displeasure.

"Oh, that's a friend of mine—someone I want you to meet." She opened the door and Isaac came inside, his neck swiveled curiously from Marissa and then to Basille.

"Isaac, this is Basille. Basille, this is Isaac. And I invited you both over so we could sit down and have a talk."

Basille slammed his drink down and sprang to his feet. "You fuckin' with another nigga? I'm not tryin' to hear that dumb shit. I'm out." He picked up his blunt and strode toward the door.

"Basille. Calm down. Just do me a favor and sit down and listen, okay?"

Turning up the side of his top lip, Basille gave Isaac a roving gaze, glowering as he looked his competitor up and down. He sucked his teeth with unmasked disdain.

Apparently the feelings were mutual, for Isaac gave Basille a long, lingering scowl.

Marissa went in the kitchen and came back with a drink for Isaac.

"Basille, I don't usually smoke weed, but tonight I thought we'd all smoke a peace pipe," she said reaching for the blunt.

"I'm not smoking that poison," Isaac fumed. "And I'm shocked that you would engage in an illegal act with this….this thug." He spat out his words.

"Yo, punk. Watch your mouth," Basille warned and then advanced toward Isaac.

"Boys! Boys!" Marissa shouted in an authoritative tone and then got in between Basille and Isaac, using her small but toned arms to keep them separated. "You both need to stop acting like children. Sit down, Basille." She nudged her head toward the sofa. "Isaac, go sit over there." She pointed to a leather recliner and then picked up Basille's drink and turned it to her lips. It was a gesture of familiarity that she knew wouldn't leave any doubt in Isaac's mind that she and Basille were intimately involved.

"Isaac, I guess you can see that Basille and I are pretty familiar with each other."

Isaac lowered his head and nodded. He grimaced as if in pain. Basille straightened his shoulders, puffed out his chest triumphantly and blew out a thick cloud of smoke.

Then, Marissa walked to the kitchen and returned with her own drink. "Shall we make a toast?"

"A toast!" Both men exclaimed. "A toast to what?" Isaac asked incredulously.

"To honesty," Marissa said.

"Aw, here comes the bullshit," Basille muttered discontentedly, his face twisted in disgust.

"Seems more like a lot of deceit, if you ask me," Isaac commented.

"You're right, Isaac. I've been deceptive—sneaking around with two men.But no more. I want to be honest with both of you because I can't go on like this."

"Ai'ight. So tell dude, sayonara," Basille said.

Isaac winched.

"Actually, I have to tell both of you goodbye," she said sadly as she pinched the stem of the cherry that floated in her drink, pulled the cherry out, and placed it in her mouth. She sucked the cherry seductively. She cut an eye at Basille and could see the bulge beginning to rise in his pants.

She sauntered over to the sofa and reached for the blunt with an outstretched manicured hand. As he passed the cigar to her, she made sure her fingers caressed his hand. Marissa inhaled deeply and blew out a long stream of smoke. She returned the blunt and set down her drink.

She was wearing a clingy lace gown but no bra and no panties. She glided to the middle of the living room floor and began to sway to the music. She threw back her head and, as if entranced, she closed her eyes and began to cup and then fondle her breasts. She wet her index fingers with her tongue and then drew tiny circles until her nipples peeked through the lace. Slowly, ever so slowly, she raised her gown until her dark forest was revealed. Giving Basille and Isaac an erotic show, Marissa, still swaying in time with the music, licked her finger again and this time parted her vaginal lips. She moaned in ecstasy, backed up and lowered her perfectly round bare ass onto Isaac's lap, and rotated her hips, giving him a lap dance.

She gave Basille a cautious sideways glance, thinking he might be enraged and about to leap off the sofa and stomp toward the front door. She expected him to be deeply offended, and thought she'd have to rush to him and soothe his bruised ego, but Basille stared at Marissa, mesmerized, his lips slack with carnal desire.

Marissa reached behind her and took Isaac's hand and guided it between her legs. Isaac didn't need much encouragement; he eagerly obliged. He rubbed her clit, delicately parted her pussy lips, then worked his finger in as far as it would go.

Breathing hard, Marissa humped his finger, riding it as if it were a dick. Finally, breathless, she removed his hand and began to lick the thick finger, which was coated with her own sticky honeydew.

Without preamble, Basille ventured to the other side of the room and joined the couple. Kneeling before Marissa, Basille eased her legs apart.

Marissa stayed in place on Isaac's lap as Isaac cupped her breasts and then used his fingertips to make tiny circles around her nipples until they became hard knots. She could feel Basille's warm breath on her thighs as he buried his face between her open legs. Her back arched; her breathing came in quick short rasps.

Basille's shaved head felt smooth and sensual as it grazed her thighs. The feeling was intense; it was utter bliss—an adventurous tongue in one place and strong capable hands on another.

Now Isaac was biting her neck, whispering in her ear while Basille concentrated on her clit, sucking it with his lips; licking it with his tongue while an insistent finger probed inside her, causing her to shudder—her arms to flail, her face to contort, and her head to roll back and forth as if she were possessed.

Marissa was caught up in the rapture of a fantasy come true. A fire raged inside her, starting at her neck and spreading down to her loins, making her thrash about and speak in tongue. She felt for a moment that perhaps she was going insane. The intense stimulation—it was exquisite torture—too much to bear. Her mouth formed and tried to speak the word, *stop*! But she only managed to emit an unintelligible utterance—a sound of passion. In her mind, she screamed for Isaac and Basille to stop; she had to get a grip before her body went into shock. Or worse, it would be a disgrace and the waste of a fulfilled fantasy if she couldn't hold back the orgasm that threatened to erupt.

Isaac's hands left her breast; Basille removed his head from between her legs. As Marissa struggled to catch her breath, Isaac lifted her flimsy gown and pulled it over her head. Basille cupped her butt checks while Isaac placed her upper body in the crook of his arms. Together, they lifted Marissa and gently lowered her naked body to the carpeted floor. Her locked hair spread out like a crimson crown.

Isaac and Basille, both still fully dressed, lay on opposite sides of Marissa. As if of one mind, their mouths were simultaneously drawn to her nipples. Basille captured the right nipple between his teeth and softly bit and licked while Isaac drew moist circles on the other nipple with the tip of his tongue. With one hand she caressed Basille's smooth head and with the other she ran her fingers through Isaac's thick, wavy hair.

Suddenly her hand felt nothing; her nipples were abandoned. Large, strong hands clamped her hips and moved her into a position where she was down on her hands and knees. Then,

Marissa was straddled from behind—by whom, she was not quite sure. But when she was penetrated and smacked on the ass she was able to identify the thick dick that rammed into her drenched vagina.

"Oh, yes!" She whispered and then her voice grew louder. "Fuck me hard, Basille," Marissa exclaimed. She was prepared to beg him to fuck her until it hurt, but her words were cut off by Isaac's penis, which he pushed inside her open mouth.

Marissa balanced herself on the floor with one hand and used the other to lightly scratch Isaac's balls. His tiny moans became loud groans as he drove inside her mouth with the same force he'd used if he were inside her vagina.

They were all in a sexual frenzy. Their passionate cries—intermingled with pounding flesh, slapping, and sucking created—a cacophony of erotic sounds.

Unexpectedly, the two men switched positions. "Want some chocolate, baby?" Basille asked Marissa, his tone, low and guttural.

Overcome with emotion, Marissa found she was unable to speak; nodding her head was the best she could do. Finally, the words that were forming in her mind found their way to her throat and were released in a wanton scream, "Yes, baby. Give me some of that good dick."

Obliging, Basille gave Marissa a mouthful of chocolate. At some point, Isaac crept behind her and pressed against her writhing body. Isaac's penis sought out her hidden opening and penetrated; his lips kissed her back, his teeth scraped against her skin. Marissa's body was under the command of Basille and Isaac. She wanted the scene to last forever; she couldn't bear for it to end because nothing had ever felt as good as this. It was forbidden love. But in their world there were no rules.

She wondered if she would ever again be satisfied with just one man. She doubted it—not after the sweet taste of three-way lust.

Having two men panting and pumping dick in separate orifices was surreal—like a dream. It was so good, she thought she'd collapse from delirious pleasure.

Waves of pleasure coursed through her. The feeling began at the tip of her toes and then moved slowly, creeping up her legs, her thighs, tantalizing her loins, making her love muscles go wild. Her clenching muscles took Isaac over the edge. His penis throbbed, but she fought to hold on—she wasn't ready to cum.

Apparently sensing that a premature eruption loomed, Basille stopped moving, but his dick continued to pulsate and demand attention. Unable to restrain herself, Marissa couldn't keep still. She rotated her hips and pushed backward, yielding to him, silently instructing Isaac to finish what he'd started. Her hungry lips worked on Basille. She sucked until he rhythmically began to undulate inside her juicy mouth.

And then she felt it, that familiar hot feeling that began in pit of her stomach and then coursed through her entire body, leaving a trail of raw nerve endings until the hotness worked its way to her loins. With their three bodies in sync, they all clenched and tightened themselves as they braced for the inevitable explosion.

* * *

The long and audible moan that escaped her lips surprised her, causing the door key to slip from her fingers and clatter down to the tiled floor outside her apartment door. The sound of the ringing telephone instantly erupted, bringing her out of her reverie. How long had she been standing there enjoying her fantasy?

Feeling panicked, Marissa bent down and quickly picked up the key. With trembling fingers, she fit the key into the lock and hurriedly turned it.

She rushed inside her apartment and raced to get to the phone. When she reached it, she snatched the receiver off the base. "Hello?" she said in a frail, desperate voice. But there was silence on the other end. Marissa hadn't reached the phone in time; the caller had hung up. Feeling dejected, she hung up and cast a frantic glance to the caller ID. *Restricted.* The word mocked her; told her she was a fool.

The caller had to have been RJ, her elusive lover. He never left messages and always called from various undisclosed places—pay phones, blocked cell phones and, although it pained her to admit it, she knew he also called from the homes of his other women.

RJ was the love of her life, her sexual addiction. He went by many aliases: RJ, Black, Basille, Isaac, and even Mustard (because he was so smooth). But Marissa preferred calling him Sweetie or Boo.

Damn, she hated the fact that she'd missed her baby's call. There was just no telling when she'd hear from him again. He might call again in the next hour. It was hard to predict. Sometimes weeks would go by without a word from him. There'd been times when he'd eluded her and deprived her of his sweet meat for months at a time.

RJ was always on the move—on the go; he was a veteran of the streets. He had that hard-to-get dick, and she was so hopelessly addicted; no other dick could satisfy her. Her desire for him consumed her to the core.

It was a damn shame the way she let him treat her. He gave her love in small doses, doling out dick as if there was a high demand for it and a short supply.

But damn, when he came through, the chocolate tasted so sweet and felt so good, it was worth the torturous, long wait.

Marissa released a deep sigh of regret. She supposed she'd have to please herself until the next time she was in the arms of her thugaliscious chocolate lover.

But in the meantime, she'd continue to fantasize about the sexual fulfillment and emotional freedom of being a woman who treated herself to the pleasure of two sweet and tasty lovers.

Damn, she sure wished could grip up RJ and clone him.

Headhunter

Anna J.

"So, what time can I meet up with him?"

"Tonight at eight o'clock, and make sure you wear that sexy red dress we picked out."

Being me can be so wonderful at times. I mean, what better job to have than a Headhunter? I get to pick my own schedule, and I come and go as I please. My clientele is made up of women that know exactly what they want—a nice long dick with a strong back attached to it. What better way to start your day?

I travel nationwide to give them exactly what they are looking for. Now, my family thinks I work for the airlines; that's why I'm always gone. But, in all actuality, I'm "working" the airlines on a more personal level. Let's just say when you develop a relationship with a couple of pilots, you get to fly for free. Feel me?

Everything I do is real discreet, so the last thing you have to worry about is your business getting out. I usually get my clients from hearsay . . . my clients telling their girl-friends, etc. My services are not cheap by a long shot; that's why I perform like I'm doing it for TV. You just tell me what you are looking for in a man—or woman if you just want some tongue game—and I headhunt for you. Now, I'm not guaranteeing a relationship or marriage, but I can insure a night of total satisfaction.

Right now I'm on my way to meet Sadiq, who is a Cuban, Haitian, and Africa- American bundle of muscle. Standing six feet even, and weighing in at two-forty, man, I almost kept him for damn myself. He has to have the whitest teeth I've ever seen on a man so chocolate. Impressed, my client, put in such an order; but more important, she requested he have at least a foot-long tool. Honestly I thought that would be the hardest part of my job, but you'd be surprised at how many men don't mind showing you what they're working with.

I met Sadiq in Jamaica at a Hedonism event. I don't usually participate, I'm more of a voyeur. At events like this it's strictly business. I go to look for *potentials* for my client base so that I know whom to pass off to. In a setting like this, I can see them in action and see what they are packing. That way, when someone has a request, I know whom to call.

When I saw Sadiq my mouth fell open involuntarily. I was coming from the pool, and was on my way to change for brunch, when I walked past his room. The only rule I think they have is if you are engaging in sex you have to leave the door open. I saw him from the back at first, and I had to step back and look again because I liked his skin tone.

Sadiq had a sexy little Latino woman twisted like a damn pretzel. From my position at the door, I could see him driving into her with so much force I almost came—and he wasn't even sexing me. Getting bold with it, I took a seat in the room and took notes on the stationary that was sitting on the desk.

His body had a light sheen of sweat that made him personify melting chocolate on her skin. His nipples were about two shades darker than his complexion, and he sported a nipple ring on the right that looked scrumptious. His jet-black hair and full goatee was the same color, and I couldn't take my eyes off him.

He moved inside of her with long, slow strokes that had my walls pulsating and had my clit jumping against the fabric of my bathing suit. The entire time he was inside of her our eyes locked. The Latino woman moaned like she hoped it never ended, and I wished we could swap positions.

I just sat back and enjoyed the performance as he worked it out something serious. He got up on his knees and leaned back so that his butt touched his calves. Then, he took her by her waist and positioned her so that they met pelvis to pelvis. I inched a little closer to the bed so that I could really see what he had going on, and, damn, was I shocked.

Sadiq was the proud owner of twelve marvelous inches. It looked smooth in texture, and I really had to refrain from reaching out and touching it. The head had a nice mushroom shape, and he donned a hood piercing that looked like it caused all kinds of havoc if rubbed against your clit. I took my seat again and allowed him to continue.

He took her nipples into his mouth one at a time, then both together, periodically giving me a glimpse of his pink tongue. The muscles in his back did a dance of their own as he quickened is pace, damn near knocking the bottom out of her pussy. He was killing the game, taking her legs and holding her off the bed by her ankles while he tried to push all of himself in her. I was holding on to the arms of the chairs like I was on a roller coaster waiting to get to the top.

And, man, when we got there and the roller coaster tipped over and went down the other side, the ride was phenomenal. He flipped her over on her stomach like she was a damn rag doll and dug all into her. I found myself short of breath on a few occasions, especially when he pulled her to the edge of the bed, and squatted under her like she was riding him from the edge. He moved in and out of her so slow, it was like they were moving in slow motion. Just before he lay down to let her ride, I gave him my business card and my room number so that I could get some more information from him. I had to have him on my roster; it was a must.

I would be on the island for four days, so I planned to make the most of it. Early in the morning, just as the sun is coming up, I go running on the beach as my daily exercise. Gotta keep the body firm in my line of business. But don't get it twisted; I deal with women that weigh anywhere between eight and eight hundred pounds. Big girls need love, too; and from what a lot of men tell me, they have the tightest, juiciest pussies out there, so don't sleep.

Every morning, for the past two days, I've been crossing paths with this guy that looks good enough to eat. He looks like a native, though. His pecan skin and curly hair gives him the appearance of maybe being from Brazil, but when he speaks I can hear the islands in his tone. All he ever said was good morning, but it doesn't take much.

Well, it just so happens, the hotel has a personal massage parlor that comes complimentary with your stay. So after I ate a light lunch, I went to get the stress rubbed out of my body. I signed in and stripped naked, putting on the robe that they supplied. A few minutes later, a woman, dressed in a sexy wrap skirt and bikini top escorted me to a room where I would be serviced. I requested a masseur, and she assured me he would be in to work his magic in a few. I hung up the robe and made myself comfortable on the table as she lit the aromatherapy candles.

Just as she was leaving, my friend from the beach walks in and washes his hands. I smiled on the inside as he got the oils together and turned on the radio to some soothing tunes. I closed my eyes the instant his hands made contact with my skin. With hands as big as his, you'd think they'd be rough, but his hands were as soft as a baby's ass, and I was loving it. I was putty in his hands as he worked the stress out of my body with strong yet gentle strokes on my skin.

He paid special attention to each foot before moving his hands up my legs. When he reached the space between my thighs, I felt his finger trace the lips of my vagina before he moved to massage my thighs. My body tensed for a split second as I made an effort to pretend like what he had just done didn't faze me, but my hormones were filled to capacity and just waiting to burst out.

I was ready to give it to him. Hell, I was already on my stomach so it would take nothing for me to be in my favorite position. I could be face down, ass up for days if it were at all possible. I started to spread my legs wider, but my head was in the opening of the massage table, preventing my sight of any action—and I liked to watch. I thought about just rising up on my knees, too, but I didn't want to jeopardize his job for a quick moment of pleasure. Besides, I was here for business of my own, so ain't no use in starting something I can't finish, anyway.

I was so busy daydreaming, the masseur had to tell me twice to turn over before I obliged. Once the cool air in the room hit the front of my body, my nipples stood at attention instantly. Goose bumps ran the entire length of my body, and my pussy pulsated in anticipation of feeling his hands work magic on my skin again.

The sheet covered my mid section, and his hands warmed my breast. I closed my eyes and enjoyed the journey his fingers took across my body. My skin felt hot like cayenne pepper, and I wanted him inside of me so bad.

I kept my eyes closed as he removed the sheet and covered my treasure with his mouth. His arms and tongue circled my exotic pearl repeatedly, building cream up inside of me. I let him control the flow and didn't hesitate to rest the heels of my feet on the upper part of his back, right between his shoulder blades.

He grabbed me by my waist and hoisted my body up on his shoulders. I took hold of the slow-moving ceiling fan to maintain my balance, and he walked me around in a circle, never loosing contact with my panic button. I let go of the fan long enough for him to lower me down onto his length and pin my back against the wall. I could feel his testicles slap against my ass every time our bodies met. My nectar ran down his length and began forming a puddle underneath us. He was doing the damn thing to me, and for the first time in ages I was speechless.

For the remainder of my stay, he took care of me. I swear if I could've stuck him in one of my suitcases I would've. It was a sad goodbye, but I made sure to get his information for later use. He escorted me to my plane, and I made sure to give him one of my business cards so that we could keep in touch.

On the flight back to the states, I was seated next to an exceptionally sexy man that I had trouble keeping my eyes off. Really, I tried to keep business as just that, but from the way he looked I would soon be getting my initiation into the mile high club—if I had anything to do with it. I was partial to vanilla, but this man made me want to dip into the lighter side of the rainbow. He was definitely a pretty boy, and an ideal date for Marsha, one of my clients from Jersey, but I had to at least see what he was working with before I passed him on.

After the plane lifted off and leveled out, and after we were able to move about freely in the air, I made it my business to show this man all of my assets. Suddenly happy that I had decided to wear nothing under the short skirt I had on, I practically sat in his lap as I scooted out into the aisle to go to the restroom. I wanted to take him with me, but I made sure he got a view of my ass on the slide-by before I switched my hips down the aisle as if I were on a catwalk.

After checking my makeup and making sure everything was cool down below I went back to my seat, scooting closer to him this time, wanting him to test my Brazilian wax job. I smiled a sly smile before turning toward the window and placing the blanket over my lap that I had asked the stewardess for on my way to the ladies' room. I wished, for a brief second, that I had packed one of my toys in my carry-on bag, but for now I would have to work it without props.

I caught him looking at me from time to time, but both of us would just blush and turn the other way. Once the movie got started, I snuggled in deeper under the cover and leaned into him a little, as if I didn't notice I was on his side of the seat. I closed my eyes and waited for him to say something because I could sense his eyes watching me.

"So, what's your name?" the handsome stranger asked with a deep baritone voice. He definitely didn't sound like he was from Philly, and a part of me wanted to say he was from the Big Apple. It's just something about that New York accent that made me wet beyond my control.

"Excuse me?" I asked him like I hadn't heard what the question. I was playing hard to get, but not too hard; I want to try him before the flight was over.

"I asked what your name was, if that was okay with you," he responded, flashing me a bright Colgate smile that could only be achieved with excellent dental care. I melted more from the sight.

"I'm Celeste, and you?"

"I'm hungry."

I knew exactly what he meant, and before I commented I discreetly checked his hand for any sign of a wedding band. Not that married men were off limits, it just made a situation more difficult than it had to be. The last thing I needed was an angry wife busting in on one of my clients.

"I see . . . So what do you do when you're hungry?" I asked, satisfied that he didn't have any telltale signs of being married. I'd find out better once I got his information and was able to do some research on him. The computer never lies.

"I eat."

Without saying a word, I took his left hand and placed it between my thighs, allowing his fingers to explore my warmth. He traced my clit with the tip of his finger before dipping down into my slit and finding its way into my opening. I opened my legs a little more so that he could spread my lips and have easier access to what he was looking for. Afterwards, he pulled his finger out of me and stuck it in his mouth, sucking all of my honey off of it.

"Meet me in the bathroom."

Now, the good thing about first class was we had our own private restroom, and there wasn't usually anyone seated in that area. I waited about three minutes before I joined him and pushed the occupied button for the door.

The bathroom was kind of small, and we really didn't have a lot of space to work with. We were able to maneuver around so that I could be placed on the sink, and he could stand in front of it. I pulled my skirt all the way up so that I could see him at work. When he pulled out what he was working with, I let out a slight gasp at the sight. He had a nice thick yellow stick with a hook in it that I'm sure was voodoo. My legs involuntarily spread wider after he put a condom on, but instead of him sliding into home base he went down on me instead.

My body began to shake the instant his lips made contact with my clit. I held my lips open for him so that he wouldn't have a problem accessing all of my goodies. He was neat with his eating, and I liked that. He did what he had to do to make me cum, and I didn't feel like I had an entire jar of Vaseline applied to my private area. Once he was done, he wiped his face with a paper towel and proceeded to enter me.

He was *thick* beyond reason, so he had to work it in slowly until he was able to fit most of it in. I thought for sure my insides would be wrapped around the head of his dick when he pulled out. It hurt like hell, but it felt so good at the same time. I heard Janet singing about the pleasure principal as he rocked my world for the next hour. My legs were so weak by the time I got off the sink, I had to lean back against the wall, and let him clean me up the best way he could before we returned to our seats. Flying first class was definitely the way to go.

I went to my seat first, and a few minutes later he returned. We made jokes about the obvious stares we got from a few of the occupants around us when we got back, but I could care less. He gave me his business card, and I gave him mine promising to keep in touch. I knew if I did nothing else when I got home, I would be finding out what I could about him. He would make an excellent addition to my team.

Once I was off the plane, I practically ran to get my luggage and my car so that I could make it back to my house in time for me to freshen up and change. I had to meet my client at the restaurant.

I didn't sit at the table with them, or anything like that, but I sat so that I could have a bird's-eye view, and only stayed long enough to ensure the date was off to a good start. I always had my clients meet their dates for the first time *at* the restaurant. That way, if things didn't work out she wouldn't have to worry about him showing up at her house unexpectedly.

In record time, even for me, I was showered and dressed in a form-fitting one-piece that hugged the hip and flared out down to the floor. The dress was jack black, and I topped it off with simple diamond and silver accessories so that I could blend into the crowd easily. After grabbing my bag, I took my hair rollers out and hopped into my car, letting the top down on my S-Class Mercedes and allowing the wind to tussle my curls until I rolled up to the valet parking at *Mirror Mirror*. The handsome valet stepped over and opened the door for me. After giving my wind-swept curls a little attention, I stepped out of the vehicle, and made my way into the most beautiful restaurant on this side of Drexel Hill.

As I was being escorted to my seat by my handsome waiter, I saw my client's date out of the corner of my eye, but I didn't acknowledge his presence. It wasn't until after I was seated, and the menu was up to my face, did I peep the entire scene. He was looking extremely scrumptious in his Ralph Lauren suit. I took note of the single calla lily he had sitting in front of him on the table. That was my client's signal that he was the right guy.

Promptly at eight o'clock, my client walked in looking extremely wonderful in the red dress that I had picked out. I saw from my table that the quick lesson I gave her on applying makeup paid off, and the jewels we picked out matched perfectly. Her date was a gentleman, rising from his seat as she approached the table, and didn't take his until she was seated comfortably. I waited a few more minutes, just in case an uncomfortable situation arose, then I discreetly made my way out of the restaurant, winking my eye at my client on the way by. She simply smiled in my direction and finished her conversation. Now, all I had to do was wait for her report in the morning or, if things went as I planned, the afternoon.

After some much-needed rest, I woke up the next day refreshed and ready to work. Every so often one of my clients may request the company of the same sex. Now, I only deal with female clientele, so it was my job to get the client what they asked for. On a personal note, I was weary of those kinds of situations; but money talked and so does bills, so I had to do what I had to do.

Later on tonight I will be meeting up with potential date number one. My client, Symphony, a femme herself, requested a feminine woman with perky breast and a flat stomach. She had to have shoulder-length hair, and it had to be her own. She also requested that the woman have full lips, a pretty smile, and a caramel, almost light-skinned tone. Her number one request was that she be a freak in the bedroom.

Now, women come on to me all the time, but I needed someone that I could see in action, someone that I could do a background check on. I don't have time to be dealing with criminals in my line of work. A good friend of mine told me about an upscale gentleman's club over in Jersey City where the owner only hired premium women to work his spot. After exhausting all of my resources, I made my way over the bridge to see what was happening on that side of town.

The club was in a high-class neighborhood and was so discreet you could only hear the music as you drove by, but the minute you got to the corner of the block there was silence. I parked my Expedition in the dimly lit lot and made my way into the building, ready to see some action.

This place was very classy, and the women there were all on point. These women weren't like the ones you saw around the way with black ash on their stomachs and stretch marks from having ten kids. These women were beautiful without a flaw on their bodies. Maybe it was the lighting, maybe not, but these chicks were on point. I took a seat in the corner and ordered a drink from the topless waitress that came to take my order. She was back in no time with my tequila sunrise, and I paid and tipped her nicely, afterwards sitting back and enjoying the show.

There was a girl exiting the stage, and she spent at least five minutes picking up all the money that covered the stage floor. The men in this establishment were dressed to the nines in business suits, and I spotted several briefcases resting by their stools on the floor, so I'm sure they were spending some money up in here. Once the performer left the stage, the topless waitress that served my drink was wiping down the pole and removing scattered items that were left by the previous dancer.

Soon after, the lights in the club went lower, and just about every man in the house that wasn't already occupied was gathered around the stage as the deejay announced *Like Silk* to the stage. Jamie Foxx's *Do What It Do* could be heard in the surround-sound speakers, and a hush fell over the crowd as she made her presence on to the stage.

I kept my eyes on the stage as I listened to the lyrics of Jamie's song while watching her body dance to the beat. I felt myself getting hot under the collar and had to check myself, reminding myself that women were not my thing. The lyrics boomed in my ears and the way Like Silk's body twisted and turned on the stage had my thong soaked, and I couldn't help myself.

Whatcha wanna do? You wanna get high? You wanna get fired up?

As the music played, Like Silk moved her body in a slow wind, slowly twirling around the pole in her cowgirl outfit. She had on a black studded crotchless thong and a top with a whip attached to her hip. Her ten-gallon hat was black with her stage name spelled out in rhinestones around the middle, all matching her thigh-high boots. I was stuck with my mouth wide open at the way she performed.

Whatcha wanna do? You wanna get sexed? You wanna get tied up?

As she worked the pole, I rocked back in forth in my seat enjoying the show. She grabbed the pole, and spun around it in a quick motion, landing almost at the top with only her legs wrapped around the pole. She came down in a slow circle, popping one butt cheek then the other, all the way down until her back touched the floor. I was speechless.

Get your rodeo ride up, baby girl lift those thighs up.

She moved her body around the stage floor like she didn't have any bones in her back. The floor sparkled from the body glitter trail she left behind. I sat in amazement at what she was doing, and knew I had to talk to her before I left here. She snaked her body into a standing position, leaving her cowgirl boots laid on the floor. Using the whip that was attached to her hip, she performed several tricks as if we were in a real-live rodeo, keeping to the beat at the same time.

I think you better wise up, 'cause I'm about to rise up.

The men on the stage went wild as she jumped through the hoops she made with the whip then came out of her top. Her breasts looked to be about a 40DD, but they stood up perfectly and were kissed with chocolate nipples that even made my mouth water. Grinding her body down to the floor, she ran the handle of the whip up her leg and inserted the top of it into her vagina, afterwards taking it out and allowing one of the many men around the stage to lick her honey from it. Money was flying everywhere as if it were falling from the ceiling; and while they were occupied, I went to talk to the owner about letting me speak to her privately. After insuring him that I wasn't scouting her for another spot, he allowed me to wait for her in her dressing room.

I only had to wait a good ten minutes before she came in holding her props and a handful of money. She dropped some of her belongings when she opened the door and saw me in the room. I rushed over, and helped her pick up some things, my hands coming into contact with her baby-soft skin in the process. I don't know what I was expecting her to smell like, but she had a light floral scent emanating from her that put me at ease.

I explained to her why I was in the room, giving her a little background on what I did for a living and why I wanted her on my list. At first she was hesitant, but I assured her that what I did was private and she didn't have to worry about her reputation being put out on the line. It took a little enticing, but when I started talking dollars and how much she could make in one session, she was all for it.

"Okay, but before you go, I do have one request."

"And what's that?" I said, stopping mid-pose as I was moving to get down off the table.

Instead of her answering, she walked over to where I was standing and kissed me on the lips. I had never been with a woman before, and I wasn't sure I wanted to be with her now; but Like Silk was quick, and before I could protest, she had my shirt unbuttoned and my short skirt high up around my waist. She was kissing me and backing me up onto the table at the same time, and I couldn't do anything to stop it. I didn't want to.

I closed my eyes and opened my legs so that she could stand between them, her mouth moving from my lips to my pebble-hard nipples. A slight gasp left my mouth when her soft tongue made contact with my already hot skin, and the handle of her whip parted my lower lips. The pearl handle felt cool against my clit as she rubbed it quickly in a side-to-side motion, causing me to cum almost immediately. Just when I thought I couldn't take it anymore, she slid the handle into me until it reached the back, and worked it slowly in and out of me.

If someone had told me a stripper would be freaking me this morning I wouldn't have believed them, but she moved with the same skill as she did on the stage, and I knew I would have to charge top dollar for her. I was losing my breath slowly, and what little air I had in my lungs rushed out when I felt her tongue touch my clit. She never moved the handle out, and her tongue worked me until I was practically screaming for her to let up. By the time she was done, my hair was plastered to my forehead, and my lipstick was gone.

"Make sure you get top dollar," she whispered into my ear right before she ushered me out of the room. I got all of her information from the owner, and once I got home I made sure to call Symphony with the news.

A few days went by before I heard from my client. She told me dinner was a smash, and she hadn't had a chance to call because they had been getting buck wild in his condo for the past couple of days. She was just now getting home. Those are the things I like to hear when I set a client up. A few of my clients went on to marry their dates, and a lot of those same married couples asked me to headhunt other couples that were in the swinging business.

Dr. Charles and Cynthia Montgomery was my reason for being up at six in the morning and rushing to catch a flight out to California. They were recommended to me from another couple that I helped out a few months ago, and her husband was the sole source behind this donkey that I'm toting around.

Anyway, they lived in a beautiful mini mansion in Bel Air, and in their line of business it wasn't that simple for them to approach a couple in the matter. A good friend of mine told me about a swing party that was going down in one of the mansions not too far from their house, and I wanted them to be there.

As mentioned, total discretion has to be in effect at all times because the people that I dealt with had lives to go back to once all of the sexing was over. So, I had to ensure that my sources were accurate, and that everything ran smoothly.

Once I exited the plane, there was a driver waiting outside for me. He was a nice, tall, handsome white guy with eyes the color of the ocean in Jamaica, and looked just as clean as the shiny cream stretch Rolls Royce that was parked behind him. The expression on his face must to have mirrored mine because I liked what I saw, and he looked as if he felt the same. He took my bags from the cart I had pushed through the airport and loaded them in the trunk of the town car.

"Make yourself comfortable, we have at least an hour's ride in this traffic before we arrive at the estate", he said in a deep baritone voice that, if I had closed my eyes, would have easily made me think the late great Barry White had spoken to me.

I didn't say anything; I just moved to the door he opened for me and melted into the butter-soft interior of the sweet-smelling car. Periodically I caught his eye watching me through the rearview mirror. After about the fifth time, I decided to give him a show. By now we were about forty-five minutes into the drive, and I would definitely make that last fifteen very entertaining.

Moving to the edge of the spacious seat, I pulled my flare skirt up and folded it across my stomach. I removed my thong panties so that my entire lower half was exposed. I started by sucking on my finger and using the moisture left on it from my mouth to rub across my clit. I smiled a wicked smile as I watched him try to drive the car straight and watch me at the same time.

Using my other hand to open my lips, I used my free hand to finger myself, moaning out loud and tossing my head from side to side. Spotting the bottle of Dom resting in the ice bucket, I first grabbed an ice cube, pushed it inside, and used my walls to push it back out repeatedly until the ice was gone. When I set up to grab the bottle out I saw that he had took the liberty of releasing his erection from the confines of his pants and was stroking his length with one hand while he controlled the wheel with the other.

I smiled at him, and leaned back again. The top of the bottle was smooth, and the bottle was a little heavy, but I worked it the best way I could. I first rubbed the smooth cap over my clit and down my slit until the top was at my opening. I began pushing the bottle in slowly, and the driver swerved to the right, almost banging into the car next to us. He quickly regained control of the vehicle, and I finished my show.

I moved the bottle in and out of me at a snail's pace, and I closed my eyes listening to his heavy breathing and picturing a real dick inside of me. We must have exploded at the same time, because I heard him moan loudly, and when I sat up I could see his cream covering the steering wheel and the front of his suit jacket. We were at the gates of the house by then, and from my positioning in the back I could see him wiping his mess up with a handkerchief. I rose up, and wiped my juices from the bottle and set it back in the ice bucket as if nothing had happened, afterwards straightening my clothes and primping in the mirror to make sure I looked good.

The good doctor and his wife greeted me with open arms, and after a brief tour of their estate I was shown to my suite, where I would be for the next couple of days. Later that night I would be escorting them to the swing party, and I needed my beauty rest because those parties always get wild.

By nine we were dressed and in the car, on our way to a night of pleasure. Dr. Montgomery cracked open the bottle of Dom as soon as we got in the car, and I smiled and glanced at the driver as I held my cup over for a drink. Mrs. Montgomery was a nervous wreck, but I assured her she would be fine, and to just relax and have a good time.

My connection met us at the door, and after a brief introduction we were escorted into the main foyer for the party. Now, most people expect to walk into a swing party and see people having sex all over the place, and everyone walking around naked. Don't get me wrong, though; in some establishments it is exactly that way. But normally when you have a private party it's a little more structured, and although by the end of the night it may be a wild encounter, you have time to warm up.

We walked in, me on one arm, his wife on the other. I greeted a few people that I recognized and peeped out a few men and women that would be great for my team. Most of the people came as couples, but there were a few singles floating around, such as myself. We mixed and mingled and were having a good time. When I saw the Montgomerys walk off to a room with another couple, that was my time to do some investigating.

I must say, I was still curious about the driver. I didn't immediately rush out to him, and I made a couple of connections while inside. Stuffing the business cards that I collected into my clutch, I snuck out of the front door discreetly and walked down the lit trail to the car.

The driver was watching a small television when I got up to the car. He didn't notice me until I got right up on the car and tapped on the window. He jumped a little and rolled down the window when he recognized my face.

"Hello, madam. Are you leaving the party so soon? We just got here under an hour ago."

"Actually," I said with a devilish grin lighting my face. "I came to see if we could finish what we started earlier. Maybe roll around the back near the garden where no one can see us."

He turned the television off quickly and was out of the car and in my face before I could change my mind. I didn't say anything; I just led him around the side of the mansion and toward the gazebo that I had spied from the balcony when I was in the house. This garden looked just like something out of a fairy tale, a lake with swans floating in it and everything.

I had opted to leave my panties at home because I knew I would try to get back with the driver before the night was over. We found a nice, heavily wooded area where we could see if someone was approaching, but they wouldn't see us until they got up close.

I stood taking in the beauty of the garden, and the driver dropped to his knees in the grass and put my leg up over his shoulder. He didn't waste any time connecting his tongue with my clit, and I held my gown up with one hand and his head with the other, keeping my balance. I had to stop him and pull the dress off so that I could lie down in the grass and enjoy the tongue bath I was receiving.

He fucked me with his tongue and fingers, and I was just about going crazy. I wanted him inside of me so bad. Before I could ask, he pulled a condom out of his pants pocket and slid it on. For a white boy he was beyond blessed, and soon after I was able to feel that blessing inside of my walls.

He dug in me deep, and it took all of the strength I had to be as quiet as possible so that we wouldn't get any attention from the house. He sat down in the grass and pulled me on top of him, and I rode him without mercy while I held onto him around his neck. He had it going on like that, and I was thoroughly satisfied with his skills.

We rushed and got dressed when we were done, and I snuck back into the house to check on the Montgomery couple I got in just in time to see them coming out of the room. Mrs. Montgomery's hair was tussled all over the place, and both wore satisfying smiles on their faces that mirrored the couple opposite of them. I took Mr. Montgomery's other arm, and we made our exit. We were home in no time.

I enjoyed the stay—and the driver—for the rest of the weekend, and was sad I had to leave when Monday came around. I didn't count the money they paid me until I was back on the plane, and they paid me more than triple what I charged them for the setup. When I moved the money envelope, to turn my phone off as the stewardess had instructed, the drivers card fell off it and in my lap. I smiled to myself and programmed his number into the phone before shutting it off. I would definitely be contacting him again.

Once I got home I was able to relax, but only for a couple of days. A surgeon that I had met in D.C. contacted me about a date for Saturday night, giving me only a day and a half to come up with someone. After taking his call, and finding out exactly what he was looking for, I went to pack a bag for D.C. As always, the job of a headhunter is never done.

Cater To You

Danielle Santiago

"Auntie, I don't want to ever in my life hear about how you suck Davie's dick. You done fucked up my whole mental," Ricky said with her tiny, cute, mocha-colored round face screwed up. She tried desperately to erase the image of her Aunt Miranda performing oral sex on her Uncle Davie.

"I'm just trying to tell your little ass what you need to know about keeping a nigga. It ain't all about staying in shape and keeping your hair and nails done. All that shit is a plus, but you gotta keep your man satisfied, if not . . ."

"What you mean, *if not*?"

"Ricky, what's the one thing Auntie told you on your wedding day when your mother was kicking all that sentimental shit?"

A smile crept across Ricky's face as she quoted her aunt's favorite line, "Never let your man leave the house hungry or horny—"

Cutting Ricky off, Miranda jumped in finishing the sentence, "'Cause another bitch will surely feed 'em and fuck 'em. Now have Ming Lee drop them kids off over here so you and Quentin can have some alone time."

"Auntie, our nanny's name is Anna, not Ming Lee *or* Sue Chin."

"Whatever her name is, have her drop them chaps off over here. You need to do like them little Destiny Child girls said, and spend some time catering to your man."

"Alright, Auntie. I'll have her bring them over. I'll be by to pick them up first thing in the morning."

"Let them stay until Sunday evening. Spend the entire weekend with your man. I don't want you to call me ever again crying because your husband says that you're not taking care of his needs."

"Bye, Auntie! Bye!"

"Bye, baby, love you."

"Love you, too." Tossing her Blackberry over onto the passenger seat, Ricky turned the stereo up blasting the sound of Faith Evans. Feeling what Faith was singing, she began singing along, "*Even though my money changed, I tried my best to stay the same. But you know with more money more problems came.*" Tears burned the outer corners of Ricky's eyes. begging to be released, all because Faith's lyrics were hitting so close to home. *It was all good before the money; I swear it was,* Ricky thought, mashing harder on the gas, pushing her brand new Benz truck faster down I-485. It was one of the luxuries that her career as a national bestselling author had afforded her. Buying that truck had been the highlight of her month. It was a beautiful mint green 2006 ML500. She'd walked right into the Mercedes dealer and paid cash for it two weeks earlier.

Now she felt like the same money that had allowed her to do such a wonderful thing was causing problems in her marriage. Before the money they were so happy. As she drove, Ricky reflected on their relationship before the seven- and eight-figure deals, before the expensive cars, before the beautiful house in the exclusive Ballantyne section of Charlotte. The sex that Quentin now felt deprived of use to be hot, heavy, and regular. Their heated conversation from earlier in the day played over and over in her head. "You don't even have time to give a nigga head no more." Quentin had said, lying in the bed, his erection poking through the top sheet as he watched her getting dressed.

"Not now, Quentin. I'm late for an important writer's conference."

"You're always in a rush to go somewhere when I wanna fuck."

"Well, I wouldn't be in a fuckin' rush if I hadn't overslept. And if you're wondering why I overslept, it's because I was up 'til three a.m. waiting for your ass to come home. And maybe had you come in at a reasonable hour you could have gotten some *ass*!"

"Yeah, right." Quentin laughed, rising up from the bed revealing his beautiful six-four nude body with skin the same color of the richest dark chocolate. His curly brownish-black hair wildly tousled upon his head from his sleep. He walked toward Ricky. She stood in their huge walk-in closet, which was the size of most people's bedroom. His large brown dick was rock hard and pointed right at her. "I sat in this fucking house until ten o'clock waiting for you. But I guess you forgot that we were supposed to go to the movies, 'cause you were too busy hanging with your author friends." Slipping on a pair of Carolina basketball shorts, he walked out of the closet and into their bathroom.

Ricky followed closely behind, getting right in his ear, "Hell no! Don't you even try to flip this shit on me? We both have careers that keep us away from home. But when we're both here at the same time, you always find time to run the damn streets with your niggas rather than spend quality time with me."

Standing over the toilet, Quentin sighed as he began to urinate, one hand on his hip, the other holding dick. Staring at the ceiling he responded, "Oh God, you back on your shit again."

"What the fuck does that suppose to mean?"

"You always on the go; then, when you stop you think that the whole damn world is supposed to stop for you. And let me not forget that it's always my fault."

"I *do not* think that. What I do think is that when our schedule does permit us to be in the same city at the same time, my husband should have the fuckin' common courtesy to spend time with his wife." Ricky turned to walk back into the bedroom, but stopped. Turning back to Quentin, she said, "By the way, when I'm running across the globe, I'm earning money and throwing bricks at a dream that I thought we were building together."

"That still don't have shit to do with me getting my dick taken care of. That's cool, though, 'cause ain't shit you can say when I get someone else to take of it."

He didn't go there . . . I know he did not just go there, Ricky thought before blowing up at him. "Go get you another bitch to take care of that dick. I hope she suck it better than I do. And I hope she can deal with all the bullshit baggage that comes with being in a relationship with you."

"What bullshit baggage?"

"All the shit I had to go through with you in the beginning. Where do you want me to begin? Let's see, I could start with your other bitch calling me all day and night. Or I could start with all those days you left me alone while you were on the come up. Yeah, what about all those days? You weren't worried about if I was satisfied sexually, were you? And I never once threatened to go out and get someone else. But what if . . . what if I told you I *did* have someone to satisfy me all those lonely nights and how he made me cum back to back?"

Suddenly Ricky found Quentin's hand wrapped around her neck and shoving her out of the bathroom and into the closet. She had gone too far and now was terrified of the outcome. Quentin had never laid a hand on her before. Still holding Ricky by her neck, he leaned over talking through clenched teeth, "What are you telling me, Raquel? Are you telling me that you was fucking another nigga behind my back?"

With her heart pounding like a small child jumping on her chest, Ricky answered, "I would never cheat on you. I just said what if so you'd know just how it feels to imagine your spouse fucking someone else. Now could you please remove your hand from my neck?"

Slowly Quentin removed his hand from her neck, then he slammed it against the wall right next to her head. Ricky slid down the wall with tears pouring from her eyes. She wrapped her arms around her knees pulling them close to her chest. In the fetal position, she pressed her face against her knees, smearing make-up all over her beige dress slacks. Quentin went back into the restroom, brushed his teeth, and washed his face. Stepping over Ricky, he threw on a T-shirt, sweat pants, and pair of sneakers. Without saying a word to Ricky, he left the house.

After thirty minutes of crying, Ricky finally got up off the floor. She was beyond late for the writer's workshop. Without a doubt she decided against going. Slipping out of her pant suit, Ricky put on a white *Lacoste* polo-style shirt and a pair of *Paper Denim* jeans. Without really knowing where she was going, she grabbed her large red *Hermes Birkin* bag off the dresser and headed for the door.

Strangely, when she got outside Quentin was still there. Sitting in his Black Hummer H2, he was smoking a *Newport* while talking on his cell phone. When he saw Ricky they locked eyes. Without trying to hide it his disgust for her spread across his face. Starting the ignition in his truck, he cut his eyes at her and sped away.

Tears of confusion escaped her eyes. What had went so wrong? Why now? When Ricky saw her reflection in the driver's side window, she was horrified by what she saw. Hers eyes were red and puffy. She quickly covered them with her *Dior* shades. Right then she knew exactly what she needed to get through her already turbulent day—the spa!

After a day of full body pampering, champagne, and a good old-fashioned heart-to-heart talk with Aunt Miranda. Sitting in her driveway, she was still confused as to why her marriage was suddenly falling apart. Her reflection of the day's events was interrupted by the ringing of her cell phone. Ricky's heart pounded a little faster when she saw that it was Quentin. Composing herself, she answered, "Yeah."

"That's how you greet me now?"

He can't be serious. "You think you deserve better?"

"I don't even wanna get into with you li'l mama. I called to apologize. I was way out of line for all that shit that happened this morning. I'm really sorry about putting my hands on you. You know that's not even me. That will *never* happen again."

Ricky sat silently with the phone pressed against her ear, thinking about her Aunt Miranda's advice.

"So you're not going to say anything?" Quentin questioned.

Knowing that she was guilty to some extent for the problems in their relationship, she answered, "I accept your apology…but let me also apologize for neglecting your needs and our relationship. And if you ever feel that I'm doing those things again could you come to me before it gets to the point that it got to this morning?"

"Of course. You know I love you, girl."

"I love you, too, sweetie. Why don't you come on home so I can show you just how much?"

"I'm at the Y. We getting ready to hoop; then, I'll be home. We still taking the kids to *Celebration Station*?"

"Nah, Aunt Miranda has them for the weekend."

"Alright, baby. Well, I'll see you in a couple of hours."

"Bye, Quentin." Ricky closed her phone. A *couple of hours is just what I need.* She decided to give in to her man's pleasures in a way that she hadn't in a long while. And taking heed to Miranda's advice, she decided that she would cater to him.

* * *

That night, when Quentin walked into the house, all the lights were out. Hundreds of candles of all sizes illuminated the huge home. Destiny's Child's *Cater to You* poured from the speakers that were hidden in the walls throughout the house. Smiling, Quentin wondered exactly what Ricky was up to. Quietly, he walked through the house looking for her. When he found her in the kitchen, his dick instantly stiffened. She was wearing an ultra-sexy grey maid's uniform, complete with the white apron. It was so short that the bottom of her round ass was peeking below the hem of her skirt. The four-inch black pumps that she wore on her feet elongated her five-foot-five frame, making her body look long and sensual. Her long red weave was slicked back and pinned in a neat little bun at the nape of her neck.

Stirring a pot of pasta, Ricky swayed side to side while singing along with the music, "*Let me cater to you, 'cause baby this is your day. Do anything for my man, baby, you blow me away. I got your slippers, your—*"

"Look at my princess," Quentin said, startling Ricky.

"Hi, sweetie. You scared me I didn't here you come in." She sashayed over to him. Wrapping her arms around him, she placed a nice wet kiss on his lips.

Tasting her lip, he could tell that she'd been drinking vodka. The sweet smell of her perfume made his erection grow. "You smell so good," he said fondling her breast.

Stepping back, Ricky told him, "And you smell so sweet. Come on, your bath is waiting."

"*My bath is waiting*? What is this all about? Don't get me wrong; I like it and all—"

Ricky placed her finger on his lips, quieting him. "Baby relax. Aren't you listening to the song? Tonight I just want to *cater* to you." She grabbed him by the hand and led him up the stairs.

Upstairs, in the master bathroom Ricky poured exotic bath salts and oils into the bubbling water while Quentin undressed. Ricky placed a fluffy towel, fresh out of the dryer, next to the oversized tub. She placed a neatly folded pair of his pajamas on the vanity.

The combination of the hot water and the jets relaxed Quentin's aching muscles as soon as his body slid into the tub. "Where're you going? You not getting in here with me?" he asked Ricky as she turned to leave the bathroom.

"I have to go down and finish your dinner. When you finish, come down and have a seat in the *formal* dining room."

Excited by the possibilities of what the night was to bring, Quentin didn't stay in the bath long. After fifteen minutes in the tub he got out, dried off, and slipped into the navy blue pajamas that Ricky had laid out for him. Once in the dining room Quentin sat in his usual seat at the head of the table.

Ricky walked in carrying a huge plate of Quentin's favorite dish, shrimp and lobster Alfredo. Leaning over to place his plate in front of him, she cleverly placed her cleavage right in his face. His dick became erect all over again. Taking advantage of the moment, he kissed the fleshy part of her right breast, which was exposed. He went a little further, licking her chest and palming her bare ass.

It was feeling so good that Ricky was finding it hard to resist, but it wasn't a part of her plan so she had to pull away. "Hmm. Not yet, baby."

"Why not?"

"I want you to enjoy your meal first. Now what would you like to drink with you meal."

"Bring me a *Hennessy,* li'l mama."

Ricky went over to the small bar area and returned to the table with a tall glass. "Here you go, sweetie, with two ice cubes just the way you like it. I'll be upstairs if you need anything else."

"You're not eating with me?"

"No, I'm not hungry for food right now." Ricky winked her eye while licking her lips. As she turned to walk away, Quentin gave her a smack on the ass and watched the wonderful jiggling effect. "Hmm you know I like it like that, *daddy*," Ricky said with a sexually charged laugh. "When you're finished eating, meet me in the bonus room."

Quentin's eyes were fixated on her ass until she was out of sight.

Filled with so much anticipation Quentin only ate half the food on his plate. After tossing back his drink he stood up, ready to see what his wife had in store for him. Trying his best to stay smooth and composed, he walked up the stairs slowly. When he got to the bonus room at the end of the hall the door was cracked. Quentin peered in and smiled at what he saw.

Ricky had changed into a pink see-through, lace, micro-mini dress from *Victoria's Secret*. She'd unpinned her hair and her long red tresses hung down to the middle of her back. In the center of the room Ricky had created a canopy with sheer curtains that hung from the ceiling. The bed was surrounded with multiple rows of candles. "Come on in, Q. I know you're standing out there." Ricky smiled as she lit the last candle. She was really ready for him; the three chocolate martinis she'd drunk had her feeling super horny.

When Ricky looked up, Quentin was still standing in the doorway. She walked over, grabbed his hand. "Why you still standing there?"

"Just watching you." He replied, unable to take his eyes off her. He was still amazed at how good Ricky's body still looked after having had three kids. Looking into her eyes, Quentin stroked the right side of her face with the palm of his hand. "I love you."

Ricky removed his hand from her face and kissed his palm. "I love you too, baby. Enough of the mushy shit." Ricky smirked, leading him over to the foot of the bed. Slowly she began to undress Quentin. First she removed his shirt and planted wet kisses all over his chest. Next Ricky slid his pajama pants down and got on her knees. Seductively she kissed her husband's ankles and licked his calves, working her way up to his thighs where she sucked hard enough to leave a hicky. With the tip of her tongue, Ricky began teasing Quentin's balls which was driving him crazy. The sensation of her tongue made him moan softly.

Ricky gently sucked on his balls one at a time, popping them in and out her mouth, sending waves of pleasure through Quentin's body. She licked his shaft vigorously before wrapping her warm, moist mouth around the head of his dick. Ricky moved her head up and down at a smooth pace, tightening her jaws with each stroke.

"Oh shit! Ricky, damn, baby." Quentin moaned loudly as Ricky deep-throated his large dick. With a little force she pushed her hands against his waist, easing his body back onto the bed, while she continued to suck him off. Bobbing her head up and down, she licked the head of his dick.

Ricky brought him right to the point of ecstasy then abruptly stopped pulling her mouth off of his dick.

Quentin looked at her, perplexed. "Why you stop?"

"Maybe 'cause I want to cum when you cum." Ricky stood up and turned around so that her ample ass was right in his face. She pulled her dress over her head leaving on her thong and heels. Teasingly she squatted and grinded her soft, plump ass on his lap.

Quentin began stroking his dick with his right hand and massaging Ricky's breasts with his left.

Ricky slid her thong to the side and grabbed Quentin's dick. She held it steady as she spread her legs a little wider and inserted his manhood inside of her. "Hmm," she moaned as she began riding him backwards. "Like that daddy?" Ricky panted over her shoulder.

"You know I love it," Quentin replied, now massaging her breasts with both hands and placing soft kisses all over her back. Their moans became louder as Ricky picked up the pace, gyrating her pelvis wildly as she went up and down on his shaft.

Quentin held her by the waist to control her movement. "Slow down, baby; stop rushing."

"I can't," Ricky moaned, "I'm cumin'." Only seconds later her rich, warm, creamy liquid gushed out drenching his thighs. Ricky sat still for a few seconds trying to control her legs, which were shaking from her orgasm.

Quentin gently stroked her hair, removing it from her face. "You okay?"

"Yes. I just needed a moment," Ricky replied as she slowly lifted her body, sliding off his rock-hard dick. She took off what little she was wearing. Now, completely nude, she turned to Quentin. "Slide up, honey."

Quentin wasted no time placing himself in the middle of the king-sized bed. She got onto the bed and crawled towards him lustfully. Her movements only matched by those of a panther on the prowl. Once she reached him she mounted him with her thick, cappuccino-colored thighs and got right back into position, placing him right back inside of her. Ricky kissed and sucked his neck as she moved her wide hips back forth, stroking his cock at a nice smooth pace. "You been missing this, daddy?"

"*Have I*?" Quentin said, his voice dripping with sarcasm.

With actual feelings of guilt coming over her, Ricky began to cry. "Please say you forgive me?"

Holding her tightly by the waist he began thrusting upwards' sending waves of pleasure through her body. "I already forgave you, sweetheart."

Ricky pressed her body closer to Quentin's and held onto his shoulder slightly as she began to ride him forcefully. She began to moan louder as her inner walls moistened even more with each stroke.

Quentin hugged her tighter as the pleasure he was feeling heightened. "Ooh shit."

"Like that?"

"Yes, baby girl . . . don't stop." Quentin slightly jerked as he began to climax. He held Ricky tightly so that she couldn't move. Ricky could feel the cum as it moved through his shaft, giving her a wonderful sensation that sent her squirting all over again.

Ricky continued to lie on top of Quentin, her ear on his chest, listening to the rhythm of his heart. She lifted her head and looked into Quentin's eyes. "Man, I love you."

Quentin kissed Ricky on the nose. "And I love you back, baby."

Ricky rolled off of Quentin and on to her side.

He turned to face her. "That was beautiful, Ricky."

"It was definitely all that, baby." Ricky threw her leg over Quentin's thigh. "I'm ready for round two right now."

"Girl, I done told you I'm not twenty-six anymore; now stop being fast. Slide a little closer and let daddy hold you."

Ricky smiled and did as she was told, snuggling her butt right into his midsection; as always, it was a perfect fit.

Quentin ran the tip of his tongue up the back of her neck softly. "Ricky."

"Yes, baby," she answered with her eyes closed, enjoying the feeling on her neck tremendously.

"Was any truth to that shit you said this morning?"

"What shit, honey?"

"About fucking another nigga when I couldn't be there for you back in the day."

"No, Quentin, there was no truth to any of that. I just said that to piss you off' cause your little slick-mouth comment 'bout getting someone else to take care of your dick hurt me."

"I hate I said that. I'm sorry." He gave her a little squeeze. "So, since we've been together, way before we got married, you've never been with another man?"

Slightly irritated, Ricky looked over her shoulder. "Quentin, like I've told you before, I've never cheated on you. Not while we were dating, not while we were engaged, and I'm definitely not going to forsake my vows."

"I'm glad. Man, the thought of another man just touching you—"

"Why don't you just focus on *you* touching me, and stop worrying about what has never and will never happen." Ricky turned to face him. Before he could say another word she slipped her tongue into his mouth, wrapped her small hand around his shaft and began stroking him until he was fully erect.

"Hmm, turn over, girl."

Ricky turned over on her side.

"Not like that. Lay on your stomach; put that ass in the air," he demanded.

Ricky loved it when he took charge. "Like this?" She asked looking back at Quentin with her chest flat to the mattress and plump ass high in the air.

"No, like this," He pulled her up by the shoulders, pinning her body against the headboard, and entered her. Quentin began pumping her at a nice rhythmic pace, almost like a slow wind. Although it felt very good, Ricky wanted it a little rougher. Ricky gripped the headboard tightly and poked her booty out firmly. "Ooh," she moaned. "Fuck me, baby. Fuck me hard."

Quentin picked up his pace and began thrusting his dick into her. "That's how you want it?"

"Yes, baby, yes. Fuck me just like that."

He gripped her hips tighter and continued giving it to her roughly. "I love you, Ricky." he said, biting down on her neck, sucking hard.

"Ohhhh, baby!" she cried out in pleasure as her juices came down and coated his dick.

The extreme warm wetness and the contracting of Ricky's pussy muscles made it hard for Quentin to fight the oncoming nut. Each stroke became faster and faster. "Ah, ah, ah, shit. *Ahhhh*." He screamed as he exploded inside his wife. "I love you, oh Ricky, I love you . . . hmm."

"I love you, too, baby."

After a few more rounds of mind-blowing sex, and more intimate yet humorous pillow talk, Ricky fell into a coma-like sleep wrapped in her husband's arms, something she hadn't done in months.

* * *

The following morning, Ricky awoke to find herself alone in the bed. All of the candles from the night before had been cleaned up. Ricky looked over at the clock and was shocked to find out that it was past noon. *Damn, I must've been worn out.* Ricky sat up and stretched, wondering, *How did Quentin clean all them damn candles without waking me*? With the kids away, the house was unusually quiet for a Saturday afternoon. "Quentin," Ricky called out.

"Yo, Q, what are you doing?"

When he didn't respond for a second time, Ricky got up from the bed. She checked each room upstairs looking for him. *Where is this nigga at?* Ricky grabbed her black silk robe and covered her nude body just in case Quentin was downstairs with company. All of the candles she had had out in the foyer and on the staircase were gone. The entire house was clean, and there was no sign of Quentin.

A note on the refrigerator door caught Ricky's attention as she entered the kitchen. She walked over and removed the angel figurine magnet that was pinning the note to the door. Ricky unfolded the note, a smile spread across her face as she read her husband's handwriting.

Hey Princess,

Didn't want to wake you. I knew you had to be tired after all your hard work last night. I really enjoyed myself. Thanks for catering to me. Everything was beautiful. Tonight I want you to relax and let me take care of you. Meet me in the secret garden at eight. Wear that little white dress that I like. I'm going to workout and run a few errands. Oh yeah, call Aunt Miranda. See you tonight, Q.

Ricky pulled up to her aunt's brick home and tapped the horn lightly. In a matter seconds Miranda came out of the house. Ricky silently admired her as she walked toward the car doing her signature strut. Miranda's lovely, tanned brown skin glowed in the afternoon sun. Her shoulder-length bob was neatly braided to the back. The powder blue cardigan set and jeans from the *Banana Republic* fit her medium size frame perfectly. She properly accessorized her outfit with a pair of ultra-soft navy blue Italian leather loafers and a navy blue leather coach bag. At forty-six, Miranda's body gave most women half her age a run for their money.

"Hey, baby girl," Miranda said, getting into the car.

Ricky leaned over and kissed Miranda on her cheek. "Hi, Auntie. Where did Uncle Davie take the kids?"

"Li'l Davie came over with his kids and they all went to Concord Mills to play at Jeepers and that NASCAR place." Miranda fastened her seatbelt then looked over at Ricky. "Tell me all about last night, and don't leave anything out."

"Now, you know I'm not giving you any graphic details. But I did take your advice and spent some time catering to my man."

"*Girl,* shut up! What did you do?"

Blushing, Ricky gave Miranda only the basics of the previous night's events. Miranda couldn't believe that Ricky had done all that based on her simple suggestion. "Girl, I just meant for you to go home and give your man some *good lovin',* but I see you went all out. I ain't mad at ya, either. *Shit,* I need you to bring me that maid uniform so I can cater to Davie."

"Quit playin', Auntie."

"I'm serious, girl. I'm already giving head night and day and spreading my legs whenever your uncle asks. You know our twenty-fifth wedding anniversary is this month, and I saw the meanest seven-carat tennis bracelet."

"Auntie, what you gonna do with all that ice?"

"Shine on all these old hoes."

"Twenty-five years . . . Auntie, that's a beautiful thing. I pray that Quentin and I can keep it together that long."

"And you will. You just have to take care of him at all times. Not just every now and then when it's convenient for you."

Ricky simply nodded in agreement as Miranda's words sank in.

Miranda continued on, "Trust me, Auntie knows how easy it is to give when you *want* to give. Try giving when you're too tired or when it feels impossible because you're having problems. You'll see how good it feels and how much more you're appreciated."

"I hear that, Auntie. You stay kicking that real shit."

Miranda smiled at her niece. "I know, that's why you love me. Now, turn that up that's my song."

Ricky raised the volume on the stereo as Miranda sang along with Keyshia Cole.

"There's this girl I know; she's so deep in love." Snapping her fingers, Miranda moved her head to the beat.

Watching Miranda out of the corner of her eye Ricky, smiled thinking, *I swear I want to look that good and be that cool once I'm in my forties.*

After four hours of gossip and beautification, Ricky and Miranda emerged from the salon more lovely than when they entered. Ricky dropped Miranda off at her house and drove away quickly before her kids caught sight of her. With six-thirty fastly approaching, Ricky shot over to South Park Mall to grab a special thong for the evening. By the time she arrived at home it was ten past seven. Quentin's truck was in the garage but there was no sign of him inside the house. Ricky didn't waste anytime searching for him. She took a ten-minute shower, which was quick considering she usually spent twenty to thirty minutes showering.

No wonder he loves this dress, Ricky thought, looking at her rear end in the mirror. The dress was so bright white, it was damn near virginal but the cut was definitely not. Ricky's body had made a few grown men drool, and some young boys blush in that very dress, when she had worn it to her book release party earlier that summer. The loose wide sleeves hung slightly off Ricky's shoulders. It was cut low in the front, stopping right above Ricky's navel; and the bottom of the dress clung to her frame, stopping right before her knees.

Quentin sat back and watched Ricky as she entered the garden. To him, she looked like perfection. He saw her face light up as she took in the beautiful scene that he'd created. On the grass, in the very center of the garden, lay a white chenille blanket surrounded by thousands of multicolored rose petals. A huge picnic basket sat off to the side. The sounds of John Legend filled the garden.

Ricky smiled so hard a giggle slipped out. She already loved her garden, but she knew after today she would love it more. It was actually her rose garden. It had been dubbed the *secret garden* because of the four ten-foot walls of white, yellow, pink, red, purple, and black roses. This was where Ricky escaped to when she wanted to get away from the pressures of her world. She had penned several of her novels in that garden. For her it was three hundred square feet of pure tranquility.

Quietly Quentin snuck up behind Ricky, grabbed her, and kissed the back of her neck.

Slightly startled she turned to face him. "Boy you scared me. Where did you come from?"

"Who else would be kissing your neck like this?" Quentin said, kissing her neck again.

"Only you, baby." Ricky's body shuttered as it always did whenever he placed his mouth on her neck.

"You like that, ma?"

"You know I do, daddy."

Quentin took her by the hand and led her over to the blanket. Ricky took a seat while Quentin got the picnic basket. She looked him up and down. *Look at him, with his cute self.* He had on a bright white wife beater, white shorts, and white Gucci sneakers. His goatee was lined up perfectly. The edges of his hair had been shaped up just right. Ricky's panties were getting moist just looking at him.

Quentin caught her gaze. "Why you looking at me like that?"

"You're so sexy, baby."

"I know."

"I hate you." Ricky laughed.

"It's impossible to hate somethin' this pretty." Quentin placed a plate of lobster tails, steamed asparagus, and fresh salad in front of her.

"Where did you get this food from?"

"What are you talking 'bout?" Quentin said with a you-got-me smile.

"Don't even front like you cooked this."

"Hush, girl, and take this." He handed her a goblet of her favorite wine, White Zinfandel.

As Ricky began to dig into her food, she noticed that Quentin didn't prepare a plate for himself. She eyed him as he seemingly enjoyed an ice-cold bottle of Evian in his hand. "You're not eating?"

"I'm not hungry."

"Since when do you pass up a good lobster dinner?"

"I'm straight, baby, you enjoy yourself."

Deciding to let it go, Ricky continued eating. Quentin watched his wife as she used her tongue to remove drops of butter from the tips her fingers. *Not yet. Not yet*, he told his dick as he felt his growing erection.

Ricky looked up at him. "Why are you staring at me like that?"

"You love me?"

"Do I love you? You trippin' asking me that."

Quentin reached over and began rubbing her face. "You are so beautiful sweetie. I haven't looked at you like this in a long time."

There was something in Quentin's voice, and the way he continuously stroked Ricky's face very softly, that made her curious. She looked closely at Quentin's eyes, which were jumping, and his pupils which were dilated. "Q, are you rolling?"

A sly smile crept across his face. "Huh?"

"Huh my ass. You heard me, nigga. You popped an X pill. You thought you could hide it from me. No wonder you didn't want anything to eat. You are so slick. Let me get one."

"Oh no. Uh-uhn, hell no!"

"That's so foul, yo. How you gonna be on one and tell me I can't take one."

"A'ight." Quentin gave in without much of a fuss; he really wanted her to pop a pill too.

"What kind do you have?"

"What kind do you want?" Quentin asked, pulling a small bag filled with colorful pills from pocket. "I've got green Louis Vuittons, pink hearts, or blue supermans."

"Which one got you rolling like that?"

"The Louis Vuitton."

"Well, that's the one I want." Ricky covered her food, placed it back in the basket, and slid it away. Quentin handed her the little pill and his water. She stared at it in the palm of her hand, still amazed at how something so tiny could make you feel so good. It had been a little over two years since her last encounter with an ecstasy pill. Quentin forbade her from taking them after she was hospitalized due to a serious case of dehydration. He felt that her illness was induced by the pills she popped while they'd been partying nonstop in Miami one weekend.

"You gon' pop that or make love to it with your eyes?"

"Shut up. I got this." Ricky threw her head back, tossed the pill in her mouth, and guzzled down the bottle of water. "Is you happy?" She laughed, doing her best T. I. imitation.

"I'll be real happy if you come lay right here." Quentin motioned for her to lie across his lap. Fulfilling his wish, Ricky stretched out, lying the back of her head in the center of his lap. Quentin looked down into her eyes. With his finger he traced the outline of her face. "Ricky, I'm falling in love with you all over again, sweetheart."

"Don't start with the X talk, Quentin," Ricky said, knowing very well how X had the tendency to make people run their mouths, although the majority of the time it helped people to express their true feelings easily.

"Nah, this real talk. You're still my best friend and will always be. I know I haven't told you in a while, but I'm so proud of you."

"For what?"

"You are a *great* mother, the perfect wife for me, and your career is through the roof."

"That's so sweet, honey." Ricky stretched as she began to feel the ecstasy take over her body. It was such a euphoric feeling. She looked her husband in the eye. "Quentin, I remember when all of this was a dream. Everything that I've become and every goal that I've reached I couldn't have done without you by my side. Being with you has always made me wanna be a better woman for you and the kids. God blessed me so . . . when he sent me you."

Quentin smiled at her. "Now whose doing the X talk?"

"Whatever! I love you, Quentin."

"I Love *you,* Ricky." He leaned down and engaged her in a passionate kiss.

Ricky broke the kiss when the intro to Beyonce's *Naughty Girl* came on. She stood to her feet and began winding her waist in front of her husband and singing "I'm feeling sexy, I wanna hear you call my name."

Watching her move around in the little dress had his dick at full attention, and she knew it. The ecstasy had her feeling so sexy and extra pretty. Her movements were borderline perfect. Quentin enjoyed the show thoroughly. He sat back and told her, "Take that dress off."

Ricky turned her back to Quentin, and he unzipped the back of the dress, letting it drop to her feet revealing her pearl thong. Seeing the string of pearls in her ass had his dick throbbing. "Whew! Where you get that thong from?"

"Vicki's," she answered, standing completely still while shaking her ass like a professional stripper, only inches from his face.

"I want you to give me a real show."

She turned around to face him, her hands on her hips. "What do you mean *a real show*?"

Reaching down into the picnic basket, Quentin pulled Ricky's rabbit vibrator.

She began laughing. "I see you had this planned all along." Taking the rabbit from his hand, she sat across from him and opened her legs wide, giving him a full view. "Tell me what you want to see," her voice dripped with seduction.

"Slide your thong over."

Ricky pushed the string of pearls over, revealing her ripe clitoris. She slid two of her fingers in her mouth and used them to add some extra moisture to her clit. "What else, baby?"

"You know what I like . . . let me watch you please yourself."

Ricky turned on her favorite sex toy and went to work parting her swollen vaginal lips with two fingers. She rubbed the vibrating rabbit ears back and forth against her clit. The vibration sent waves of pleasures through her entire body. She tried looking at her husband to see if he was enjoying her performance, but she was unable to, because she couldn't keep her eyes from rolling behind her head from the pleasure. Her body suddenly tensed up, jerking back and forth as she became tingly all over. She moaned loudly as the liquefied cream shot straight out of her pussy and onto the blanket.

That did it. Quentin could no longer contain himself. He crawled onto his wife, pushed her knees back to her shoulder, and pushed his hard member inside of her. He just let it sit inside of her.

Ricky looked up at him still panting from her strong orgasm. "What you doing? Why you not moving?"

"You gotta tell me you want this dick," he said, giving her a little pump.

"You know I want it."

Giving her two small forceful pumps he told her, "Then, tell me you want *this dick*."

"I want your dick, only yours, baby."

Quentin rolled his hips back forth, driving himself farther into her. The ecstasy had both of them extra sensitive, so each stroke was magnified intensely.

Ricky screamed his name out passionately as he moved in and out of her. "Ooh, baby, Quentin, baby, I love you so much."

"What else you love?"

"I love this dick, baby. I love the way you give it to me daddy."

"Hmm, I love this pussy. You acting like you don't want to give it to me, though."

"Let me get this right. You want me to really give it to you?" Ricky asked as she began throwing it at him hard, bucking her hips up and down wildly.

"Oh Ricky, damn, Ricky." Quentin kissed her wildly, biting down on her bottom lip and sucking it as they both began to climax. His body shook and jerked uncontrollably as he released himself into her. Doing her usual trick, she flexed her inner muscles around his dick, squeezing every drop out of him.

Quentin shook his head from side to side, "Whew girl, I think we might've just made our fourth baby."

"I hope not." Ricky rolled her eyes.

"Why? I thought we both wanted five."

"I meant, not right now." Ricky wrapped her arms around his neck and smiled.

"Only because I want to have plenty more nights like this in the weeks and months to come."

Knowing that it was her treat for him the night before, which had set everything in motion Quentin looked her directly in the eye and said, "Thank you, Ricky."

"For what, baby?"

"Catering to me."

Her smile became even brighter as ran her fingers through his hair and jokingly sang, "I catered to my man; now he caters to me!"

Purpose Pussy

Thomas Long

Even though it was the middle of the day, the mood was set just right for some freaky shit to go down. Delicia had the sweet mandarin-flavored scent of satsuma oil emanating throughout her apartment thanks to her oil burner. The curtains were closed shut to prevent any sunlight from entering the room. The light that came from the candles, which were strategically positioned throughout the house, was all the light needed for what she had on the agenda today. She had taken the day off from work for this special event. She had a perfectly chilled bottle of Möet waiting in an ice bucket on her coffee table in front of her plush cream-colored sofa. She programmed the CD changer to play all of Jamie Foxx's slow jams. Every song she selected was raunchy and guaranteed to get her partner in the mood for some headboard-bangin', booty-smackin', nonstop sex.

Delicia had on sexy red silk lingerie that screamed *"Come sex me right now!"* to any man that would have walked into the room with her at that moment. It hugged every curve of her voluptuous body. It was kind of a waste for her to wear it because once her special guest saw her in it, she was sure that he would be so overwhelmed by her beauty that he wouldn't hesitate to rip it off of her. She lay back on the couch and awaited her guest's arrival. She watched *Jason's Lyric* for the umpteenth time. She was at the part in the movie where Jada Pinkett and Allen Payne made love on a blanket spread out in the grass. Every time she saw that scene in the movie it got her juices flowing. She loved herself some Allen Payne ever since she saw him play G Money in *New Jack City*. She had fantasized many a nights about running her fingers through his curly hair while he was inside of her.

As she watched the movie, her hands made their way down to her sweet spot. She slid her thong to the side and teased her clitoris until it throbbed with the sexual anticipation of a man's hardness up against it. She spread her legs wide across the couch and inserted her fingers into her vagina to feel the moisture that had begun to flow. Her nipples were ripe for sucking. She took one of them into her mouth and pleased it with her tongue. Her sexual odyssey was interrupted when she heard a knock at her front door. She fixed her clothes and got up to answer the door. She turned off the television and turned on the stereo. When she opened the door, her eyes were pleasantly surprised. Her special guest wasn't Allen Payne, but he was fine enough to do her just right.

"Come on in," Delicia said. She opened the door all the way for her guest to enter her apartment. His name was James. He came into her apartment and was frozen dead in his tracks when he got a full view of her in her lingerie. He tried to play it cool, but his sinful thoughts showed all over his face.

"Very nice." James said in his smooth baritone voice. As they walked over to the couch, he couldn't take his eyes off her ass when she walked in front of him. She had an ass like Buffy the Body with a small waist and wide hips. *Damn, I'm a lucky man! I'm glad I took that 50 mg Viagra before I came over here. I'm gonna need it to handle all of this ass!* he thought.

"Do you want something to drink? I have some champagne if you're thirsty," Delicia said. She sat down on the couch and crossed her satiny smooth legs slowly and seductively.

James joined her on the couch. "Yeah, I'll have a glass," James replied. Her breasts peeked through her ensemble and made his mouth water. He took a sip of champagne to cool off.

"Let's make a toast. I wanna toast to new friendships," Delicia said.

"To new friends," James said. They tapped their glasses and devoured the champagne.

"I'm glad you stopped being scared and decided to finally take me up on my offer," Delicia said as she sipped on her third glass of champagne. She was feeling the effects of the alcohol.

"Well, I have to admit that you made it hard for me to resist," James said as he poured himself another glass of Möet. He also felt a little buzz from the champagne.

"Are you talking about little innocent ole' me? I didn't do anything but just be myself," Delicia said playfully. She seductively ran her fingers through her shoulder-length hair.

"Being you is more than enough for any man. Can I use your restroom?" James asked.

"It's right over there behind you. The light is on the left-hand side when you open the door. Don't get lost in there," Delicia said jokingly. She watched James from behind as he walked to the bathroom. *Yeah, I'ma turn this nigga out. When I'm done, he's gonna be fiendin' for this kitty kat! I got something for his ass. He just doesn't know what he done got himself into fucking with me. A bitch got major plans for him,* she thought.

James Blackmon was a young, successful brother with good looks and money in the bank. He had a medium brown complexion with thick eyebrows and a thin goatee. He wore his hair closely cut with a tight, bald fade. He was six feet tall with bulging biceps and triceps. He was always mistaken for an NFL football player due to his athletic build. He used to be a high school football star at the Baltimore Polytechnic Institute. He played the running back position and ran the forty-yard dash in 4.4 seconds flat. He led the city in rushing yards his junior and senior years. He had hundreds of athletic scholarships thrown his way in his senior year, but they all dried up once he blew his knee out in the final game of the season. With his football career over, he decided to focus on his academic pursuits.

James was graduated from the University of Baltimore School of Law at the top of his class. He managed to get a job working for the biggest law firm in town, Snyder, Lebowitz, and McMillan. They started him out with a low, six-figure salary. He drove a lightning-fast red convertible Corvette and lived in a plush estate in the Owings Mills New Town section of West Baltimore County with his wife, Arnell, and their two children. It appeared as though he had the ideal suburban family life and everything that a man could want. However, a man would always be a man—no matter how good a woman he had at home.

His wife was beautiful, but she couldn't satisfy his insatiable sexual appetite. That was why he was trying to get his freak on with a hood rat like Delicia at the moment.

James and Delicia had met at the law firm where they both worked. She was a temporary secretary hired to fill in for his full-time secretary, who was out on maternity leave. Once she saw how handsome her new boss was, Delicia had it set in her mind that she would take full advantage of this temporary job and make it into a full-time opportunity to get ahead. She did everything in her power to entice James from the first day she started work. She wore form-fitting skirts that showed off her best asset—her pear-shaped ass. She always made sure she had on a blouse that displayed her 36 C cup breasts. She rarely wore a bra and loved to stand in front of James showing off her deep dark chocolate nipples that were always rock hard. She would bend over in front of him in his office and act as though she'd accidentally dropped something so that he could get a nice view of her very spankable rear end. She knew that the attraction was mutual by the way he flirted back with her. When Delicia found out that he was married, it only increased her attraction to her new boss. The fact that he was another woman's man made her panties wet and got her competitive juices flowing. It took about two months of their flirting back before it led up to today's visit at her place.

When James returned to the living room, he wasn't prepared for what was before his eyes. Delicia was stretched out across the couch butt naked. Her legs were spread wide open in an inviting manner. Her clean-shaven private area looked tasty. She spread her pussy lips so that he could get a better view. James's heart began to race from excitement. He felt a bulge growing in his jeans. She took her finger and motioned for him to come join her. He walked towards her. He towered over her and admired her flexibility.

"Damn, you don't waste any time, do you? I like a woman that knows what she wants," James said. He grabbed the bulge in his pants and rubbed it.

"Well, I like a man that knows how to give me what I want. Bring them sexy lips over here and make me feel good," Delicia requested sexily. Delicia's enchanting hazel eyes grew wide when she saw the huge print in his jeans. His dick begged to be set free from its denim cage. She grabbed a hold of his front pocket and pulled him down towards her.

James got down between her legs and passionately kissed the insides of her thighs. He blew on the wetness that his tongue left behind. The cool air up against her skin made Delicia's stomach quiver. James slowly ran his lips and tongue up and down her hairy legs. He worked his way down to her feet and sucked on her toes one at a time. The sweet sensation made Delicia's whole body tingle. When he was done, he spread her legs apart and dove headfirst into the poonani His tongue made circles around her pussy lips. He kissed them intensely before he took her clit into his mouth. He sucked on her clit and licked it at the same time without stopping to take a breath. He took two fingers and inserted them inside of her. He worked them around with care and precision. He could tell that she was enjoying it by the way her body responded.

After thirty minutes of cunnilingus and finger-fucking her, he felt fluid erupt from Delicia's opening.

"That's right, make that cum flow, baby. You got a sick head game, nigga!" Delicia said as she held his head between her thighs. Her grip was so tight that she damn near snapped his neck. Her juices were all over his face.

"I aim to please," James said coolly. He smiled because he knew he did his job well. He took his hand and wiped her wetness from his face.

"I ain't mad at that, boo. We need to take this thing in the other room. You won round one, but I got a trick for that ass," Delicia promised. She got up off the couch and led him into her bedroom. When they entered the bedroom, she pushed James down onto her king-size bed and stood over him. She admired his muscular body. Her imagination ran wild with images of what she was about to do with this sexy black man in front of her.

"I love a woman that knows how to take charge. My wife always wants me to initiate things when we have sex," James said.

"Well, you ain't with ya wife, sweetie. You're with a woman that knows how to please a man. Now shut up and let me do what I do," Delicia commanded.

"It's your world, baby. I'm at your mercy," James said submissively.

Delicia took her tongue and ran it across his chest. The scent of his Armani Black Code cologne enticed her nostrils and increased her desire for him. She worked her way down toward his midsection and kissed his finely shaped six-pack. She clutched his penis and proceeded to bring James oral pleasure. James watched as his dick melted in her mouth and was aroused by the movements of her hand. Delicia was a bonafide head doctor. She knew what she was doing.

"Damn, baby. Your head game is right on the money, too. Work them lips, mommy!" James shouted in sheer delight. Delicia went at it even harder until her jaws got sore. She felt him about to cum and stopped.

"I wanna ride this big pole," Delicia said. She reached over and pulled a condom off her nightstand and opened the package. She took the Magnum condom out of the wrapper and slid it on his dick with her mouth. Once it was secured, she mounted his dick slowly.

"Work that dick, baby!" James yelled. They went at it like two wild animals. Delicia had that bombin', comeback pussy because once you got it, a nigga would be beggin' for a shot to come back and get some more.

"That's right, nigga; tell Mommy how good this pussy is to you. Whose dick is this?" Delicia asked James as she straddled his erect penis. She dug her fingernails into his chest lightly. She clawed at his chest playfully like a kitten.

"It's your dick, baby. This pussy is the truth. It's everything you said it was gonna be. Don't stop. Oooh, yeah, keep riding that dick, bitch!" James exclaimed.

Delicia obliged him by picking up the pace of her hip movements. She twirked that thing on him like it was nobody's business. James's rock-hard member held its own inside her garden of lust. He kept up with her every movement without missing a stroke. He lifted her ass up in the air as he pumped his hips toward and away from her. Her abdominal muscles tensed up. Cum oozed down her leg. Her toes curled up into a ball. *This nigga, James, is no joke!* she thought.

Delicia put the palms of her hands up against the wall to keep her balance as she grinded on top of him fiercely. She tightened up the muscles in her pussy walls. The friction made the head of his penis eager to release the fluid it contained. However, James wasn't going out like a five-minute brother. He did what any seasoned playa would do in this situation: He thought about something other than the good pussy he was all up in, something to prolong his erection. The fact that he was almost about to bust off didn't go unnoticed by Delicia. She could tell by how tightly he held his eyes closed and gritted his teeth every time she gyrated her hips. She knew that the slippery juices that flowed down her love canal were too much for most men to handle when she released them. Her pussy was like a spider's web: Once you got caught up in it, it was hard to get back out of the trap. James was at her mercy. She went in for the kill.

"I got your ass right where I want you. I've wanted your fine ass from the first time I saw you, but I had to make you wait to get some of this good lovin'. I told you to be careful what you wished for because once I put it on you, I was gonna make you my love slave," Delicia bragged. She wiggled that ass to the left and then to the right. She grinded on his dick so fast, you could hear her butt cheeks clap together. As good as she was with her sex game, James wasn't a slouch in the bed, either. She forced him to bring out his A game. He could talk just as much shit as she could—and back it up with his wicked long stroke.

"I can handle that phat ass, baby. You're talking loud but ain't saying nothing. Yeah, this pussy is the bomb, but I got something for that ass that will make you beg for mercy," James said just as cockily. Before she knew what was going on, James flipped her over on her side without taking his dick out the pussy. He put his dick into power-drive mode as he worked her vagina like a construction worker with a jack hammer. He looked her dead in her eyes to send her the mental message that he was serious with his shit. He took his hand and wiped the sweat from his brow. They both were drenched in each other's perspiration.

"Ooh, yeah, now that's what I'm talking about! I like a nigga that knows how to beat the pussy up. Make me sweat, baby. I love to see a man work hard for what he wants. Aaw, shit! Now you're hittin' my spot! Ohh, James, make Mommy cum all over that love stick!" Delicia screamed. Her back was covered with sweat and her hairdo was ruined. She didn't care. Gettin' some good dick and already having five orgasms was worth another trip to the hair salon. They went at it in the same position for about fifteen minutes before James got tired. He pulled his penis out her and lay back on the pillow to take a break for five minutes.

"What's wrong? You can't hang with a pro? I was just getting started with you," Delicia said.

"Nah, I'm straight. I just had to catch my breath. I wanna hit that ass from the back, baby. I wanna see it jiggle," he replied, half out of breath. He held his penis in his hand and stroked it back up to full attention.

"You can have it however you want it, baby. You know that's my shit right there!" Delicia said as she rose up on the bed and hoisted her ass up in the air. She shook her ass in such a sexy manner that you knew she had to have been a stripper in a past life. James got excited watching her do her thing. She took her hands and spread her pink full pussy lips open as wide as she could. She wanted to make sure James got a good view of the treasure chest he was about to enter in search of the ultimate prize. James inserted himself inside her and enjoyed the view of her back side bumping up against his groin. The slapping sound it created was like music to his ears.

"I wanna make that pussy talk to me. Let me hear it talk, baby!" James demanded as he slapped her on the ass. Her pussy juices made a squishing sound every time he went in and out.

"Damn that feels good, but slow down, baby. Take your time. The pussy ain't going anywhere. I wanna enjoy every minute of this," Delicia pleaded. The seven inches of human steel that James pounded her with made her go crazy. He paid her request no mind. He was in a race for every one of his thrusts to keep pace with his rapid heartbeat. The bed squeaked loudly as an indication that some hardcore lovemaking was going on.

"Oooh, this is it right here, baby! I wanna cum in this pussy! I can't hold it any longer!" James yelled. He grabbed a hold of her waist tightly.

Delicia could feel the head of his penis swell inside of her. She knew he was about to let it flow. She tightened up her vaginal muscles to prepare for the inevitable.

"That's right, James, give me all that cum! I want you to cum for me! I'm cummin' wit you, baby!" Delicia yelled as she let loose orgasm number six.

"Damn, Delicia, your ass is off the hook. I wish my wife could fuck me like you do," he said. He ripped the fluid-filled condom off his penis and held it in his hand. Delicia got up off of the bed and took him into her mouth. She licked up all of the remaining semen that dripped from his dick. She swallowed every drop. It tasted like a cold glass of grape juice going down her throat.

"That bitch can't do what I do. That's why you came to me. I can give you what you can't get at home. I know how to make a nigga feel like a man. While ya bitch is worried about messing up her hair when it's time to get busy, I ain't got no problem gettin' down and dirty with it," Delicia boasted as she wiped her mouth.

"You're a'ight with me, baby girl!" James said as a testament to her skills.

"Before you leave out of here, don't forget to show your appreciation for my services," Delicia stated firmly.

James nodded his head in acknowledgement of her statement as he made his way to the bathroom.

"I hope you ain't drowning up in that shower, James!" Delicia yelled from the other side of the bathroom door. She got up off the bed to find the remote control so that she could turn the television set on. Just as she was about to jump back onto the bed, James swung open the bathroom door. He stood in front of her, naked, with a towel in his hand. Seeing his finely sculpted physique made her clitoris throb.

"Nah, I'm good, baby. You know I had to make sure I washed up thoroughly. I can't go home smelling like sex. My wife would kill me," James reasoned.

"She better be careful before I steal ya sexy ass away from her," Delicia said in a serious tone. She looked James up and down with nothing but lustful thoughts on her mind.

"Slow down a minute. Let's not be up in here talking crazy now. We have an agreement. This was just a one time thing, remember?" James asked.

"I know what we agreed to. I'm a big girl. We're just two adults having a little fun. Are you trying to convince yourself or me that you don't wanna hit this again?" Delicia asked. She walked over to where James was and stood in front of him. She rubbed her ass up against his penis. He became hard again instantly. She took the towel out of his hand and wrapped it around her neck as she walked back over to the bed.

"Delicia, the head on my shoulders tells me that I need to get my ass outta here and go home, but the other head down there is saying we need to do this again. I think I need to be getting up outta here before I wind up spending the night sexing you in every room of this apartment. Since you took my towel, I take it you wanna finish drying me off?" James asked.

"Of course, I can do that. But once I'm done, I wanna give you a massage before you leave. I promise to stop after I do that. I'll be good." She took the towel from around her neck and proceeded to dry him off. She started at his neck and worked her way down his body making sure she got every drop of water. Her hand accidentally slipped around his penis when she reached his waist area. His penis somehow found its way into her mouth again. James didn't seem to mind this minor mishap. He closed his eyes and enjoyed every minute of it. Delicia playfully licked his balls. The tingling sensation made James laugh.

"Damn, Delicia, you are just too much. Now, you know I gotta get home soon before my wife beats me there with the kids. I can use a massage, though. We just have to make it quick," James said. Part of him felt guilty that he had cheated on his wife for the first time. He genuinely loved Arnell, but she just wasn't enough for him in the bedroom. Since Arnell had the kids, her sexual appetite gradually decreased. She just wanted to come home from work and sleep most nights, while James's sexual urges skyrocketed. Delicia did everything he had been begging his wife to do to satisfy him over the past year.

"Aaw, nigga, stop cryin'. That bitch ain't going nowhere. Get ya ass over here on this bed and lay down on ya stomach," Delicia demanded.

"You sure are demanding. I can't front, though, that shit turns me on," James admitted as he sprawled out across the bed.

Delicia did as promised and gave him a relaxing massage and sent him on his way, but not before he paid her the thousand dollars that they had agreed upon for her services. She got what she wanted for her time, and James got a chance to release some of his sexual tension. He made it home before his wife did. James and Delicia would see each other at work on Monday and act as though nothing had happened between them. None of their coworkers would be any the wiser. At least that's what James hoped would happen. Delicia had another trick up her sleeve. Hood rats like her always did when they came across a young brother with cash, like James, who was still a little wet behind the ears. She'd had him pegged from day one.

* * *

It was the Monday morning after his wild romp with Delicia. James pulled his convertible Mustang into his reserved parking spot. He was dressed in a sharp black Armani suit and Ferragamo shoes. He spoke to some of his coworkers who had arrived at the same time. He made his way into the building. He had butterflies in his stomach. All weekend long he had to battle with the guilt of cheating on his wife for the first time. He couldn't believe that he had actually paid for sex. He had never done that before in his life, because more than enough women would give him some for free. However, it was something about Delicia that just made him have to have her no matter what the cost. As he made his way to his office, he was filled with nervous energy. Although they had an agreement to act as though nothing had happened between them, he wasn't exactly one hundred percent sure that Delicia would stick to the deal. He got his answer as soon he reached her desk. As soon as he laid eyes on her, he was instantly reminded of how fine she was and why he craved her so badly.

"Hello, Mr. Blackmon. How are you doing today?" Delicia asked, when he approached her desk. She loved seeing him in his professional attire. It gave him an aura of power when he walked into a room. It was what had attracted her to him initially. He looked like Denzel Washington on the cover of Ebony magazine.

"I'm doing fine, Delicia. How are you doing this beautiful Monday morning? How was your weekend?" James asked calmly. He was now at casc because she carried things exactly as they had agreed to do.

"My weekend was fun. I hung out with my girlfriends at the club. What about you?" Delicia asked as she fumbled with some papers on her desk, pretending to be doing some work. She took both of her hands and pulled her hair into a ponytail.

James began to drool at the thought of biting on the nape of her exposed neck. "I didn't do anything special. I just spent time with my wife and kids. I have a boring life," James replied.

While he stood there engaging in small talk, James got an eyeful of her nipples as they poked through her aqua blue blouse. She leaned over the desk so that he could get a better view of her breasts. Delicia came from behind her desk and walked over to the copier machine while they conversed. She made sure that he caught a glimpse of her juicy ass in her tight skirt when she walked by him. The sexual chemistry flowed between them. The longer he stood there and engaged in conversation with her, James knew, the more he would be turned on by her. His desire for her body forced him to think about violating his agreement that their sexual encounter would only be a one-time thing. Delicia knew what she was doing and knew that she had his nose open.

"James, you might be married but you hardly seem like the boring type. I bet if I met your wife she would tell me a different story," Delicia said teasingly. The mention of his wife brought James back to reality.

"Well, not to cut you off, Delicia, but I have to go do some work now. I gotta earn my keep around here. I can't keep earning my salary if I don't deliver in the courtroom." The thought of Arnell and Delicia meeting face to face frightened James. He would definitely have to make sure that never happened.

"I don't know about the court room, but you sure do deliver in the bedroom," Delicia mumbled in a low tone, loud enough for only James to hear.

"What was that you just said?" James asked. He wanted to confirm that he wasn't hearing things. He would fire her ass without hesitation if he thought she posed a threat to his job at the law firm by running her mouth about them to his coworkers.

"Oh, I didn't say anything important, James. I was just thinking out loud. I have work to do as well. I hope you have a good day," Delicia replied. She wore a big grin on her face.

"I hope you have a good day as well," James said. He walked away from her desk and into his office shaking his head.

James entered his office and hung his suit jacket on the rack by the door. He took a seat in his Italian leather executive chair behind his burl-wood-finished desk. He picked up a picture of Arnell and his two kids, and his mind began to wander. He thought about how fortunate he was to have such a beautiful wife and two healthy children. He thought to himself about how foolish he had been to cheat on her with Delicia. He let his lustful desires lead him into another woman's arms. He felt terrible inside.

Arnell wanted to be intimate with him the same night that he had had sex with Delicia, but he lied and told her he was tired and had a headache from working so many hours on the job. She didn't put up a fuss or complain like most women do when they wanna have sex and their man wasn't in the mood. In his heart, he knew that he had a good woman, but his dick couldn't control its urge to wanna sex Delicia. Not only that, if she ever found out that he'd cheated on her, Arnell could burn him up in a divorce case. James wasn't willing to throw away all of his hard work for a piece of ass. While he was caught up in his thoughts, he heard a knock at his door. It was Delicia.

"James, I didn't mean to disturb you. I thought you might've wanted your morning cup of coffee," she said as she closed and locked the door behind her. James eyed her body up and down as she stood pressed up against the door holding a cup of coffee in her hand. She walked towards him and sat the coffee on his desk.

"Thank you, Delicia," James said.

"Thank you? Is that all you have to say?" Delicia asked. She took a seat on the corner of his desk. She crossed her legs so that he could clearly see her muscular calves and shapely thighs. He couldn't take his eyes off her. She knew he wanted her. She wanted him just as much.

"Delicia, what are you doing? We agreed to keep it professional at work. Ooh, please don't do that," James said as Delicia began to unbutton her blouse. She threw her blouse on the floor.

"What's wrong, James, you can't handle the heat in here? Am I making you uncomfortable?" she asked. She got up and took a seat in his lap. She was pleased to see that her antics had worked. His hardness up against her ass let her know that she could have her way with him. She grinded her hips on top of him to get him more aroused. He used his hands to try and push her off of him. If she sat there any longer, the temptation to whip his dick out and stick it in her raw would be too hard for him to resist.

"Delicia, please don't do this. As your boss, I'm ordering you to stop!" James said forcefully. His serious tone did nothing to discourage Delicia. She was a woman on a mission. She knew that he really didn't want her to stop.

"Oooh, I love it when you talk to me with authority, daddy. Okay, I'll stop if you can honestly tell me that you don't wanna sink your teeth into this ass right here," Delicia said. She bent over his desk, hoisted up her skirt, and revealed her firm ass for him to see. A black G-string rode up in the crack of her butt.

James couldn't fight it any longer. He threw all caution to the wind. The feelings of guilt about cheating on Arnell were replaced with thoughts of having raunchy sex with Delicia. Any brother that could resist the delectable treat she offered him had to be gay.

"Aaw, fuck it. I gotta have you now!" James said anxiously as he placed his face between her ass cheeks. The sweet smell of

Mango body butter greeted his nose with a pleasant aroma. He pulled her G-string to the side and buried his tongue in her asshole. He ate her out like a fat man at a soul food buffet.

"That's right, lick that shit, James! Eat my ass, baby! Put ya tongue all up in that thing!" Delicia squealed in a low tone. It felt so good that she wanted to scream at top of her lungs, but she didn't want their coworkers to hear them. Delicia cupped her breasts in her hand and massaged her nipples. She bit them to muffle out the sounds of her moans and groans. She enjoyed every minute of him tossing her salad.

When he was done, James stood up and unzipped his pants. They fell to the floor and hung around his ankles. He whipped his dick out and was about to put it in her vagina from behind when she stopped him.

"What's wrong, baby? I know you're not teasing me. Don't get me all hot and heated and then say stop now!" James exclaimed with a hint of sexual frustration in his voice.

"Nah, it's not like that, baby. Oh, I ain't the one to let a nigga leave his job half done. You should know that from the other day. It's just that you were about to put it in the wrong hole. I know you know how to treat this pussy right. You showed me that already. I want something different this time. I wanna give you a special treat. Not every man gets a chance to do this with me. I want you to fuck me up the ass so that you can make me cum all over you," Delicia said boldly.

James couldn't believe his ears. Delicia was freakier than he thought she was.

"You want me to do what?" James asked for clarification. He had never had anal sex before in his life, but had always wanted to try it. There was no time better than the present. Delicia made the perfect partner to break him in.

"You heard me. I wanna feel you in my ass. Fuck me like the whore that I am. Fuck me, James!" Delicia pleaded.

James gave her what she wanted. He slowly slid his member into her anus without any need for lubrication. Once he was inside of her, James felt an indescribable rush go throughout his entire body. The tightness of her asshole felt ten times better than he ever felt inside of a vagina. With every stroke, he wanted to cum. Delicia tensed up her ass muscles to increase the pleasure. She buried her face on his desk and moaned her delight and approval. James slowly increased the pace of his thrusts.

"That's it, baby. Don't be gentle. Fuck that ass like it was pussy!" Delicia commanded. You could tell that she had no virgin asshole. The way she handled his dick, she had done this many times before. Her pussy leaked with the sweet fluids from the multiple orgasms she released. They went at it so hard, Delicia accidentally knocked over the picture of Arnell and the kids. James didn't notice because his eyes were closed and his mind was in another world.

"Damn, Delicia, this ass feels so good. It's so nice and tight. Back that ass up for me, baby!" James requested in a low husky voice. Delicia threw the booty on him as he requested. James knew what they were doing was wrong, but it felt oh so right. His wife never gave him pleasure to this degree. Delicia was nice with her shit. Once she was sexually satisfied, Delicia used her ass to push James backwards. He fell into his chair. She stood up and faced him.

"Now, I wanna feel you in my ass while I look you in your sexy eyes. I want you to see the expression on my face so you know how good you're fucking me!" Delicia stated. She sat down on his lap and guided his penis back into her asshole. The intense gaze she gave him as she winded her hips on his dick let James know that he was hitting the right spots. He fucked her pussy with his fingers while she humped up and down on his dick. He used his thumb to stimulate her clit. He had to cover her mouth with his hand to muffle her screams so that nobody could hear them. Delicia rode him nonstop for ten minutes before he released a gigantic explosion in her ass. They both trembled with pleasure from the exhilarating experience. The scent of hot, sweaty, funky sex filled the room. They both panted like two dogs in heat. Sensing that James was a little vulnerable from getting some more of that comeback pussy, Delicia decided to throw some salt in the game.

"James, we need a new arrangement. I think I wanna keep you for myself. I don't care if you're married. As long as you fuck me like this twice a week and take care of me financially, we can have a good thing between us. You got any problems with me being ya mistress?" Delicia asked as she licked her lips.

"That's not a good idea. I love my wife. It's true that I did enjoy the sex, but this has to stop. We can't do this anymore, Delicia. You're gonna have to find another job. This is just too risky for me," James said bluntly as he pulled his pants up.

"James, stop playing. You know damn well you want me as much as I want you. I like to get what I want," Delicia said as she attempted to fix her clothes. She was no longer smiling.

"I know, and that's the problem. I want your ass too much. I have a wife and kids. I can't lose my family. You have to find another job. I can't give you what you want."

"Are you serious? You want me to quit that badly?" Delicia asked. She put her hands on her hips to display her disapproval of his request.

"Yes, I'm dead serious," James said with no emotion. His rational mind was now back in force. His sexual thirst was quenched.

"Well, fine then, but if you wanna get rid of me it's gonna cost you. I don't handle rejection too well. I need to be compensated for my time," Delicia demanded. She wanted to call his bluff. If he wanted to make her go away, then he would have to pay through the nose.

"Exactly, how much money are you talking about?" James asked.

"You pay me five grand now and you'll never hear from me again," Delicia said.

"It's a done deal. Hand in your letter of resignation today. I'll tell everybody that you found another job. You can take the rest of the day off with pay. I'll even give you a good reference if you need it," James said feeling relieved that she agreed to his request.

"I don't need shit else from you but my money," Delicia said rather coldly.

"You've got it. I'll bring the cash by your house tonight. What time is good for you?" James asked. Five grand was a small price for him to pay to get her out of his life.

"You can come by around eight o'clock tonight. You just don't know what you will be missing out on. You could've had this ass anytime you wanted it. Go be with your boring wife. You won't have me to turn to when you get horny and need satisfaction. You'll regret the choice that you just made for the rest of your life," Delicia threatened as she walked out of his office. *This nigga is gonna regret dissin' me in more ways than one,* she thought as she packed her things.

That bitch is off the fucking chains! Damn, that was some bombin' ass! I'ma miss fucking that whore! James thought as he watched her walk out of his office and his life. A few minutes after Delicia left out of his office, his cell phone rung. It was Arnell. His feelings of guilt and shame returned.

"Hey, baby, what's up?' James asked.

"Nothing much, honey. I was just checking up on my favorite man. I wanted to see if you might be free for dinner and a movie tonight. My mother agreed to watch the kids so that we could go out tonight," Arnell replied.

"I would love to baby, but I have to work late tonight. Can I get a rain check for another night? There's nothing that I enjoy more than spending a quiet evening on the town with my beautiful wife," James said sounding sincere.

"Aaw, James, I was really looking forward to spending the evening unwinding in your arms. I know I haven't been attentive to your needs lately and I wanted to make it up to you. Is there any way you could get off a little earlier?" Arnell pleaded.

"I would if I could, baby, but I can't. I have a big case coming up and I have to be prepared. If I wanna move up in this firm, then I gotta always be on my P's and Q's," James replied.

"Okay, I guess I'll have to take you up on that rain check ASAP. What time do you think you'll be home?" Arnell asked.

"I should be done with everything by ten at the latest. As soon as I'm done, I'm on my way home to you so that we can make this a memorable night," James said. He had to make sure he gave himself enough time to drop the money off at Delicia's house and make it home at a halfway decent hour so as not to arouse Arnell's suspicion.

"Ok, I'll see you when you get here. I love you," Arnell said.

"I love you, too" James replied. He gathered himself together as he left out of his office headed to the locker room of the fitness center in the lobby of the building. He needed to take a quick shower to wash off the stench of sex. James planned to go to the bank on his lunch break to get the money to pay Delicia. Once their transaction was done, he hoped she would be out of his life for good.

* * *

James pulled up to Delicia's house fifteen minutes early. He got out of his car and walked toward her apartment building. He entered the building and proceeded to the third floor. When he reached her apartment, he knocked on the door. He was shocked when a tall, muscle-bound brother with dreads in his head answered the door with attitude. James wasn't a small dude, but this cat outweighed him by a good fifty pounds. He was buffed for real.

"Who the fuck is you and why are you knocking at my girl's door, nigga?" the man asked him. He eyed James up and down and hoped he said something wrong outta his mouth to give him a reason to stretch him out.

James had to think fast or risk getting his ass kicked. "Slow ya roll, bro. I'm not here to cause any problems. My name is James. I'm Delicia's boss. Today was her last day and I offered to drop off her last paycheck so that she wouldn't have to make another trip to the office. She knows that I'm coming by," James said calmly. He hoped that his act worked.

"My bad, dude. My name is Rock. I thought you were some dude trying to push up on my girl. She's the wild type. As fine as she is, I gotta always get some wreck in on a nigga because she can't keep from flirting and leading niggas on. She's a handful to deal with, bro. She's the type that likes a nigga to go upside her head to feel like she's loved. Man to man, I know you've seen that type before, playa. Come on in, James. Delicia, your old boss is out here!" Rock said as he opened the door to let James come in.

James had a seat on the same couch that he had just sexed Delicia on a few days ago. He exhaled and couldn't wait to get this whole deal over with. A few minutes later, Delicia walked into the room. She was dressed in a wife beater and a pair of Daisy Duke shorts.

"Hey, James, what's up? Thank you for stopping by to bring me my check. I see you've met my crazy boyfriend, Rock. We've been together for five years and plan to get married next year," Delicia said as she sat in his lap. She kissed Rock on his forehead.

"Yeah, we're getting married if you act right," Rock chimed in.

"It's not a problem at all. I have your check right here. Oops, I must have left it in the car," James said as he searched his suit jacket. He didn't want to give Delicia five grand in cash in front of her man because he would know that something wasn't right. He wanted her to come outside to get the money with no drama so that he could be on his way. He hoped Delicia would take the cue.

"That's no problem. I'll walk out with you to get it. Rock, watch the food on the stove while I go outside to get my check," Delicia said. She followed James out the door toward the parking lot. When they reached his car, Delicia reached out her hand and grabbed his ass. James slapped her hand away. She just giggled at him.

"Woman, are you crazy? Your man is right up them stairs. You didn't tell me you had a boyfriend or that he lived with you. You had me up in there with you, and he could've come home and killed both of us!" James said angrily. When he reached his car, he leaned up against the passenger-side car door and took the envelope containing the money out of his suit jacket inside pocket. He handed it to Delicia. She took the envelope and checked to make sure that all of the money was there. Once she saw that it was five grand in the envelope, she was content.

"Be easy, Mr. Tight Ass. Rock was outta town and I knew that he wasn't coming home until the next day. Besides, that ain't none of ya business. You've got a wife at home ya self. Anyway, as bad as you wanted to fuck me, you would've still came over if I had told you that I had a man. Tell me that I'm lying," Delicia demanded boldly. She leaned forward and pressed her body up against his.

"That's beside the point. Anyway, I hope this concludes our business agreement," James said.

"Not quite. I need one more thing from you," Delicia said as she took his hands and rested them on her *derrière.* James couldn't resist squeezing her Charmin-soft rear end.

"And what's that?" James asked.

"Since this is the last time I will see you, I want a goodbye kiss," Delicia replied. Before he could respond, she pressed her lips up against his. The connection between their lips felt so good, James found his tongue wrapped around hers in a kinky French kiss. Delicia began to fondle his private area. When James felt his nature rising, he pulled back.

"Nah, you ain't getting me with that one again. You've got your money and now I'm outta here," James said. His body was hesitant to pull away, but his mind knew that if he stayed there a minute longer, Delicia would be sprawled across the hood of his car getting all seven inches of his manhood shoved up inside of her for the whole neighborhood to see. He pushed Delicia off him and walked over to the driver's door.

"Have it your way, James. It was nice knowing you. Excuse me, I mean, fucking you," Delicia said as she walked back to her apartment. James sped off to get home as soon as possible. When Delicia got back to her apartment, Rock greeted her at the door.

"Did you get the money, bitch?" he asked.

"Hell yeah, I got every penny. Oh, and watch who you're calling a bitch, nigga. You can only call me that when you're fucking the taste outta my mouth," Delicia replied. She handed him the envelope so that he could count it for himself.

"That was a sweet-ass lick you pulled off, baby. You made five grand just for fucking a nigga twice. I might have to put you out on the track like the rest of my hoes," Rock said as he smacked her on her bottom. Rock was a pimp and Delicia was his main bitch. She didn't have to work the streets like his other girls. He used her for special projects. They had been running scams like this for years.

"Not a chance. I ain't walking the streets for nobody anymore. Those days are over for me," Delicia said.

"Yeah, well get that ass in that bedroom and show Daddy why he shouldn't put you back out on the streets," Rock commanded.

"Anything for you, Big Poppa," Delicia responded. She strutted into the bedroom and Rock followed right behind her. She was gonna do what she did best—work her magic on a man to make him do whatever she wanted him to do.

* * *

When James put his key into the door, the house was totally dark except for the TV in the living room. He walked into the living room expecting to find Arnell waiting for him. He saw several boxes positioned all over the room. Arnell lay across the couch fully dressed with tears flowing down her cheeks.

"Baby, what's wrong? Why are you crying?" James asked in a concerned tone. He walked over to the couch to comfort her. When he tried to hug her, she pushed him away.

"Where have you been, James? I called your office and nobody answered. If you were there, why didn't you answer the phone?" Arnell asked angrily as she wiped her eyes with tissue.

"Baby, I was there all night. I didn't answer the phone because I didn't want to be disturbed while I completed my work on the case," James lied with a straight face.

"Oh really? I came by your office and I didn't see your car parked in your reserved parking space. How do you explain that?" she asked with attitude.

"My car was parked in my space, baby. Are you sure that you were in the right parking lot? Where are all these crazy questions coming from?" James asked. He was calling her bluff to see if she really did come by the office or was just fishing for him to confess to doing something wrong.

"James, you know what? I didn't come past your job. I just wanted to see if you could be honest with me. When I got home tonight, there was a package under the door addressed to me. I opened it up and boy was I surprised to see what was in it," Arnell confessed.

"What was in the package?" James asked curiously.

Arnell didn't respond. She grabbed the remote control off the couch and pressed play on the VCR. When the tape began to play, his jaw dropped onto the floor. It was a tape of him and Delicia's sexcapade from the other day. He didn't know what to do.

"Baby, I can explain. I am so sorry. I never meant for this to happen. It was a mistake. It only happened once. I swear. Baby, please forgive me!" James pleaded. He got down on knees in front of Arnell. She laughed at his futile attempts at being regretful for his actions.

"It only happened once? Is that right? Well, then why did Ms. Delicia include a note with the tape saying she fucked you today in your office?" Arnell asked.

"Baby, she's lying. I only cheated on you once. I swear, that's the truth! You've gotta forgive me, Arnell!" James pleaded.

"James, I know you're lying and I know that you weren't at work tonight. She also said in her letter that you were coming by her house tonight to pay her money to quit her job and for her silence about your affair. Do you deny that as well?" Arnell asked angrily.

"No, it's all true," James admitted in a defeated tone. He was straight busted. He held his face in hands as he wept.

"Good. Well, now I want you to leave. I took the liberty of packing your clothes while you were out. Anything that I forgot, I'll send to your mother's house. You have twenty minutes to get ya shit outta here!" Arnell screamed.

"Baby, please don't do this! Don't throw away everything we've built. This was my first time and it will never happen again!" James said.

"I know it won't happen again. I loved you with all of my heart, James. I gave you two beautiful children. I won't give you another chance to hurt me like this. You better hurry up and get ya shit together. The clock is ticking," Arnell said coldly. She walked out of the room then up the stairs to her bedroom. She wanted to mourn in private.

James began loading the boxes into his car. Once he was done, he headed for a hotel to spend the night. He had wrecked his marriage over a piece of pussy. He wanted to kick himself for being so stupid. He knew that the chances of Arnell forgiving him were slim to none. His life had been turned upside down by a lowlife chick like Delicia. He was pissed that he'd paid her what she wanted and she still fucked him over. Wanting to vent his rage, he called her on her cell phone. She answered on the second ring.

"Hey, James, what's up, boo? Are you calling me because your wife got that little package I sent her?" Delicia asked.

"That was so fucked up for you to do that to me. How could you ruin my life? What did I ever do to you? If I ever see you again, I swear I'ma kill you, bitch!" James yelled into the phone.

"Aaw, James, you ain't gonna do nothing. You don't have the balls to kill nobody. Soft niggas like you talk the talk but can't walk the walk. Remember, I did tell you that I hate to be rejected. You should've took me up on my offer to become your mistress and everything would have been fine. Since you didn't, I had to make you pay for not doing what I wanted. Payback is a bitch. Oh, yeah, and if you think about coming after me, I have Rock right here as my witness that you threatened me so that I can have you arrested for harassment. You know the law and how easy it is for a woman to jam a nigga up on that type of charge. If that doesn't work, Rock will have no problem stomping a mud hole in ya ass if you try to harm one hair on his baby's pretty lil' head. Let this be the last time you call me, motherfucker!" she said and hung up the phone.

I am a fucking asshole! I'm going through all of this shit because I couldn't keep my dick in my pants. I'm gonna lose everything I worked to build because of a piece of ghetto ass. I gotta get Arnell back! She's gotta come back to me! James said to himself as he contemplated how he could put the pieces of his fucked up life back together.

Coming After School

Keisha Ervin

Part One

Beep . . . Beep . . . Beep!

Opening her eyes, thankful for another day, Sharice Cummings arose ready for war. Knowing that it was going to take a mountain and a mole hill to get her kids up and ready for school, she headed down the flight of steps to the kitchen. Twisting open the window shade, she gazed out and welcomed another dreary day. Fed up and tired were not the words to describe the way she felt. It was almost five years since her divorce from her children's father, Lester, and nothing in her life had changed.

Everyday the routine remained the same; wake up, cook, kids, work, cook, clean, kids, sleep. The order was always the same. Life for her ex, however, seemed to be getting better and better. After dedicating thirteen years of her life to him and their children, he up and left her for none other than her best friend, Tammy. Now, happily married, he and Tammy live in a $700,000 home; he has been promoted to partner at the law firm; and Tammy is pregnant with their first child.

T*hem hoes on Desperate Housewives ain't got nothing on me.* She smiled. With hopes of getting a minute or two of, more sleep she folded her arms across her chest and closed her eyes. Only the sound of coffee drips draining from the filter filled her mind. Instead of sleeping, she found herself counting each drop. Still groggy and yawning, she headed back upstairs with her cup of coffee. Inhaling deeply she stood in front of Mason's door, her eighteen-year-old son and prepared for war.

"Mason, it's 5:52, time to get up!" she yelled.

Placing her ear to the door, she listened for any sound of movement being made. Not hearing any, she rolled her eyes again and headed to the bathroom for her morning shower.

Towel-drying her hair on the way out of the shower, she checked the clock; it read 6:09. Grabbing her robe, she slid into it and tied it gently around her waist.

Staring at herself in the full-length mirror, she made a mental note to lose five pounds. Marching past Mason's room, she yelled for him to get up once more. Beating on Mya's door, her twelve-year-old daughter, Sharice called out for her to get up as well.

Waking Mya up was never a problem; it was her slowness and lolley-gagging that drove Sharice crazy. Twenty minutes passed and everyone in the house was up and running around. Standing in front of her walk-in closet, Mya couldn't make up her mind on what she wanted to wear. Catching her as she walked by' Sharice yelled, "Quit pussyfootin' around, girl, and come on!"

"I ain't got nothing to wear," Mya yelled back.

"Mya all them clothes in that closet and you can't find nothing to wear? Girl, you better quit playin' wit me and come on!"

Checking her watch Sharice noticed that she had only fifteen minutes to get Mason to school. "Mason are you dressed yet?" she shouted as she walked past his room putting makeup on.

"Yeah, but I can't get in the bathroom, 'cause yo' slow-ass daughter is in there."

"You better watch yo' damn mouth, boy!"

"Hurry up, Mya!"

"Wait!" she laughed, taking her precious time.

"You ain't gon' look no better so hurry up," Mason said while beating on the bathroom door.

Swinging the door open, Mya pushed him in the chest. Yanking her by the arm, Mason grabbed the back of her neck and put her in a headlock.

"Momma!" Mya yelled.

"Mason, quit playin' and let your sister go!"

Easing his grip on her neck, Mason let her up, only to kick her in the butt.

"Punk," Mya spat.

"Ho!"

"Momma, Mason called me a ho!"

"Mason, I'm gon' beat yo' ass if you say one mo' cuss word in my house," Sharice yelled while putting on her heels.

Another five minutes passed by and they still were no closer to being dressed and ready to leave. Besides getting the kids to school she had an eight-o'clock meeting with a couple looking to buy a home. Sharice was a realtor and a damn good one at that. She sold real estate to some of the richest people in the Show Me State.

Sharice loved her job. Everyday she got the chance to see how the other half lived. Sometimes she would catch herself gazing at the homes, wishing that one day, she would have one of her own. She told herself that one day she would be able to afford her dream house. Only being in the business for a year and a half, Sharice had already sold more than forty homes.

Besides her job, her kids filled up her life. To Sharice, her life was complete; she had no room for anything else. She would sometimes have drinks with the girls, but that didn't happen too often. And a man, what about one? Sharice hadn't been around one of those in years.

The betrayal, mixed with heartache that Lester had left behind, nearly killed her. After talking to a psychologist, her wounds healed, only to be reopened. Three years after her divorce and Sharice had finally gotten the courage to date again.

Her first time out in years, she lucked up and met a fine gentleman by the name of Nathan. He approached her with a slick-ass line and she fell for it, hook, line, and sinker.

He told her he was a journalist for one of the local newspapers, and that he had no children of his own. He told her he was engaged once but it was called off after he caught his fiancée in bed with his best friend. To Sharice, Nathan seemed to be heavensent. Not only had they suffered humiliation and heartache at the hands of a loved one, but she found him to be funny, smart, and sensitive. Sharice found him so appealing that after their third date they wound up at the Holiday Inn together. Sharice hadn't had sex in years, and her body desperately needed to feel a man on top of her.

They weren't even halfway in the door before she began to rip into his clothes. Picking Sharice up, Nathan palmed her ass and carried her over to the bed. Lying on top of her, he caressed Sharice's body from her head down to her feet. Lifting her left leg up, he fondled her toes with his tongue. Laughing and moaning at the same time, Sharice smiled. Locking eyes with her, he circled his tongue around her baby toe and sucked.

Inhaling slowly, she bit down into her lower lip. Sharice could have sworn that she saw the stars, the sun, and the moon spinning above her. Swept up in the moment, he massaged her feet while trailing kisses down the inner part of her thighs. Reaching her knee he stopped. Lifting her up, Nathan unzipped the back of her dress. Standing back, she let him watch, as her dress hit the floor. Sharice wanted him to see that even though she was thirty-five, she still had it going on.

Admiring her honey-colored skin, he gently placed Sharice back onto the bed and turned her over. Pulling her lavender Victoria Secret panties down, he massaged her buttock. Slipping his tongue between her ass cheeks, he slid his tongue up the crease of her ass. Playing with her hole he licked until she bucked from pleasure.

Resuming his kissing game with her thighs allowed him to familiarize himself with the areas that hadn't been awakened in years. Wanting him to taste her, Sharice spread her thighs as far as they could go. Getting the hint, Nathan placed her on all fours and lay underneath her opened legs. Holding her creamy thighs, he lifted his head up and sucked her pearl-shaped clit.

"Oooh…just like that," Sharice panted, holding onto the sheets.

"You like that?"

"Yeah," she squealed as he flicked his tongue across her clit faster.

"Oh Baby, make me cum," she begged.

Scooting down some, he spread her labia even wider. Tasting her juices, he let them slide down his face. Teasingly Nathan inserted his tongue inside of Sharice, while lapping up her juices, drinking over and over again.

"You like the way I taste, Baby?" she asked.

"Sharice, Baby, you taste like caramel."

"Oooh . . . Nathan, make me cum."

The faster he licked the more she begged. Taking his fingers, he placed two inside of her, while still sucking on her clit. The combination caused Sharice to buck and moan. Every time she bucked he slapped her ass roughly.

"I can't take it!"

"You can't take it?" he asked.

"No . . . I'm gon' cum but I don't want to cum yet!"

Sliding from underneath, he quickly put on a condom and entered her.

"Oh Nathan, fuck me!"

Sharice couldn't believe she had gone three years without having sex. As soon as Nathan entered her, her legs began to shake. Gripping her waist, he forcefully grinded his way around, until her walls loosened up. Juices began flowing out of Sharice that she didn't even know she had. Massaging her clit, she played in her own wetness.

"Oooh Baby, fuck me! Fuck me, Daddy! Fuck me!" she called out.

"Damn, Baby," Nathan said while slapping her ass with force.

"Don't move, baby! You hitting my spot!"

"That's it right there?" He stroked harder, making his balls slap against her ass.

"Yeah . . . right there! Ahh, yeah, Baby, keep it right there!"

Holding her waist, Nathan pumped until he felt himself about to explode. Pulling out, he snatched off the condom and jerked off into the crack of Sharice's ass. Watching, as his love juices slid down the crease of her ass, he slapped it once more. Still playing with her clit, Sharice felt herself nearing an orgasm.

"Shit!" she yelled into the air as she came all over her hand.

With one of her ass cheeks in his hand, Nathan massaged his juices into her skin. Out of breath and still moaning, Sharice lay flat on the bed, trying to catch her breath.

Nathan continued to wine and dine her for months, until his goal of getting into her house was met.

At first she was a little weary about letting a man around her kids, but she was in love so she began letting him spend the night. It wasn't even a good week and things in Sharice's house started coming up missing. She first started noticing that her wallet would come up short a couple of dollars each day. Sharice tried telling herself that Nathan would not steal from her.

She even went as far as blaming Mason. But when her four-carat wedding ring came up missing, she knew that Nathan was the culprit. Picking up the phone, she dialed his cell but was met with a *'M02 35, Welcome to AT&T Wireless Services. We're sorry but your call cannot be completed as dialed. Please try your call again.'* Sharice felt like a complete fool. Never once had she been to his house, and she never bothered to ask which newspaper he worked for.

Defeated, she threw the phone across the room and cried. That one incident caused all men to be looked upon as dogs in her eyes. Sharice hasn't trusted a man ever since.

Gathering her suitcase and laptop, she headed for the door with the kids in tow. As usual, they arrived at Mason's school a minute before the final bell rang.

After dropping Mya off at the middle school, she headed to work.

The day seemed to drag on, and for the first time in almost two years, Sharice wasn't successful in showing a house. Tired and disappointed she headed to Mason's school for a parent-teacher conference. Going to his school was the last thing that she wanted to do. It wasn't like her plate wasn't full enough. Dinner still had to be prepared, clothes had to be dropped off at the cleaners, Mya had piano lessons, and, on top of that, Sharice had to go back up to the high school to pick Mason up from football practice.

Fortunately for Sharice, Mason's teachers had wonderful things to say about him.

Back at home she whipped up a casserole and threw it in the oven. Running to each of the kids' rooms, she picked out all of the clothes they would need pressed for the week.

The dry cleaners were unusually packed for a Monday afternoon, so Sharice was forced to take a number. Getting the number 46 out of the machine, she looked up and saw they were only on number 30.

Her usual five-minute stop at the cleaners ended up being twenty-five minutes. On the way back home she called to make sure that her ex-husband, Lester, had picked Mya up from school.

"Hello," Tammy, her ex-best friend and now the new Mrs. Cummings, answered.

"Did Lester pick Mya up from school?" Sharice asked, annoyed that Tammy answered the phone.

"Hi to you too, Sharice. Yes, he picked her up from school."

"Alright then, that's all I wanted," Sharice responded with an attitude.

"Sharice, it's been five years, when are you going to get past this? I mean, we were best friends and I want you to be my son's godmother."

"Bitch, is you crazy? I will get past this when the both of you rot in hell! You were supposed to be my best friend, Tammy, and you slept with my husband! I can't forgive you for that! Now you have the audacity to ask me to be your child's godmother? You ain't working wit a full deck, are you?"

"*Look* Sharice, I'm trying to be nice to you! It ain't my fault that Lester left you for me!"

"Tammy, don't make me come over there and kick yo' narrow, pregnant behind! You should have tried telling me that my husband wasn't happy instead of sleeping with him! That's what you should have done! So don't come telling me that you tried! You tried to get my man, that's what you tried to do!"

"Whatever, Sharice, I'm tired of arguing with you about this. At least I tried. If you can't forgive me then, oh well," Tammy said while hanging up.

Slamming her flip phone shut, Sharice tried her hardest not to let her tear filled eyes cry. It was bad enough that she was still hurt over what Lester and Tammy had done, but to have Tammy throw their relationship in her face every time they spoke tore her up inside. Counting to ten, Sharice inhaled deeply and tried to calm herself down. Leaning over the seat to get her purse, she caught a reflection of herself in the rearview mirror.

The dark circles and bags under her eyes revealed a woman under stress. Nevertheless, Sharice was beautiful. Tan complexioned, slanted eyes, heart-shaped lips, shoulder-length, sandy-brown hair, and a size eight body defined her essence. Searching through her Coach bag, she grabbed her M.A.C. concealer and foundation and dabbed some around her eyes. Noticing a few stray hairs, Sharice tucked them behind her ear, while smoothing the rest up into a ponytail. Walking across the field, she watched as Mason made a pass to one of his teammates. Smiling to herself, she clapped and cheered him on.

"Go, Mason, go!" she shouted, jumping up and down.

"He's one of my best players," a voice said from behind.

Turning around to find the face that went with the voice, she found a young man, who looked to be in his twenties, standing behind her. Tall, with an athletic build, he towered over Sharice. The late afternoon sun seemed to shine down on his peanut butter complexioned skin. His round eyes, full lips, square chin, and low haircut demanded her attention. White shirt, baggy shorts, and Air Force Ones made up his outfit, and Sharice was turned on by just the sight of him.

'Your brother, Mason, he's one of my star players," he spoke again not sure if she had heard him the first time.

"I'm sorry, have we met before?" she asked while pieces of her hair flew into her face.

"I'm the new assistant coach, Coach Rainey, but you can call me Maliq," he said, extending his hand.

"Nice to meet you, Coach Rainey; I'm Mason's mother, Sharice," she smiled shaking his hand.

"I'm sorry, Mason told me he had a younger sister, so I assumed you were her."

"No, I'm his mother," she smirked, rolling her eyes. Sharice knew he was trying to run game on her.

"If you don't mind me saying, you are absolutely breathtaking."

"Thank you, but I do mind," Sharice checked him, trying to smooth down her hair once again.

"Forgive me. Are you married?"

"No, I'm not."

"Then what's the problem?"

"Boy, I'm old enough to be your mother," she laughed.

Reaching out his hand, Maliq took a piece of hair that strayed and gently tucked it behind Sharice's ear. Startled by the touch of his hand against her skin, she grabbed his hand. For a second, Sharice let herself feel what she'd denied for years—the touch of a man. Silently they stood, for the sexual attraction between the two was evident. Needing room to breathe, she took a step back.

"Haven't you heard, age ain't nothing but a number?"

"Yes, I have, but your age and my age don't even come close to mixing."

"You can't be any older than thirty-three."

"I'm thirty-seven," she said, trying not to blush.

"Okay, I'm twenty-six; that's not that big of an age difference."

"It is for me." Tired of the conversation, Sharice turned her back on him and called out for Mason. "It was nice meeting you, Coach Rainey," Sharice replied as she walked back to her car.

"Nice meeting you, too," Maliq said while eyeing her hips as they swayed from left to right. Watching as she and Mason got into the car, he told himself that he had to have her, no matter what.

Part Two

A couple of days passed and the weekend finally arrived. Mason was out on a date with his girlfriend, and Mya was at Lester's for the weekend. Carl Thomas's '*Summer Rain'* filled the room, and Sharice lay in bed, legs spread wide open, with her vibrator in hand. Licking her lips she clicked it on and glided it in slowly. The friction between her thighs caused her back to arch as she moaned. Using her free hand she played with her nipples.

Twisting and pulling she stroked her breasts until her nipples were ripe and erect. Taking one in her mouth she licked and sucked. Gliding her wet tongue over her nipples she pretended as if her lips were Maliq's. Loving the way her nipples tasted she sucked harder. Taking the vibrator out, she slid her fingers inside of her warm sugar walls. Stroking herself until her fingers were wet enough she took them out and began caressing her eager clit.

Placing the vibrator back in as far as it could go, she found her spot and moaned. Letting it sit there, Sharice continued toying with her clit, causing herself to be stimulated inside and out. Picturing Maliq's face, she envisioned him opening up her pussy lips and licking her nice and slow. Slowing down the pace of her fingers, she rocked to the beat of a slow grind.

"Maliq, go slow," she moaned. "Yeah, Baby, right there; keep it right there. Oooh that feels good. Yeah! Yeah!" Sharice screamed, feeling herself cumming. As her body began to spasm she imagined Maliq cumming with her. Calling out his name, Sharice begged for more.

"Oh yes, fuck me, Daddy! Yeah! Yes! Yes!" she screamed, bucking and shaking.

Pinching down on her nipples Sharice tossed and turned from sheer pleasure. Rubbing her breasts, she pushed back and forth as if he were inside of her. Sweating and panting, she lay there still playing in her wetness. Taking her fingers, she tasted her juices and agreed that she did taste like caramel.

Finally able to open her eyes, Sharice realized that she was alone, and that Maliq was nowhere to be found. Staring up at the popcorn ceiling, she wondered how much longer she would have to go on pleasuring herself. Touching herself had become a normal thing. On a good day, Sharice was able to masturbate at least twice. During a hectic week she could maybe slide in one finger session.

The kids never knew. Most of the time she got off in the shower, but on days like today, when the kids weren't home, that's when she would go all out. Setting the scene, Sharice would light candles, turn on a little music, and slip on something nice, all to please herself. To Sharice, a man couldn't satisfy her body like she could. Since she spent so much time getting to know herself, she'd learned all of the spots on her body that turned her on.

Teaching a man all of her spots, and how to work them, would take forever in her mind. And besides, never in her life had she had an orgasm while having intercourse. The only way Sharice was able to cum was by stimulating her clit. During the divorce, Lester told her that that was one of the things that drove him away. He said that her satisfying herself during sex made him feel less of a man.

It wasn't her fault that he wasn't able to take her mind, body, and soul to a place of forbidden ecstasy. Nathan came close but he still wasn't able to seal the deal. Sharice wanted a man that could take control. Someone that could teach her body things it never even knew it could feel. She wanted a man that would turn her out and have her screaming for mercy.

High from the orgasm, she jumped into the shower and pressed the shower head against her still-throbbing pussy. The pressure from the water massaging against her flesh drove her wild. Letting the feeling flow through her vaginal walls, she came once more. After lathering soap all over her wet, tight body, she dried off, dressed, and headed out for a day of window shopping.

With jeans that fit like a glove, Sharice sashayed through the mall like a woman of half her age. Unbeknownst to her, she garnered attention from the male species daily. If you let Sharice tell it, she never got hit on or looked at. Finding a table in a deserted part of the food court, she sat alone, licking on an ice cream cone while reading *Chyna Black* by Keisha Ervin. A couple of pages into the book, Sharice noticed someone standing in front of her. Looking up, she saw Coach Rainey.

"Good book?"

"Yeah, it was until you interrupted me," she replied with a hint of sarcasm in her voice.

"My bad, you just looked so lonely over here all by yourself," he said as he took a seat across from her.

"Please sit down," she said, annoyed that he hadn't asked.

"I just keep on fucking up, don't I?"

"Watch your mouth!" she yelled like he was her child.

"Last time I checked, I was a grown ass man," Maliq shot back, checking her.

"I'm sorry, you just remind me so much of my son," Sharice teased.

"That's cold," he laughed.

"I'm just playing." She laughed too.

"You look nice today," he said while eyeing her frame.

"You just don't give up, do you?"

"Not when it comes to something that I want."

"Let me guess. You want me?"

"See, it wasn't that hard to figure out after all."

"Ha, ha, funny. Look, Maliq, you're a nice man, but you are entirely too young for me. There are plenty of beautiful young women here; why don't you try macking on one of them?"

"To me, you are the baddest chick up in here, and your age doesn't bother me one bit."

"Listen to the way you talk. We don't have anything in common. I'm old school; you're new school. The two don't coincide."

"I may be younger than you, Sharice, but I'm a man that knows what he wants, and from the first time I laid eyes on you, I knew that I had to have you. You may not feel the same way now, but eventually, you'll come around."

"You are really sure of yourself, aren't you? Sharice asked, turned on by his charm.

"It's Saturday afternoon, the sun is out; why don't you and I have dinner together?"

"But I already had dessert," she said, pointing the cone towards him.

"I haven't," he replied while gazing between her thighs.

Feeling a warm sensation blow through her legs she crossed them tightly.

"What do you say?"

"Alright, I'll have lunch with you and that's it, nothing else."

Smiling, Maliq took Sharice by the hand and helped her up. Not comfortable enough to ride with him, Sharice decided to take her car. Meeting each other in front of a restaurant called J Bucks, Sharice felt under dressed.

"I'm not sure about this, Maliq. I have on jeans and a tee shirt."

"Ma, you look fine, quit trippin'."

"Ma? Boy, I ain't none of your damn momma. You better get it together," Sharice yelled, insulted.

"Sharice, ma is a figure of speech, calm down. I'm sure you've heard Mason use the word before," Maliq laughed.

"Oh, sorry," she smiled, feeling foolish.

Maliq requested for them to be seated in the quietest area of the restaurant so they could talk. After being seated and ordering lunch, they enjoyed the presence of each other's company. Sharice never would have guessed that she and Maliq would have so much in common. Besides football, he loved reading, exercising, and quiet evenings at home. Lunch had already been served and the two had eaten, but they still were not ready to leave.

"Hey, they have a dance room across the hall; you want to go?" Maliq asked.

"I haven't danced in years."

"Come on, it'll be fun."

"Alright," Sharice answered hesitantly.

Leading her across the room, holding her hand, Maliq quickly whisked Sharice onto the dance floor. Turning her around so that her butt could rest against his dick, he grasped her waist firmly and led her hips to the groove of John Legend's '*She Don't Have to Know*'. Feeling shy and uncomfortable, Sharice swayed from left to right with caution. Knowing that her mind was taking control of her, Maliq took control of the situation by raising her arms into the air and caressing her from her hands all the way down to her waist.

Wanting to kiss her, he gently soothed the back of her neck with his tongue. Intertwining her fingers with his, they held a slow grind until Faith Evan's *'Love like This'* bumped through the loud speakers. With a surge of confidence Sharice got her groove back and bopped along with Maliq and the rest of crowd. Liking her newfound confidence, as she let herself be free. Swinging her hips from side to side while pumping her fist into the air, Sharice got into the groove of things.

Slowing it down a little bit the DJ played Bobby Valentino's *'Slow Down'*. Thinking that she was the shit, Sharice boldly approached Maliq and placed her arms around his neck. Licking her lips she shamelessly grinded against him, causing him to get a hard on. Knowing the effect she had on him, Sharice worked her hips against him even harder. Not able to take anymore, Maliq grabbed her hand, and led her to a vacant corner of the room.

"Let's go back to my crib," he said as he kissed her ear.

"Come on, let's go get a cup of coffee." She laughed as she left him standing there. After going to the bathroom to freshen up, Sharice met back up with Maliq at a quaint table by the window.

"I know this is getting off the subject, but you have a beautiful smile, Sharice."

"Thank you, Maliq; that was nice." She smiled, feeling her cheeks burn bright red.

"I see you blush very easily."

"No, I don't," she lied, trying not to blush again, but failing.

"See, I told you so," Maliq grinned.

"Whatever," Sharice grinned too.

"So what now? I mean, the night is still young; how about we go for a walk or something?"

"Maliq, we talked about this. I agreed to lunch and that was it. I'm sorry but that is all I can offer you."

"I understand," Coach Rainey said trying to believe his own lie. Every time he stared at Sharice, his dick did a dance. Checking her watch, Sharice saw that it was getting a little late. Mason would be home soon from his date with Candice, and Sharice wanted to beat him home.

"This was nice, Coach, but I have to be getting home now."

"What happened to you calling me Maliq?"

"Hey, we do have to remain professional, don't we? I can't be calling you Maliq around the kids now, can I?"

"How about you call me Coach at school, and when we're alone call me Big Daddy," Maliq whispered, now standing in front of her.

Looking into his eyes, Sharice had the unavoidable desire to haul off and kiss the hell out of Maliq but didn't.

"Um . . . thanks for dinner, Maliq, but . . . I have to go," she replied licking her lips.

"Let me walk you to your car."

Once outside of J Bucks, they stood talking.

On the other side of town, Mason and Candice fooled around on the couch.

"Put it in, Mason," Candice begged.

"I don't know, my moms might be home any minute," he said while squeezing the tip of his dick.

"Come on, Baby, please."

"First give me some head."

"Okay but don't cum in my mouth like you did the last time."

Unzipping his pants, Candice slid his boxers down just below his knees. Taking all of him in her mouth, she bobbed her head up and down. Leaning his head back on the couch, Mason enjoyed the warm sensation coming from Candice's mouth. Sucking on the head of his dick, she flicked her tongue across the tip. Staring down at her he grabbed her head and drove himself deep inside until his dick reached the back of her throat. Guiding her head with his hand, Mason listened to the sound of Candice's mouth making slurping noises.

Juggling his balls in her right hand, she massaged his dick while still sucking on the head. Not able to deny her small supple breasts anymore, Mason lifted her up and placed her gently onto his mammoth dick. Licking his lips as Candice bounced up and down on his dick, Mason grabbed a handful of ass to lift her up even higher.

"Oh Mason! Mason!" she yelled, enjoying each stroke.

"Damn, Ma, you about to make a nigga bust," Mason groaned, ramming himself even deeper. Turning around on his dick, Candice leaned over so that he could get a good view of her round, plump ass. Playing with her asshole, he inserted a finger inside.

"Oh Baby! Play with my ass! Oh Mason!"

"I'm about to bust baby!" he yelled back.

"Ahh, go deeper! Ahh yeah, go deeper!"

Gripping her waist tightly, Mason watched as cum juices poured down her thighs. Thrusting harder, he hurried his orgasm in hopes of not getting caught by his mom. The harder he pumped, the more excited he became, and the more excited he became, the more he neared cumming. Slowing down some, he stroked her until cum came flowing down from her valley. Cumming too, Mason's juices trickled down Candice's thighs, causing a clapping sound every time she eased down on his dick. Hearing a key entering the keyhole, Mason jumped up but not fast enough.

"May—" Sharice began to yell but was stopped by the sight in front of her eyes.

"Momma, it's not what you think," Mason tried to explain.

"Mason, what in the hell is going on here!?"

"Mrs. Cummings, I am so sorry," Candice apologized.

"Candice, save your apology 'cause I don't want to hear it! What you need to do is get your clothes on and get the hell out of my house!"

"Yes, ma'am," Candice sobbed as she walked past her with her hands covering her breasts.

Slapping Mason upside his head, Sharice screamed, "What in the hell were you thinking, Mason!"

"Ma, we was just fooling around! It was nothing, don't trip!"

"It sure doesn't look like nothing! Standing there wit yo' little-ass dick out! You're naked, Mason, with cum dripping down yo' leg! Does that seem like nothing to you?"

Holding his dick in his hand, he whispered, "Nah."

"I can't believe that you would disrespect my house like this!"

"I'm sorry."

"Sorry my ass, Mason! I can't trust you anymore after you pull a stunt like this! Wait until your father hears about this!"

"What you running and telling him for?" Mason yelled.

"Because he's your father, Mason, and I think he should know how his son disrespected my house, that's why!"

"What you think you telling him gon' do? I'ma grown-ass man; there ain't shit he can do to me!" Fuck him! He don't give a shit about you or me! 'Cause if he did he wouldn't have left you for Tammy! You just want to have an excuse to talk to him! Face it, he doesn't want you anymore, Ma!"

Slap!!!

"Don't you ever in your life talk to me like that again? *Do you hear me*?"

"Mason, I'm getting ready to go. I'll talk to you later," Candice said easing out of the door.

"*Do you hear me Mason Alexzander*?!"

"Yeah!" he yelled back as he left the room.

With tears forming in her eyes, Sharice picked her keys up off the floor and headed back to her car. Sitting in the car she placed her head on the steering wheel and had herself a good cry.

Part Three

About thirty minutes passed by and Sharice still sat with her arms folded underneath her tear-stained face. Lifting her head up, she wiped her eyes, and tried not to take Mason's words to heart. But that seemed to be very hard to do since everything he said was true. A part of Sharice still longed for Lester's affection. She wanted to believe that maybe deep down inside he did in fact still love her.

Sharice tried to fool herself into believing that the relationship between him and Tammy was just temporary and that he would be back. She had been lying to herself for the past five years, telling herself that dating was useless. But in fact, all she really wanted was to be back in Lester's arms. Looking at herself in the rearview mirror, Sharice realized how foolish she looked. Not wanting to see her own reflection anymore, she rummaged through her purse in search of a number.

Ring . . . Ring . . . Ring . . .

"Hello?"

"Maliq," Sharice whispered, barely getting out through the tears.

"Sharice is that you?"

"Yeah. I'm sorry, I shouldn't have called."

"Nah, it's not a problem. I'm just shocked to hear your voice' that's all. What's up? You sound like something is wrong?"

"I don't want to talk. I just want to see you. Is that okay?"

"Yeah, you want to meet up somewhere?"

"No. Your house is fine," she replied as she fixed her makeup and hair.

After getting directions, Sharice jumped on the highway and was parked in front of Maliq's house in less than ten minutes. Knocking on his door, she waited patiently, feeling a little nervous. Smoothing her hair back once more she heard the sound of his footsteps nearing the door.

"Come on in," Maliq said as he opened the door in a wife beater and jogging pants.

"You have a nice house," Sharice said as she surveyed his living room.

"Thank you."

"The color concept that you put together is really nice," she replied nervously.

"Sharice, I know you didn't come over here to discuss the décor in my home."

"You're right."

"Well then, what's up?"

"To be honest with you, I don't know why I came over here."

"Damn, that's cold," he grinned.

"I don't mean it like that. It's just that I know that I shouldn't be here."

"But you want to be here, don't you?" Maliq said, now in her personal space.

"Yes," Sharice whispered, while gazing up into his eyes.

"I want you, Sharice," Maliq kissed her neck.

"I want you too," Sharice responded, wrapping her arms around his neck.

Taking her into his arms, Maliq guided her body over to the wall behind them. Still pleasing her neck with his lips, he interlaced his fingers with hers and placed them against the wall.

"Don't move your hands," he instructed.

Lightly gliding his tongue down over her chest, he lifted her shirt over her head. Unclasping her bra, he let it slide off and threw it across the room. Feverishly tonguing her nipples, Maliq kissed them as if they were her mouth. Biting down on her bottom lip, Sharice closed her eyes tight. Letting her inhibitions go, she held on for the ride.

Sucking her nipples until they were nice and long he flicked his tongue across them while massaging her curvy waist. Trailing kisses from her breasts on down he let his tongue play with her navel. Wanting to taste her, Maliq unzipped her jeans and slid them down her voluptuous thighs. Pushing her thong to the side, he placed each of her legs on his shoulders and began to assault her pussy with his tongue.

"Oh Maliq," Sharice called out while cumming.

Tasting her warm tender flesh, he enjoyed the sweet nectar that lay in between her thighs. Fully aroused, she began to let her hands roam across her body. Stroking her breasts, she pinched and pulled as if she were alone. Looking up Maliq became even more aroused when he saw Sharice toying with her nipples. Wanting to drive her even crazier, he sucked on her clit until her legs began to vibrate. Grinding her pussy against his face, Sharice licked her fingers and placed them on her clit. Noticing what she was about to do, Maliq grabbed her hand.

"Uh-unh, Baby, ain't no need for that. I got you," he said.

Removing her legs from around his neck, he turned her around toward the wall. Spreading her ass cheeks apart, Maliq slid his tongue slowly up the crack of her ass. Loving having this done, she came again all over his mouth. Ready to feel her, Maliq stood up and undid his pants. Holding his dick in his hand, he slid it up her now moist ass as she began to shiver.

"Put it in! Baby, please," Sharice panted.

Placing the tip in, Maliq watched as her back arched. Taking it back out he watched how it went back down. Putting the head of his dick back in, Maliq watched as Sharice bit into her lip. Pulling it out once more he noticed how her face showed disappointment.

"Quit teasing me, Baby, and fuck me!" she whined as she pushed her butt up against his dick.

Carefully guiding his way in, Maliq felt how tight she was. Fucking her untamed pussy his hands invaded her pulsating clit. Enjoying her wetness, Maliq let his dick slip out. Turning around Sharice got down on her knees and took him into her wanting mouth. Not really wanting her to do that he lay on the floor. Sitting astride his long, hard, stiff dick, Sharice's insatiable appetite for dick escalated.

Using her well-toned calf muscles, she placed her feet on the floor and worked his dick like she was riding in the Kentucky Derby. Feeling like he was about to cum, Maliq picked Sharice up and placed her on the couch.

"What's wrong?" she asked, panting heavily.

"Play wit yourself."

Smiling, Sharice gladly glided her hand down and circulated her fingers around her now blossomed pussy lips.

Making sure he had a good view, Maliq sat on the opposite end of the couch and watched as she stroked herself. Connecting eyes with him, Sharice licked her finger and inserted them inside her treasure chest of pleasure. Seducing her pussy with her fingers, she watched as Maliq glided his hand up and down his rock-hard dick.

"That's it, Baby, play wit it," Maliq groaned.

"You like that, Baby?" she asked.

"Yeah, Baby suck yo' fingers for me."

Sliding her glazed fingers out, Sharice took them into her mouth and sucked.

"What it taste like?" he asked.

"It taste like caramel kisses," she smiled.

"I want to see you cum. Cum for me, Baby."

Spreading her lips apart, she stroked her clit and rotated her hips. Imagining that Maliq was tearing her shit up, she let her mind drift away and her desires seep through. Cupping her pussy with both hands she felt herself nearing another orgasm.

"Ahh yeah!" Sharice screamed.

Watching as cum poured from her vaginal walls, Maliq took his lips and caught every drop in his mouth. Lapping it up, his tongue played with her pussy, causing more electrical sparks to go off inside of her. Holding the back of her thighs, Maliq pushed them up by her head and sucked on her juicy clit. Feeling another jolt of orgasmic pleasure rip through her body, Sharice called out for God.

"Oh my God! Oh yeah! Eat it , Baby! Yeah! Like that! Just like that!"

Never in her life had Sharice cum so much. Maliq was everything that she longed for. Cumming again, Maliq buried his face deep inside her pussy so that he could taste every last drop of her juices. Taking his face into her hand, she guided him back up to her mouth.

Kissing him, Sharice licked her juices off of his face.

Squeezing the head of his dick, Maliq pushed his way back in. Fucking her slowly, his grinding increased, causing them to fall onto the floor. Laughing, they continued on as if nothing had happened.

"Damn, Ma, I can't get enough of you," Maliq moaned.

"Don't ever stop fucking me," she said, licking his neck.

Pumping like he was trying to break her back, Maliq lifted both of her legs into the air, holding on to her feet.

"Oh my God, Boy what are you doing to me?" Sharice asked, delirious.

"I'm fucking you like you ain't never been fucked before." Slapping thighs, Sharice's head bounced off the floor as she tried to find something to hold onto. With nothing in sight, she did the only thing she could do, play with her tits.

"Fuck, I'm about to cum!" Maliq yelled scrunching up his face.

"Cum inside of me," Sharice moaned.

Normally Maliq would have been concerned, but that night he didn't give a fuck. If he could have, he would have slept inside of her pussy.

"Don't move!" he yelled.

"Cum inside of me, Baby! Cum inside… Oh! Oh baby!"

"*Goddamn*! Yo' pussy feel good!" Maliq shouted, ready to bust.

Pushing him back' Sharice hungrily took him in her mouth letting his creamy cum explode all over her face. Licking all over his dick, she made sure that no trace of cum was left. Using her right hand, she rubbed up and down his shaft while sucking on the head of his dick.

Gripping the back of her head, Maliq tilted his head to the side, enjoying the sensation.

Sharice spit-coated his rock hard dick as she French kissed every pulsating inch. Wanting him to cum again in her mouth, she played with his balls. The combination of his dick in her mouth and his balls in her hand drove Maliq crazy.

Picking Sharice up off the floor, he prepared her for some more rough sex. Sliding her down onto his dick, he slapped her ass and told her to go. Taking her cue, Sharice bopped on his dick like it was a joystick. Making her butt cheeks jiggle, he grabbed her tiny waist and drove himself into the depths of her pussy.

"You gon' cum again," he grunted.

"Yes, Daddy!"

"I want you to cum all over me!"

"Ooh, I wanna cum! I wanna cum all over you!" she whined as she grinded anxiously.

Taking one of her breasts in his mouth, Maliq probed her nipples with his wet, slippery tongue. Sharice's pussy was throbbing for another orgasm.

Dropping it down on him, she made sure that his dick hit her spot. With every stroke that she gave, Maliq stroked back even harder.

"You cumming?" he asked.

"No, not yet," she panted.

"Oh, I see you wanna play games," he grinned deviously.

Flipping her over, Maliq entered her from the back. Fucking her hard and fast, he gripped one side of her ass so that he could hit another corner of her wall. Leaning down on her elbows, Sharice put a little arch in her back so that she could take in all of Maliq.

"Ahh baby just like that!"

"Damn, Baby, I love fucking you!"

"Maliq, I feel it! I'm about to cum!" she yelled with quivering lips.

"I'm about to bust too!"

"Cum on my back baby!"

"I wanna cum inside!" he pumped slow and hard.

Feeling himself become weak, Maliq let out a loud, thunderous moan. Cumming too, Sharice closed her eyes and screamed. Juices not only went inside of Sharice, it went down her butt, on the couch and on Maliq. Weak and limp, he slumped over Sharice, still grinding slow. Neither could move so they just lay there in their juices for almost an hour.

Part Four

Two weeks passed by, and Sharice had been avoiding Maliq like he was the plague. Whenever Mason had practice she would let him drive the car just so she wouldn't run into Maliq. Mason found this odd, but he didn't care as long he had the car a couple of times a week. Maliq called every day but Sharice never would answer.

He couldn't figure out what the problem was. They had had mind-blowing, kinky, animalistic sex and still he couldn't get her to change her mind about him.

Rubbing her thighs she tried to ease some of the pain that Maliq had caused weeks before. She hadn't been sore like that since high school. Hearing her cell phone ring ,she picked it up.

314-555-7252 showed on the screen; it was Maliq. She didn't know what to do. A part of her wanted desperately to give him a chance. But logical thinking always kicked in, and then she would dismiss the whole idea. Letting the phone ring until her voicemail kicked in, she waited a minute before checking it. Putting her code in Sharice listened as Maliq poured his heart out over the phone.

Yo', Ma, I miss you. I don't know why you won't answer or return my calls. I wish you would just give me a chance, Sharice. All I want to do is make you happy. If you don't want that, then I'll understand. But I can't keep on going back and forth wit you. For me to be the younger one, it seems to me like you're the one playing games. This is my last time calling you, so you can quit avoiding me cause it ain't even like that no more.

Sitting Indian style on the floor, she listened to the message five more times. Maliq was right, she was the one playing games. Looking at her calendar on the wall, she saw that Mason had practice the following day. Tomorrow she would leave all of her insecurities and doubts at the door and give her heart to Maliq.

Pulling up to the field, Sharice inhaled deeply and got out. It was kind of windy and chilly out that afternoon, so she wrapped her arms snugly under her breasts to shield herself from the wind. Finding Maliq standing alone, deep in thought, her heart began to flutter. Tapping him on the shoulder she waited to get his attention. Giving him a half smile, Sharice waited to see his reaction to seeing her again.

"What's up?" he asked with attitude.

"I got your message last night," she spoke softly.

"So, you have been avoiding me?"

"No." Giving her a look that said you're lying, she told the truth. "I mean, yes."

"I don't see what for. I told you I'm done. I ain't got time for all the games."

"That's just it; I'm not playing games. I'm just afraid, Maliq."

"Afraid of what? I told you that I wasn't gonna hurt you."

"I know that. It's just that I've been through a lot, and I'm not trying to get hurt again."

"I understand that, Sharice. I'm not like none of them other niggaz you done fucked wit."

Smiling, she laughed at the way he talked. Loving to see her smile, Maliq wrapped his arms around her and hugged her tight. Hugging him, Sharice knew that with him is where she wanted to be. Pulling her behind the outdoors restroom, Maliq passionately kissed her.

"I want to taste you right now," Maliq moaned.

"I want you to, too, but we can't," Sharice grinned.

Flicking his finger across her hard nipples, he made her moan.

"Come on, just a little taste." Not giving her enough time to answer, Maliq pushed her thong to the side and lightly licked her clit.

"Ooh, Baby, don't make me cum," Sharice moaned again.

"Come by and see me tonight," Maliq smiled, easing his way back up, now licking her neck.

"Okay," she whispered, barely able to breath.

Just as Maliq was about to lift up Sharice's skirt again, Mason appeared, startling them both.

"What the fuck you doing rubbing on my momma, nigga?" Mason yelled.

"Mason, watch your damn mouth!" Sharice yelled back.

"Nah, fuck that! What the fuck you doing wit this nigga, Ma? This is my coach!"

"I know, Baby, but Maliq and I care for each other."

"Yeah, man, me and your mom really like each other. I care for her a lot and would never do anything to hurt her," Maliq explained.

"Man, fuck what you talkin' about!" Mason said, getting up in Maliq's face.

"Don't even try it!" Sharice shouted.

"Yo' Mason, what's the deal? We can hear y'all all the way on the field," a teammate said.

"Fuck this, man, I'm out of here," Mason said, pushing past Maliq.

"I am so sorry Maliq," Sharice apologized.

"It's cool. He's just shocked. He'll be a'ight." He smiled, trying to reassure her.

"I hope so," Sharice said, still worried.

Four hours later Mason still was still M.I.A., and Sharice paced the floor awaiting his return.

"What's wrong, Ma?" Mya asked.

"Nothing. I just need to talk to your brother, that's all."

"He's probably over Candice's freaky butt house." Mya laughed. Laughing too for a second, she stopped once she heard Mason walking through the door.

"Where have you been? Mommy's been worried," Mya yelled at Mason.

"Shut up talking to me, lil' girl," Mason yelled back, not in the mood.

"I don't appreciate how you acted earlier, Mason. I raised you better than that," Sharice said.

"And I don't appreciate seeing my thirty-seven-year-old mother kissing my twenty-something-year-old coach," Mason yelled.

"Momma, you was kissing Coach Rainey?" Mya questioned.

"Yes, I was! I think the two of you forget that I am grown! There is more to my life than taking care of the two of you!"

"You go, Momma. Coach Rainey is *fine.* All the girls like him," Mya said.

"Thank you, Mya," Sharice smiled.

"She young; she don't know no better. How you think that's gon' make me look when everybody finds out that my momma is dating somebody half her age!" Mason continued to shout.

"It's not about you, Mason! This is about my happiness! Your father gets to do whatever he wants to do and I don't hear you two complaining about that! Finally, for the first time in years, I have found some kind of joy and you want to ruin it with your selfishness!"

"Of all the niggaz in the world, why it gotta be Coach Rainey!" Mason asked.

"Call him another nigga if you want to! Now I'm sick of this! You get to have football and Candice's ol' trifling ass. Your father gets to have money, the house, cars, and Tammy. And what do I get? A nine-to-five job, a mortgage, car payments, bills, and a spoiled, selfish son!"

"I don't want you seeing that nigga, Ma!"

"It's not up to you, Mason! Who I date is my business, not yours! I make my own decisions!"

"Just like you made the decision to date Nathan!" he shot back.

Before she knew it, Sharice had swung and hit Mason in the face twice. A knot was already beginning to form on his forehead.

Holding his head, he looked at his mother and cried.

"I'm sorry, Mason, I didn't mean to do it," she said ashamed of her actions.

"It's cool, gon' ahead and be wit that nigga! But when he hurt you, don't come running to me 'cause I ain't got nothing for you," Mason said as he turned to go upstairs to his room.

Crying too, Sharice slumped down on the couch and let the tears flow.

"It's okay, Mommy, I'm happy for you," Mya said while holding her mother.

"Thank you, Mya."

"If I was you, I would've hit him again." Mya laughed.

"I know you would have, Mya." Sharice laughed too.

Later that night, after hours of contemplation, Sharice made the call that her heart dreaded making. Slowly dialing the seven digits, she lifted the phone up to her ear and listed for the rings.

"Hello?" Maliq said, half sleep.

"Hi," Sharice said, clearing her voice.

"Hey, beautiful, how are you?"

"I'm okay, but…"

"But what," he asked, hearing the hesitation in her voice.

"I need to talk to you."

"About what?"

"Us," she whispered while tears formed in her eyes.

"What about us, Sharice?"

"I've been thinking that maybe seeing each other isn't a good idea after all."

"Is this because of what happened today between you and Mason?"

"Yes and no. I mean, he's really hurt by this and I have already hurt him once before. I will not do that to my son again."

"So you're just going to let your kids run your life?" Maliq asked, upset.

"Mason is not running my life. I run my life," she said, not believing her own words.

"Yeah, a'ight, whatever, Sharice. When you grow up come holla at me," Maliq said, hanging up in her ear.

Still holding the phone to her ear, she listened to the dial tone, shocked and hurt. After a while, she hung up the phone and curled up into a ball, crying herself to sleep.

The next couple of days seemed to go by like a cloud of smoke. Sharice went to work, did stuff for the kids, cooked, cleaned, and cried.

Her heart hadn't hurt so bad since Lester had left her for Tammy. Often at night she would toy with the idea of calling Maliq but would always punk-out. The night they had spent together replayed over and over again in her mind. Every single detail of their encounter was remembered accurately. From the feel of his tongue, to the way he looked in her eyes.

Maliq brought out things in Sharice that she didn't even know existed. She prayed for years that she would meet someone who could satisfy her every sexual desire. She never knew what good dick felt like until meeting Maliq. Another month was approaching and she had not spoken to Maliq in weeks.

He hadn't tried calling her, seeing her, or anything. Sharice figured that he might have moved on. Mason was happier than ever. He had gotten his way once again. The more she looked at him the more she resented her decision. The more time passed by, the more she wanted to live for herself.

On the weekends, when Mya was home, the two would go shopping and get manicures and pedicures. Mya even gotten her mother to dress hipper. Even though she enjoyed her time with her daughter, Sharice's heart still ached for Maliq.

Sometimes at night she would ride past his house to see if he was there. She held her breath each time, hoping that another car wasn't in the driveway. Her heart couldn't take it if she found out that he was seeing another woman so soon. One day while they were out, Mya gave her mother some advice.

"Momma, I know you miss Coach Rainey."

"How you figure that," Sharice questioned back.

"It's written all over you. I can look in your eyes and tell."

"I do miss him a lot, but I don't think he misses me as much," Sharice explained.

"Momma, just because he ain't called you don't mean that he don't miss you. You told him to step, didn't you?"

"Yeah."

"Well then. Men don't take rejection well, Momma. If you want Coach Rainey back, you are going to have to go out and get him," Mya said knowingly.

"But what about your brother?"

"What about him? You got to do you, Ma."

"Girl, you are too grown for your own good." Sharice laughed.

"I know I am but I'm right. Watching Oprah has taught me a lot." Mya grinned.

"What am I gonna do wit you?" Sharice smiled, hugging her daughter.

The next day after picking Mason up from practice, Sharice made her way over to Maliq's house. When he opened the door, he was surprised to find Sharice standing there in a tight pink Baby Phat shirt and jeans.

"I know that I should've called first, but I didn't have my phone on me," she lied.

"It's a'ight," he said, playing it cool.

"Can I come in?" she asked.

Holding the door open for her, he didn't answer. Without a word, Sharice grabbed Maliq's face and kissed his lips. Missing her just as much as she missed him, he kissed her back with intensity. Tearing into each other's clothes, Maliq quickly inserted himself deep into her warm pussy.

"Damn, you feel good."

"You too."

"Ooh, I missed you," Maliq moaned.

"I missed you too baby," she said while kissing his soft lips.

"You feel just as good as last time," he panted, pumping in and out of her feverishly.

"Ooh Maliq, fuck me!"

"Like that?" Maliq asked giving her the death stroke.

"Ooh yes, just like that!"

"I can't live without you, Ma."

"I can't live without you, Pa," she smiled.

Smiling too, he fucked her even harder. Biting down on her nipples, he licked and sucked until they burned a deep red. Every time Maliq stroked he drowned in the wetness of her pussy.

"Damn you wet! You must've really missed me!"

"I missed you so much, Daddy! Ahh! Fuck this pussy, Baby!"

"I'm getting ready to cum!" Maliq grunted.

"Me too, Baby! I love you!"

"Promise me you'll give us a chance," he said.

"I promise," Sharice yelled as cum dripped down from her caramel coated walls.

Lady Scorpio

Michael T. Owens

She hadn't had sex since leaving that sorry Negro in February. That was three months ago—ninety whole days without *it.* She didn't necessarily miss *him* but she did miss those big hands on her thighs, that magical tongue, the heat of his body on hers, and that long, smooth, chocolaty . . . She didn't want to think about it anymore, didn't want to get too hot and bothered at work. He wasn't much of a boyfriend, but the man definitely had a gift and he knew how to use it. The only problem was he used it on anything with legs and a slit. At thirty-three years of age, Debra Clark didn't have time for that. But it was getting ridiculous. Simply put, she needed to get a piece, something thick and juicy. Her girls said it would relieve stress and free her mind. But they didn't have to tell her about the therapeutic powers of sex. She was a Scorpio, a lady Scorpio, the most intense, most sexual zodiac sign, she already knew. Before this drought, she had more sex than all of her friends combined. Those were the days. At anytime, she could get a man; men loved a light-skinned woman, especially a busty one; that wasn't an issue. But she wanted to honor the promise she'd made to herself: no more casual sex. She knew it would be hard. To ease her mind, she convinced herself that sex was overrated, that most men didn't satisfy her, and that going without sex wasn't a big deal. Those lies quickly faded. Often she caught herself fantasizing about men she had sexed and men she wanted to sex, kinky things she wanted to try, etc. However, a promise was a promise. No casual sex. She knew it would take all she had to resist Mr. Jameer Lovett. He recently transferred from another Orlando district, and today was his first day. He would be reporting directly to her.

It was Monday morning, 11:45 sharp. Jameer walked inside Debra's office as if he owned the world. It immediately turned her on. He was definitely attractive with his freshly edged and trimmed hair. Although he looked young for his age, his physique was something to behold—the upper body of a middleweight boxer, the lower body of a runner, and smooth Brazilian nut skin. The small scar on his cheek seemed more like a beauty mark than a blemish; it rounded out his rugged prettyboy look, made him even sexier. Debra had heard about his reputation for being a cocky, smart-alecky jock, but she'd dealt with his kind before. Her last boyfriend fit the same bad boy mold. For some reason she was attracted to that type, but she reminded herself that he was off limits. Everything had to be kept professional. Besides, her sexual toys served her just fine—although they weren't anything like the real thing. She knew the real thing when she saw it, when she felt it. Part of her wanted to know if Jameer was the real thing.

"I'm Ms. Clark. Nice to meet you," Debra extended her hand.

Jameer shook it reluctantly. "I know."

"Sit," she said, in a slightly commanding tone. She knew his kind had issues with women in authority—unless it was in bed. She planned on using it to get under his skin just for fun, just because she could. Browsing through a manila folder on the desk, she said, "I've heard about you, Mr. Lovett. You're some piece of work."

"Whatever you heard is all true." He smiled slowly.

Debra closed the folder. "You're proud of this?"

"Why am I in here? What we meeting for?"

"What *are* we meeting for is the proper English, Mr. Lovett."

"Is that you?" Jameer asked, looking at Debra's picture on the desk. "Nice picture, *real* nice . . ."

He had known her less than sixty seconds and was already making moves. Typical.

Debra took a sip of Pepsi and cleared her throat. "You should know up front that I'm nothing like the people you've dealt with. I don't mess around. I can make this a miserable place if you don't cooperate. Understand?"

Jameer picked at his nails and smiled.

Debra stood. "We're done, Mr. Lovett, but I want you to check in Mondays, Wednesdays, and Fridays until you're acclimated."

"Check in? What kind of place is this?"

"Like I said, I don't play games."

"Okay, Deb."

"Ms. Clark!"

"I have some work to do. See you Wednesday . . . *Ms. Clark*," he smiled deviously.

Debra licked her lips at the shapeliness of his butt as he left. It looked juicy but firm. She wanted to slap it, squeeze it, lick it, bite it—she wanted to do everything. He was the macho type but she could handle that. His attitude sent sexual thoughts through her head: various sex positions and locales; she could use her entire arsenal of toys, or maybe even do some role-playing. Oh what fun they could have but only in a fantasy world. Nothing could ever happen in reality—or could it? She took another sip of Pepsi to cool off. Two years at her job and finally, she had some eye-candy, something she could look forward to. Wednesday couldn't come soon enough.

* * *

Debra woke up thirty minutes early to get ready on Wednesday. She had a red skirt with a matching blouse that she had been dying to wear but never did. The outfit accentuated the curves of her chest, hips, and butt, and it tested the rules of acceptable and unacceptable work attire. She convinced herself that being sent home was the worst that could happen. Why not live on the edge for once? Besides, she wanted to catch Jameer's attention. She had no real intentions other than showing him she wasn't conservative in appearance. That was just her work persona. Outside of work, she could mix things up and get loose like the next person.

Just before lunch time, she worked feverishly on an excel spreadsheet. She hoped to finish before Jameer arrived. A few times she glanced at the clock, anticipating him. Before she knew it, he stood in her office looking good, smelling good. If she didn't know any better, she would have thought that he too had put extra effort in his appearance today. He said hello with a crooked smirk. He appeared as though he knew she had been thinking of him, knew she dressed up to impress him.

"Wow, 11:45 on the dot," she said.

He tapped his watch. "I believe in being on time."

"That's a good quality," she said flatly. She didn't want to acknowledge any of his flirting attempts. "I have some forms I need you to fill out."

"Can I borrow your pen?"

Debra's pen accidentally fell on the floor as she handed it to him.

"I'll get it," he said, ducking underneath the desk.

"Ahh!" she jumped when his arm brushed her leg.

"Sorry, my bad. Why are you so jumpy?"

"I wasn't expecting that. You scared me."

"I can see if it was my tongue but it was just my arm . . ."

"That was an inappropriate comment, Mr. Lovett."

Jameer laughed.

"Um . . . did you find the pen yet?" she asked uneasily.

"Nope, still looking." He caught sight of her smooth, slender legs and hadn't stopped staring. His eyes moved from the tip of her red pumps, up her calves, to her crossed caramel thighs. He wondered what kind of goodies she hid under her skirt. He felt himself getting hard. "Still . . . looking . . . "

Debra could feel him looking at her under the desk. " . . . Maybe I need to help you."

"No!" He grabbed her legs before she could stand. "I have it under control." He moved his hands across her calves. "How do you get your skin so soft?"

"Mr. Lovett, this is extremely unpro . . . " she felt his tongue, moist and warm, moving up the back of her left leg. "Unprofessional . . . "

"You're right, Ms. Clark," his voice was muffled under the desk. "I guess . . . I should . . . stop . . . " He slowly uncrossed her legs, raised her skirt just enough to expose her lower thighs. His tongue moved slow and controlled, then wild and fast, almost as if playing tic-tac-toe on her skin. "If you want me to stop just say so."

"Huh?" Debra swallowed the lump in her throat and exhaled slowly. *This is wrong, so wrong but it feels so good,* she thought. And he was no where close to her goodies yet.

"Tell me to stop if that's what you want."

"Huh?"

"Do-you-want-me to stop?" He slid his hand up the opening of her skirt, across the trail of saliva he made.

" . . . Huh?" she said again, even though she'd heard him perfectly the first two times. Her voice was weaker, almost trembling.

Using his index finger, Jameer lightly tapped the moist center of her panties. "I asked you a question; don't be rude, Ms. Clark."

Feeling him under the desk without actually seeing him drove her crazy. It was mysterious, adventurous, and stimulating. Without saying a word, she slid her skirt up as far as it would go and spread her legs wide. He was free to do whatever he wanted, however he wanted, as long as he wanted.

He licked his lips, nodded, and smiled. "That's what I thought . . . " He reached under her skirt and slowly pulled her panties down her legs.

She shifted her body so he would have no difficulty.

"This is what you wanted, right?"

She said nothing.

"Ms. Clark!"

"Huh? What?" Debra snapped out of her short-lived fantasy.

"This is what you wanted, right? You wanted to see my work." Jameer walked to the desk and handed her a folder.

"Oh, yes. Thank you."

"You looked zoned out for a minute. You all right?"

"I'm fine. Just a little tired. I need more caffeine." She rubbed her eyes then took a sip of Pepsi. "I drink too much soda . . . "

"Maybe you should get some rest tonight. Pretty women should always get their rest . . . "

Debra stared for a moment before the comment registered in her head. She wasn't that easy! He would need more than that to impress the Lady Scorpio. She decided not to comment. Instead she said, "I'll look this over and get it back to you ASAP."

Debra stayed at work for a few more hours before leaving. Attending numerous staff meetings, preparing a presentation for a conference, daily office duties, and general administrative work began taking its toll. Not getting enough sleep wasn't good for a light-skinned woman like her; dark circles would easily show under her eyes. Her plan, when she got home, was to eat, shower, finish Michael T. Owens' latest book, and go to bed early.

When she made it home, she noticed all the things she meant to do but hadn't: take out the trash, load the dishwasher, and open the mail on the counter.

"I'm too tired. I'll do that later," she said out loud, looking over the place. She kicked off her shoes, let her plum highlighted hair down, and slipped out of her clothes. She looked over her naked body in the mirror: five-seven, a size eight, and curvy where she needed curves, slim where she needed to be. She turned to the side to look at the small scorpion tattoo on her left shoulder blade. It had the words "Lady Scorpio" below it. Her ex thought it was sexy. "You had a good woman," she said, grabbing her breasts while thinking about him. "I know you miss this."

Thoughts of those hot and steamy nights made her nipples stiffen. Moving her hands across her chest, down her sides, and between her thighs, she then thought about the fantasy from earlier. At first she refused to let her mind take that path. Jameer was younger and probably inexperienced—she wasn't in the business of training anyone. As she touched herself, all she kept hearing in her head was: *Do you want me to stop?*

She pulled one of her pleasure toys from the closet. It was long, thick, and flexible. It was her favorite and even had a remote control. Propping herself on two pillows, she began stimulating herself. Slow, soft, and steady—something her ex never mastered. Fast and hard was all he seemed to know. She was moist now, ready for her treat. Seductively, she licked her toy, covering it with saliva before pushing it inside. No remote was needed; she would do it manually this time.

"Mmmm . . . " She slid it in.

She slid it out. "Ohh . . ."

In. "Unghh . . ."

"Ahhh . . ." Out.

Her mind drifted to Jameer and the casual innuendos he had made: *Is that you? Nice picture, real nice . . . Maybe you should get some rest tonight. Pretty women should always get their rest . . .*

For a moment, she felt awkward because she rarely let anyone or anything at work affect her personal life. *Oh well. It's just a silly fantasy,* she reminded herself. *It's not real. It's all in fun.* Once she convinced herself, it was back to the matter at hand.

"Yeahh. Hmm Mmm. I . . . I'll control you like a-a-a little dog," she said to an imaginary Jameer. "You think you're sooo . . . b . . . bad, huh? Mmmm . . ."

In.

Out.

IN.

OUT.

"Yep," she heard him say. "I'll have you worshipping the ground I walk on . . ." He pushed deeper inside, his testicles squishing against her, his chest against her breast.

Sweat on sweat.

Heat on heat.

Thrust after thrust.

"You're just a little boy to me! I'll break you in h-h-haaalf—oohh . . ."

"Yeah?" He pulled her hair while thrusting harder. "A little boy?"

"Y-Yeah—ooooooooh . . . ah . . ."

He gripped underneath her chin with his hand, looked dead into her teary eyes, and then removed himself.

"Wha? What are you doing? Put it back in!"

He licked his lips. "Nope."

"*Put it back innnnnn now*!"

Jameer wiped his sweaty forehead and smiled. "What's the magic word?"

"Pleeease! Pleeeeeeeeease put it—" Before she could finish, he was already inside churning diagonal, up, down, and side to side. He left no area untouched.

"Do you want me to stop?" she heard his voice in her ears again.

This time she answered quickly. "Noooo! I don't want you to stop . . ."

"Didn't-think-so!" Jameer's three deep thrusts lit her insides.

"Mmmm . . . oh…my . . . goddddddd, that feels so . . . " Her sentence was cut short by an internal tidal wave of pleasure gushing from her body onto the sheets. She eased her toy from her body, sitting it aside while she caught her breath. Fantasy over. Looking up at the ceiling, she lay on the sweaty sheets thinking about what had just happened. It made her laugh out loud. "I can't believe I just did that!"

* * *

Debra felt uneasy when Jameer walked into her office Friday. Wednesday night she pleased herself while thinking of him, and today it was back to being professional. It just didn't seem right, but it sure felt good!

"How are things going, Mr. Lovett. Are you adjusting to your new environment?"

"I'm doing all right. I'll tell you one thing, the ladies around here are crazy!"

"What do you mean?"

"I don't want to sound like I'm bragging, but they keep throwing themselves at me."

"I thought guys liked that."

"Immature women don't do anything for me." He leaned in close, walking his fingers across her desk. "I like mature women. Women who know what they want and aren't afraid to get it."

Debra adjusted her hair, even though it didn't need it. It threw her off every time he talked like that, especially since she was his superior. How was she supposed to reply to his comment? "Well, Mr. Lovett, that's good. Uh, I read over your work and—"

"How come you're not married?"

"Excuse me?"

"How come you don't have a husband? You seem like a nice woman."

"That's none of your business, Mr. Lovett."

"It's just a simple question. Why you getting so uptight?"

Debra ignored his question. "Your work was surprisingly good. It flowed well and your analysis of the—"

"All the things you heard about me made you think I was dumb?"

"No. No, that's not it at all. I didn't mean it that way."

"Tell me how you meant it, then." He leaned back in his chair and waited for an answer.

"Well . . ."

"Why aren't you looking me in the face?"

Debra couldn't look him in the face because of fantasies she'd had. But she couldn't tell him that. Usually Scorpios were good at hiding emotions, but her face hinted of guilt. "Mr. Lovett . . ."

"It's okay. People doubted me my whole life; I'm use to it," his voice rose. "They doubted my cousin, too, and now he's out in L.A. making moves."

She cleared her throat. "All I was saying is—"

"I'll see you Monday." He stood up and sarcastically said, "Have a good weekend."

He walked out.

Debra stared at the door, trying her best to figure out what just happened. One minute she was talking about his work, the next minute he was asking about her personal life, the next minute he was gone. *I think I hurt his feelings*, she said to herself. Seeing flashes of his sensitive side made her curious—more curious than she already was. She already wanted to know basic things like: *What size is penis? Is he a two-minute man or a marathon man in bed? Are his orgasms silent or loud?* Now she wondered who Jameer Lovett really was. What made him tick? And why did seeing him get upset turn her on?

Late that night Debra awoke with an insatiable craving for something sweet: key lime pie, lemon pound cake and ice-cream, or Jameer would do. In addition to her cravings, her breasts felt tender, and she had been feeling hornier than usual. She knew it was close to that time of month. She felt clammy and hot inside, heat flashes were another monthly symptom of hers. To cool down, she slipped out of her panties and Mickey Mouse T-shirt, opting to sleep in the nude. Maybe she could fall back to sleep.

Fifteen minutes later she was still awake, staring at the numbers on her digital clock: 10:52PM. 10:52PM on a Friday night and she was in bed. Back in the days, she would be getting ready to hit the club. She rolled on her back. Every little sound seemed ten times louder than usual. The crickets outside sounded like an orchestra. The cars driving by sounded like trains. Even with those miscellaneous noises, her room still seemed lonely—and Scorpios didn't like being alone. She had gotten use to it, but around this time of the month it bothered her. If she could just get to sleep she would be fine. A good, body-rocking orgasm would knock her out for the night. But she tried to avoid any sexual thoughts; it would only make matters worse. Instead, she counted backwards from one hundred. By the time she reached the seventies, her eyes were fluttering.

Seventy-eight . . .

Seventy-sev . . .

Seventy-si . . .

She yawned twice and off to dreamland she went.

A noise from her squeaky bedroom door woke her an hour into her slumber. Standing in the doorway was a shadowy male figure. He stood motionless with his arms folded. She jumped from the pillow, covering her breasts with the sheets.

"Who are you?" she asked. "How did you get pass the alarm?"

The figure stepped forward. Looking harder, she realized it was Jameer. "Shhh," he said. "It's the middle of the night, why you talking so loud?"

"How did you get in my house?"

"The front door, how else?"

"What do you want?"

"Do you always sleep naked?"

"Answer me!"

"I want what you want . . . " He smiled and took off his shirt.

"Leave!"

"That's not what you want . . . " He loosened his belt, dropped his pants and boxers to the floor. "Playtime is over," he said, walking closer to the bed. "I know what you *really* want." His body was more muscular than she had imagined. And that big trophy hanging between his thighs sent lustful thoughts through her mind. "Touch it. You know you want to."

She bit her top lip. He looked good and tasty, thick and juicy—just what she liked. It took all she had to keep from attacking him.

"I said touch it!" Using his lower muscles, Jameer bounced his manhood up and down, enticing her to take it into her hands, mouth, or wherever else. Seeing his "talent" was all it took. In one motion, she pulled him to her face, taking as much of him in her mouth as possible, grabbing his butt for leverage. She feasted on him while he stroked her hair, smiling with pleasure as her head moved as if bobbing for apples. Using her warm tongue, she made spiral designs up, down, and around his crown. She trapped it between her tongue and the roof of her mouth, pressed her lips together and squeezed. Every time he moaned, she got wetter. Every time he groaned, she licked, slurped, and sucked harder.

"Mmm gooood . . . " she moaned. With a loud popping sound, she removed her lips and looked at him. His facial expression, squinted eyes, and open mouth begged for more, though he said nothing. She took a deep breath and returned to her post.

"Look at you. So greedy." He smiled.

"Unh huh . . ." she mumbled.

He felt a bubbling sensation building in his abdomen. Debra sucked with great determination, as if charming it out of him against his will. His muscles constricted as he buckled forward. Grabbing her head, he tried to push her away. She refused. She would not move until she was ready. He grunted, cursed, shook his head while the pressure seeped downward, swelling in his loins.

"That's enough!" He snatched himself from her wet mouth before her job was done. He pulled up his pants.

"Where are you going? Don't leave!"

"Bye."

"Don't leave . . . don't leave . . . don't l—"

Debra opened her eyes and looked around the room. The bedspread was laying on the floor; her pillows were sideways. The clock read: 1:17AM. She put a hand on her forehead. She was hot and sweaty, and her thighs were moist. The dream seemed so real, she smacked her lips to see if she tasted anything unusual.

* * *

Debra never understood the weather in Orlando. An hour ago the sun shined brightly; now it was pouring rain. When would it stop? Why was it ruining her Saturday night? If she had a man, it would be fine. The sound, smell, feel, and even the sight of rain used to put her in a relaxed and often sexual state of mind. To distract herself, she sipped a little wine. During a brief moment of insanity, she scrolled through the few male telephone numbers in her cell phone. She had deleted most of her old flame's numbers because she didn't want temptations during her abstinence kick. Besides, they were *old* flames for a reason—they were no good. If she could get some without dealing with them she would, but there was no way to do that. And she would have to talk to them. What torture that would be. She didn't feel like hearing the customary I miss yous, the come back to mess, the you're the best thing to ever happen to mes, or the I didn't realize what I hads. All she wanted was sex. Couldn't they understand that? She didn't want to get back together; she didn't want to hang out, didn't want to go anywhere with them—she just wanted sex. *Sex. Sex. Sex.* She loved how the word sounded in her mind. Just like men, sometimes women just wanted sex and nothing else. But if she let them feel the bedroom sting of the Lady Scorpio again, they would assume they were back in her life. They would think it would be a regular thing. That meant more drama and she would end up pissed, especially if she didn't get off. She set the phone aside; it wasn't worth it. Being a do-it-yourselfer still had its appeal. Recently she had purchased a new sex toy. It was neon green and it glowed in the dark. Tonight would be a good night to try it out.

Her toy hid on the top shelf of her walk-in closet. She had to stand on her tip-toes to reach it. It looked like it would be fun. She imagined all the things she could do with it. As her mind drifted, Jameer peeked through her blouses hanging on the rack. He was completely naked and fine.

"Peek-a-boo!"

"Oh my god, Jameer! You almost made me piss in my pants."

"Sorry, baby."

"What are you doing here?"

He came from behind the blouses. "You . . . "

He kissed her before she could reply. As horny as she was, she didn't resist. He moved so fast, she didn't have time even if she wanted. Their tongues moved wildly, licking each other's lips, noses, cheeks, chins. They didn't discriminate.

"Baby, you don't know how horny I am," Jameer said.

"No, you don't know how horny *I am*!" Debra's clothes slid off effortlessly as if her skin were made of Teflon. Jameer took a few seconds to admire her body before lifting her up and pinning her against the closet wall. He was stronger than she had imagined; his body wedged between her legs, his hands under her butt, all of his weight pushing against her. She squirmed when the cool wall touched her naked back, but she heated up quickly.

"Boy, if you don't hurry up and give it to me, I'm going to, I'm going to . . . " She didn't know what she would do, but he had better give it to her. And he did. His manhood burned so hot, he had to extinguish it inside of her—immediately. She squealed when the tip reached her, and moaned when the rest followed. The power in his thrusts along with his guttural grunting was the barbaric savagery that made her curse and scream. Hopefully the neighbors didn't hear. They might have called the police, thinking she was being assaulted. An assault *was* taking place—a full frontal assault by Jameer. With both arms wrapped around him, she felt the tension in his back muscles flexing and contracting. How he managed to thrust so many times and still have the strength to keep her pinned surprised her. She was speechless. Neither of them spoke, their actions spoke; for them. And how in the world was he hitting her spot every single time? Ecstasy was inevitable. It arrived with the force of a monsoon blowing through her body. Closing her eyes hard, savoring each stroke, she screamed so loud, she may have awakened the entire subdivision. When her eyes opened, she was against the closet wall. Alone, breathing heavy, with her new glow-in-the-dark sex toy in hand.

She shook her head, rubbing the hairs on the back of her neck. "Mmm. Mmm. Mmm." No longer did guilt plague her mind. She wasn't ashamed of anything. The Lady Scorpio was a grown woman with grown woman needs. She would satisfy them by any means, fulfilling her desires however she wanted, as many times as she pleased. That's right. Once she gained her breath, she prepared to let Jameer work his magic again.

On the edge of the bed, she sat twirling her neon toy to a ballad playing on the radio. The Quiet Storm always set the mood. She lit a single aromatherapy candle, placed it in the center of the dresser. It released a mild earthy fragrance that soothed the mind. It added to the ambiance she created. After the rough and rugged session in the closet, her goal was to finish the night in a romantic environment, mellow and cozy. Using her sex toy, she seductively guided it from her lips, to her breasts, abdomen, and finally her inner thighs.

"Mmm, Jameer . . . " she moaned, summoning him to join her. "I love it when you touch me like that . . . "

She teased herself with the neon tip while Jameer softly caressed her breasts. Last time he was aggressive; this time he was smooth and sensual. "You look so sexy. I want to watch you," he said, looking at the sex toy between Debra's legs.

Biting her lip, she looked at him while standing naked, skin silhouetted by candle light. ". . . You do?"

He put his lips on hers and whispered, "I do."

She slid to the center of the bed to give herself more room. He moved beside her for a front row seat. Debra placed her neon toy in her mouth and worked her tongue around the tip, down the sides, moaning and cooing as if it were real. The way she cut her eyes at Jameer gave him second thoughts about being in the audience—he wanted to be a part of the show. Every time he reached for her, she playfully smacked his hand.

"No . . . you wanted to watch, so watch me, baby . . ."

His manhood saluted instantaneously, but sooner or later, he knew, he would be satisfied. So he watched, horny and hard.

And watched.

Gritted his teeth.

And watched.

Now the sex toy had sunken deeper into her moistness. She pleased herself many times before but never felt so aroused. Jameer was the reason. He looked at her liked she was the most desirable object on earth. It had been a while since she'd last felt that way. She thought of him and the mind-blowing things they would do tonight.

Jameer reached for her again.

"Not yet!" She wouldn't allow him to touch her just yet, so he did the next best thing: touched himself.

"Mmmm . . ." he sighed, switching his eyes between her face, the sex toy, and the solidness between his legs. He squeezed himself to release the pressure. When he let go, it returned. He looked impatient, couldn't wait any longer. In quick motions, he began stroking himself to the pinnacle of passion. Debra became as excited watching him as he did her. Her hand flickered between her legs in exact unison with Jameer's hand. Together they pleased themselves, racing toward sexual nirvana. Simultaneously they expelled liquid lust on their hands and sheets. When it was over, Debra let her toy soak in her juices, imagining it was Jameer, just as she had imagined him being there. But he wasn't, never had been. It was only soft music, one candle, and a relaxed yet puzzled, Lady Scorpio present. *What's wrong with me? Why do I keep fantasizing about him?* she questioned herself. *I have to do something about this.*

* * *

Debra stayed in her office all Monday morning. It gave the appearance of working diligently; however, she spent most of the time with her head in her hands and asking herself question after question: *Do I really want Jameer, or is this a subconscious reaction to being sexless? Why is he in my head? Is this drought worse than I thought? What if my coworkers found out about this? What would they think?* The whole situation had bugged her all weekend, especially after the dream she'd had. Something had to be done. Stopping the meetings with him was the only thing she could think of. As a professional, she felt it was the best thing to do. If he was out of sight, he would be out of mind. She planned on telling him as soon as he came to her office today.

Like clockwork, he walked in at 11:45am.

"Mr. Lovett, about last week . . . I'm sorry about what hap—"

He cut her apology short. "Don't worry about it, Ms. Clark. How was your weekend?"

"It was okay."

"Catch up on that sleep you've been missing?"

"Not like I wanted to. We need to talk, Mr. Lovett."

"Okay."

"There's no need to check in with me anymore," she said without hesitation. "You seem to be fitting in with no problem."

"It's only been a week."

"I know but . . . I just feel it's the best thing to do."

Jameer looked suspiciously at her. "Am I missing something? Is there something you're not telling me?"

"No, that's it."

"Sure?"

She sighed. "Some inappropriate behavior has gone on between us. I should've stopped it immediately."

"What are you talking about? Are you talking about the comments I made?"

"Yes. I mean, no. I mean, sort of. Look, if you need help with anything, let me know. But these meetings aren't necessary."

"I brought you something." He handed her a small gift bag.

"What is it?"

"Look and see."

Debra looked in the bag and pulled out a small bottle. "What is this?"

"Ginseng tea."

"Ginseng tea? What's it for?"

"It gives you energy, and it's good for your mind, body…and your sex life . . . "

"Why are you giving it to me?"

"Well, you looked so tired last time I saw you, I figured I'd help you out."

She handed the bottle back to him. "Thanks, but no th—"

"Keep it. I sure don't need it. I have plenty of energy and my sex life is all good!"

"See, that's the very behavior I'm talking about, Mr. Lovett. That comment was completely uncalled for."

"Ah, come on. You're a grown woman; you can handle it."

"That's not the point. This is a professional environment."

"You're human just like me, right?"

"Yes, I am."

"You get horny just like me, right?"

"Mr. Lovett, that's enough!"

"Call me Jameer from now on. Now do you or don't you?"

"I have no response for that."

"Don't worry. I know you do. I see how you look at me."

Debra sat up in her chair. "What on earth are you talking about, Mr. Lov—Jameer?"

"We're not little kids. I don't care if you look at me. I look at you too."

The office seemed to get hotter. Debra took a deep breath. If there was a way to hide under her desk without looking stupid, she would. "This conversation isn't going like I planned . . ."

"I see you didn't deny it. You *do* look at me!"

She stood up from the desk. "You can go now, Mr. Lovett."

"Jameer!"

"You can go now, Jameer."

"I thought you were the type of woman that could handle her business. I guess I was wrong."

"If only you knew . . . " she mumbled, tuning out everything he said after that. She floated away to her own world. Understanding what had been happening to her lately was still a mystery. She liked researching and mystery-solving, but this was one she couldn't crack. How did she just let him dominate the conversation? When it came to men, she controlled the conversations, she controlled the relationships. The odd thing was that they didn't even realize it. That was the key: make them think they ran the show when, in actuality, she did. Sometimes being the dominant mate was tiring. Although she would never admit it to anyone, deep down she wondered how the submissive role felt. How did it feel to be controlled? She received a quick taste when Jameer had her fumbling over her words. It made her uncomfortable. It was also shocking. No man had put her in her place in a long time. Most were afraid of a "woman's wrath". Jameer didn't seem fazed. He had a domineering personality that probably carried over into bed. He probably yelled out commands like a drill sergeant: Faster! Slower! Left! Right! *What would it really be like?* Debra wondered as her imagination took over.

"Get over here!" Jameer demanded.

"Yes, Jameer, my Nubian king."

"Take your clothes off. I want to see you naked . . . "

She quickly began removing her clothes. "As you wish Jameer, my Nubian king."

"Slower! I want you to tease me."

Her blouse and skirt were already on the floor, leaving her in a bra and panties. She unsnapped the back and slid one shoulder from the strap. She winked at him before slipping out the other shoulder. Holding the loose bra to her chest, she slowly turned in a circle.

"Drop the bra!"

Debra did as he said.

"Come here."

She walked to him.

"Get on your knees."

"Yes, Jameer, my Nubian ki—"

"Shut up! Did I tell you to speak?"

She nodded her head.

He looked at her while she kneeled before him. He pulled her forward by her hair.

"Ouchhhh . . . ouch . . . "

"I said shut up!"

"Yes, Jameer, my Nu—"

"*Shut up!*" He lifted his fist. Debra closed her eyes, anticipating the worst. Jameer laughed. "Open your eyes; I'm not going to hit you." As soon as she opened her eyes, he faked like he was going to slap her. "Got'cha." He laughed again. "You like being on your knees, don't you?"

She was unsure about what to do. Should she speak even though he had told her to shut up? If she didn't obey him, he might strike her for real. She could ignore him, but that would be the worse of all the options. There was no telling what he would do then. "Do you like being on your knees?" he repeated.

"Yes, Jameer, my Nubian king." She quickly bowed her head, not knowing what to expect.

Jameer opened his legs, grabbed his crotch. "Good, because I got something for you to do . . . "

She knew he was speaking of oral sex. All men loved it. She loved giving it. She rubbed her hands up his thighs and then reached for his zipper.

"What are you doing? That's not what I want." He kicked off his sneakers. "I want you to lick my feet. Lick them until I'm satisfied . . . "

Debra froze. In all her sexual encounters, she had never licked a man's feet. She was always on the receiving end—plenty men licked and sucked her feet but she was never a giver. And he had been walking around in those shoes all day! His feet were undoubtedly sweaty, musty, and just nasty. Oh well. Her job was to please him. With that thought, she lifted his left leg, rolled off his sock, and raised his foot to her mouth. He actually had pretty feet for a guy. Starting from the ball of his heel, she licked toward his pinky toe, and then worked across the others, sucking, and licking like he'd commanded.

"Suck them good, too! Don't stop until I say so!" His hand was inside of his pants while he watched her. It wasn't as bad as she thought. His reaction made her want to do it more. Ironically, being submissive made her feel powerful. She controlled his pleasure, his responses, and all his involuntary facial expressions and sounds. "Oh, baby . . . oh . . . girl . . . " he moaned. He sounded like a baby.

Debra smiled devilishly.

"What's so funny?" Jameer asked. The sharpness of his voice snapped her out of her fantasy world.

"Nothing, Jameer, my Nu—nothing." She took a sip of Pepsi because it was something else to focus on—not because she was thirsty.

"So you're serious. We're done?" Jameer asked. "No more meetings?"

"Correct."

"Can you do me one favor?"

"What is it, Jameer?"

"For once will you look me in the eyes when you talk?"

"Um…sure…okay." She felt tiny beads of sweat forming on her forehead. She looked him directly in the eyes, but no words left her mouth. All of her previous fantasies came to the front of her mind. "I . . ." she sighed. "I . . . I have a lunch meeting to attend." She didn't wait for him to leave before getting her things.

He caught her arm as she walked by. "You're cute when you're nervous."

"Who said I was nervous? And let go of my arm!"

He pulled her hand to his nose. "You smell so good. I love a woman that smells good . . ." He moved her hand across his torso. Debra wondered if his penis was as hard as his chest. She almost drifted into another fantasy with him standing right there, but she caught herself.

"Jameer, this is—"

"Shhhhh . . . "

She felt the bulge through his jeans when he pulled her closer. The mystery was solved; his penis was definitely just as hard as his chest. Her hormones leaped inside as if lit by fire. Her mind raced. *What if someone walks in?*

"You sure you want to stop meeting?" He spoke firm and seductively, purposely breathing in her face. His breath smelled like the cinnamon gum he was chewing.

"Th . . . This is wrong. This shouldn't be hap . . ."

He kissed her. Three months of suppressed desires were unleashed. Fantasies created in her mind were becoming a reality. No more wondering if Jameer Lovett was the real thing. He was. When his lips touched hers, she knew. They felt as though they were specially designed, molded and crafted for hers; their touch, feel—everything seemed perfect. He tasted like a rare delicacy that only she could eat. *What am I doing?—oh, forget it,* she thought, ending her resistance.

Gripping the side of his head, she whispered in his ear. "You a sexy nigga; you know that?" It felt good finally letting it out. No more secrets. No more hiding her feelings.

Jameer's eyes widened. He never heard her talk that way. It sounded strange and unbelievably sexy at the same time. From the waist down, it electrified his body. Bolts of excitement and disbelief shot from his toes to his thighs. He was actually about to hit it. In only a week of knowing her, he was about to bang Ms. Clark's brains out. Wait until his homeboys heard about that—true playa status for life. "I knew you wanted me!"

"Unh huh . . ." She shoved half of her arm down his pants before she reached the tip of his manhood. She squeezed it and smiled. It was big just like in her fantasies. Leaning into him; she licked inside his ears and down his neck, and collarbone. He responded by dropping his jeans and boxers and reaching underneath her skirt for her panties.

"Wait!" She fumbled through her purse, pulled out a condom she'd had for over three months. Jameer grinned. There was no turning back. They kissed sloppily as she backed him up against the leather swivel chair. He sat down looking up at her while she stood in front of him. His pants and boxers were crumpled at his ankles. Her panties were somewhere; she had just slung them across the room.

Quickly hiking up her skirt, she eased in his lap with her back facing him. He was glad her wardrobe consisted of mostly skirt because it made things easier. Immediately he began exploring between her legs with his fingers. She was so wet, her juices dripped down his knuckles. He looked at his hand in awe because he had never seen anything like it. He continued enticing her with his fingers until she was unable to withstand it any longer.

"I want it in me!" She said through clenched teeth, reaching for him, barely allowing time to put on the condom. "I want it right now!" She lifted her moist rump above his lap before making a smooth landing. "Eeeuaaaaah," she moaned, loving the heat she had been missing for months.

He held her by the waist while she rose up and snapped down on him. She was so wet, so warm, and it felt so, so good, he knew he wouldn't last long. Her nipples pressed against her blouse and pointed straight toward the wall. He caressed them from behind. As she rocked in his pelvis, Jameer leaned her forward; he made sure she took all of him. She felt the heat in her stomach and chest. *What the*? Was it in her throat too? She inhaled through her mouth because her nose couldn't take in air quick enough. To make sure her mouth didn't dry out, she rolled her tongue between cheeks to keep saliva circulating.

Being on him was like riding a roller coaster at Islands of Adventure. She decided if she were to get caught, she should at least get ultimate enjoyment. Now she wanted to face him, see the pleasure she gave. She quickly got up, turned around, hiked her skirt again, and returned to her perch.

He gripped her butt hard, locking her in place in his lap. She loved it. He loved it. The sloshing sound of latex and wet flesh excited both of them. With his left leg, he spun the chair around in a circle. She concentrated on keeping rhythm and balance while the office swirled.

Around.

Around.

"I'll-make-your-head-spin, baaaaby," he said, pulling her hair. When the chair stopped, he spun it around again.

Despite lightheadedness and an unbalanced equilibrium, Debra kept grinding closer toward the moment of complete ecstasy. "Ohh . . . mmm, sp-spin it . . . unggghhh, spin it, niggaaa . . . " She gripped his neck with her fingernails while her body jerked. Being dizzy, horny, and sweaty was an orgasm-inducing sensation. Her muscles loosened and relaxed as the juices flowed. She felt him throbbing within her. It wouldn't be long before he

got his too. He spun the chair around again while she grinded harder than ever. That was it.

"Owwwhooah . . ." He exploded with such force, his lower muscles hurt. His shoulders buckled as if sneezing. His eyes rolled to the right as the swivel chair came to a complete stop.

Reality hit Debra as soon as he went limp. As if in a hypnotic trance, she got up, fixed her skirt, and found her panties sitting on the electric pencil sharpener. Jameer was slumped in the chair with his eyes barely open. He finally caught his breath enough to toss the condom and pull his pants up over his sweaty legs.

"Whew!" He watched Debra fix her clothes until she was presentable. If she weren't there, he would have patted himself on the back for a job well done—even though she had done most of the work. His homeboys would definitely hear about the chair, and how he spun her around, made her climax while she was dizzy. And how soaking wet she was. He wished he had a camera phone. They probably wouldn't believe him otherwise.

Debra's arms hung by her sides like lead rods. She looked depressed. Why did she have to be such a Scorpio? She'd broken her no-casual-sex rule for a ten-minute quickie in her office? Was she that weak? It wasn't even great—okay, but not great. What would happen now? The whole thing with Jameer was a huge mistake. She couldn't imagine what repercussions lay ahead. "You need to get out of here. I have a meeting at 12:30," she said.

He buckled his belt. "Yeah . . . "

"Before you go. Can we talk for a minute?"

Jameer sighed. He knew every time a woman wanted to "talk", it usually wasn't good. He figured something was wrong but didn't care to find out what. He was still shocked that she'd even gotten involved with him. Now his ego was bigger than ever. If this never happened again, it didn't matter; he already got his.

"Okay, let's talk."

She sat down behind her desk. "Well . . . this was wrong from the beginning. None of it should've happened. I can't express how ashamed I am."

"Why?"

"... Because as your high school guidance counselor, it's my job to make sure you get promoted to the twelfth grade—not to have sex with you, Jameer."

Fantasy

Beneath Her Nose

Brittani Williams

It had been a week since the last time I'd been able to so much as smell the scent of Daron's cologne. I was feening for his touch, though I knew it is was forbidden. Each time we met I was left longing for more. The feeling of being the other woman was part excitement but part pain. The excitement coming from sneaking behind his woman's back any chance I got but the pain resulting from the idea that I would never be much more than a jump-off. Countless times I thought about walking up to her and revealing our affair, but I knew that I would lose any chance of a future with him if I did. So, for now I was satisfied with boning; I would make him love me later.

I walked into my bathroom and drew a tub full of hot water with lilac-scented candles lit to relax. I was horny, and the hot water against my skin would give me the illusion of his warm body on top of me. I slid down into the water and grabbed my cordless phone off the floor. I hesitated before dialing his number but I needed a fix, and hearing his voice would have to suffice. It took a few rings before he answered. I almost burst hearing his deep tone through the receiver.

"Hey, baby, are you busy?" I quizzed as I rubbed my hand over my left leg.

"I'm just sitting here watching a movie with Lana. What's up?" he asked, obviously attempting to throw me a hint. "I miss you." I couldn't resist letting out that tad bit of information.

"Really? So, did you need me to do something for you?" he asked, trying to cut the conversation short. I wasn't about to get off of the phone that easily. "Actually I do," I said lowering my voice to a seductive whisper. "I want to make love to your ear!"

"What's that?" he was attempting to dodge my comment.

"I want you to listen while I imagine you here with me. Is that okay?"

"Who, Lana? She's right here lying across my lap," he said trying to rein form me of her presence.

"I know she's there; you already told me that. All you have to do is listen."

"Okay, go ahead and tell me what happened," he responded, giving me my cue to move forward.

I continued using that seductive tone that caught him in the first place. This tone was enough to make any man as hard as a brick. I was aware of my talents long ago and had been able to snag many men in the past—even men that were attached.

"I wish you were here so I could feel you caressing me. You begin to remove your clothing to join me. I sit in the hot water watching as the steam rises from the tub. I'm getting excited as each part of your muscular body is revealed. Damn, I want you and I lick my lips anticipating tasting you. Once you are fully undressed you fondle your manhood as I continue to pant, waiting for your hardness to meet my lips. You take your time moving closer to me, forcing me to wait a little longer. I part my lips widely enough to make way for you, and you slowly push your thickness inside of my wet mouth. My tongue massaging your shaft forces you to let out a sigh. I begin to massage my clit with one hand as I use the other one to play with your balls. You taste so good as I feel your hands on the back of my head, easing me into a deep-throating routine. I stick two fingers inside of my tunnel as I crave you inside of me. Can you feel me, baby?" I asked as I caressed myself imagining the scene that I was describing.

"Yeah, I feel you. What happened next?" he spoke quickly.

"You retrieve your manhood from my oral cavity, and its missing your presence already. You stroke your length from end to end and pull me from the tub. I follow your lead and you kiss me long and sensually as I feel your member pressed against my body. Damn, I want you inside of me and I grab hold of it to let you know just how much. You bend me over with my hands using the tub to brace myself, and you slide in from behind. Your shaft has been missed, and I moan with satisfaction as you

fill me up completely. The sound of you moving in and out of me intensifies the excitement. My tunnel quickly provides more lubrication as you increase your speed. I scream 'I love this dick' over and over again, the way you like it, and you tell me exactly how much you love this pussy as you push down on my back to create a deeper arch. Are you feeling me, baby?" I ask as I continue to move my fingers in and out of my wetness.

"Oh yeah! So then what?" he asked excitedly.

"You remove your length once more, long enough to pick me up and sit me on the edge of the sink. With much force you dig deep inside of me with my legs opened wide, allowing you the space to fit all ten inches inside. I wrap my arms around your neck and look into your eyes. I raise up to get close enough to lick your lips. I savor the taste as I beg for you to go faster. You oblige and I am satisfied with the tempo. I yell 'fuck this pussy' over and over again as you continue to keep up the pace. I don't want you to stop and I pray that you can hold on a little while longer. I can feel myself nearing an orgasm as you go to a slow stroke with circles, hitting my G-spot. I moan for you to keep it right there as you continue the movement. I can feel you throbbing inside of me, letting me know that you are close to your peak. I want us to cum together, so I wrap my legs around you, giving you a direct hit of my spot. I feel it, baby, I'm cuming, I'm cuming, I yell as you explode inside of me. We stand there holding onto each other as I know that I am completely satisfied. Are you satisfied, baby?" I ask as I remove my cum-covered fingers from my burrow.

"Most definitely," he spoke honestly.

"Who is that, baby? I thought that we were going to watch the movie together," Lana spoke in the background.

"We are," he responded.

"Well, go ahead and tend to wifey. I don't want to get you in any trouble. I'll talk to you later; I'm about to go hit the mall."

"Cool. Thanks for letting me know what happened. I appreciate that."

"No problem." I said smiling before hanging up the phone. I had never had phone sex prior to tonight but afterwards I felt so satisfied I knew it wouldn't be the last time. I washed myself off

before letting the water out of the tub. I had made plans to go out to the club with my girls this weekend, and I need to pick the perfect outfit. Though it was only Monday, I had to go now or I would be at the store the day of, still looking. I threw on a pair of jogging shorts and fixed my hair. It was about 4:30 and I needed to be back home by at least seven to have dinner with my girls tonight. At the beginning of each week we usually pick a restaurant out of the hat and go there to eat. It had become a weekly ritual for us, since we were all usually tied up until the weekends. I went out to the parking garage to find my car. I seemed to always forget where I parked so, it always took me at least 10 minutes to find it. I lived in a condo that has a high-rise parking garage. I was glad that it was daylight because I hated searching for my car in the dark. I noticed someone standing next to my car, and I was instantly nervous. In the past I'd had a few ex's, and I hoped that is wasn't one of them waiting to get me back for running out on them. I got closer and I still couldn't tell who it was from behind. I took a deep breath before I spoke, since I didn't want to offend anyone by asking why the hell they were leaning on my car.

"Excuse me, can I help you with something?" I said in a non-confrontational tone.

"You sure can." Daron said smiling as he turned around.

"Oh my god, Daron, you scared the shit out of me. What are you doing here? I thought you were watching flicks with wifey," I said, walking closer to hug him.

"You fucked me up earlier with that phone call. My dick was hard as hell; I was hoping that Lana didn't notice. I couldn't even watch the movie after that shit I had to come see you."

"Oh really? So that's all I have to do for you to come see me. Shit, I wish I would have known that before, because I'd be calling you every day with a new scene," I said as we both began to laugh.

"But on some real shit, Kima, I missed you. I just couldn't peel away from her."

"I understand completely, baby. I definitely don't want to break up a happy home!" I lied.

"Come here," he said, licking his lips, motioning me to come closer.

I walked over to him and stood between his legs as he slouched down against the car. He stared at me before kissing me. I was in heaven as our tongues got reacquainted. I was getting extremely wet as he rubbed his hands across my back.

"I want you." he spoke into my ear as he continued to feel me up.

"Let's go upstairs, then." I spoke.

"No, I want you right here, right now" he spoke as he slowly put his hands into my shorts.

"Its broad daylight, Daron; anyone can drive up and see us."

"I thought you missed me?" he said rubbing his fingers against my clit through my panties.

"You know I missed you; I just . . . " I could no longer speak. He continued to caress me down below, forcing me to lose my words. I moaned as he kissed my neck. I could hear cars driving through the parking lot, but soon I was deaf to the sounds around me. It was turning me on realizing what we were about to do. He turned me around and boosted me up onto the hood of the car. He nudged me a little, forcing me to lie down. He raised my legs up, placing them over his shoulders. He pulled my jogging shorts and panties to the side and slowly licked my clit. I hadn't forgotten how good he could make me feel, but it had been a while since he touched me and it was worth the wait.

He continued to lick my clit and would occasionally pause to suck on it while slowly letting it slip from the grips of his lips. He stuck two fingers inside of me and made love to me with them. It didn't take long for me to climax, and I could feel him taking in the juices as they were released. I almost lost my concentration as a car drove by and slowed down to enjoy a quick glance at our lust. Daron stood up and licked his lips while staring at me. He unzipped his pants to release his hardness, which was about to bust through his jeans. Once it was freed he rubbed the head of it on my wetness, causing more juices to flow.

"Fuck me, please," I begged, because my body was yearning for him. He slowly inserted his pole but stopping just as my

tunnel was wrapped around the tip. I moved my hips to massage it with my wet mound. He rammed it inside of me with force—the way I loved it. He placed his hands on my shoulders to aid him in digging deeper inside of my passageway. I called his name to reassure him that he was doing the job well, and I voiced this along with how extremely wet I was.

He gained more momentum. "I'm not ready to come yet!" he yelled before removing his full length.

He pulled me off the car and got on the hood, instructing me to straddle him. I took off my shoes before climbing on top and got in a squatting position on top of him. I rose up and down a few times, taking in only the tip before pushing it deep inside. He moaned as I worked in circles. I could hear the echo of my ass slapping against his legs as I picked up speed. Cars continued to drive by, and I kept riding him as if they were invisible. I was anxious to reach that climax, and I could care less who was watching. I continued bouncing up and down on his extremely stiff member. As I neared an orgasm, I pushed down and moved in circles close to his body. He grabbed hold of my ass and held on tight as we both exploded. I bent down to kiss him before reality set in.

"I can't believe we just did that," I said as I climbed off him and fixed my clothing.

"I had a hell of a time. We need to do things like that more often," he said, getting up off the hood to straighten out his clothing.

"You know I'm down; I want to see you as often as possible."

"Well you know I try my best to see you as much as I can."

"I know you do; I just miss you, that's all."

"At least now you have something to remember me by until the next time I am able to see you," he said before grabbing hold of my waist to embrace me. I didn't want him to release his grip. I was falling in love with him more each time we were together. I had purposely put dating on hold so that he would be the only man I was with. I knew that I was a fool for believing that one day he would be mine and we could live happily ever after since he was genuinely in love with his wife. I never set out to fall for

him; hell, I never even set out to be with him. You know that saying, "It just happened!" well that's the story with us.

I was all about the thugs. I could spot the niggas with paper from a mile away. I was known for taking them for everything they had and walking away. Shit, everything I had was bought for me from random ballers. *Love* was a word that wasn't even in my vocabulary until I met him.

See, Daron was the owner of one of Philly's most exclusive nightclubs. *Top of the Night* was the name of the decked out club he'd purchased, courtesy of his drug dealing days. I frequented the club often after I turned 21. I was excited about finally reaching the age where I could use my own ID to get in instead of borrowing someone else's that resembled me. I knew Daron long before his wife and had had sex once or twice with him before they were together. She never knew about our past sexual endeavors, and I wanted to keep it that way.

Daron was fine as hell, and he knew that shit all too well. His body was sculpted perfectly; you could see the definition even when he was fully dressed. His hair was jet black with waves that appeared to be never ending. He had teeth that shined even in the dark, and his perfectly trimmed mustache accented his mocha-colored skin. He had one of the sexiest asses I had ever seen on a man, and let's not mention what he was packing down below. All I could say was that the punch was powerful and was capable of knocking you out in round one!

I never knew what Daron saw in her. She was cute in the face but that was basically where her attractiveness stopped. She was tall and lanky. She had hair that was hard to manage, so she wore weave all of the time to cover up the disarray. Back in high school the guys ignored her, and it wasn't until she graduated college and got a job at a big time law firm that men paid her any attention. The new job boosted her confidence and she walked around with a new swagger that somehow caught the men's attention. I was definitely not impressed since I knew what lay underneath. I wasn't going to bad-mouth her to Daron, so when their relationship was revealed I had no choice but to leave him alone. I wasn't about to fight anyone over a man, especially a man that would only break my heart in the long run.

Lana was warned many times about Daron's manners. She didn't fit the mold of the women that he could show off as an accomplishment. Even after all of the lavish things he threw at her, she didn't illustrate the excellence he wanted. I knew that, had she not pulled the pregnancy stunt, he would have dropped her as soon as he figured out that she wasn't worthy of being his wife.

* * *

I tried to keep my distance for a big part of their relationship, and it wasn't until a year after they had been married that an awkward situation landed me in his arms again. I was having my 25th birthday party, and I decided to give his club some play to bring him in a little more cash flow as well. I called and left a message regarding my ideas and waited for him to call. I went down to the club to meet him to make all of the arrangements, and as I was leaving he suddenly asked me to wait.

"Kima, wait! I have something to ask you."

"What's that?" I asked, letting the handle of the door loose from my grip.

"Do you ever think about what life would be like if you and I would have gotten together instead of me dealing with Lana?"

"I think about it all the time, but it doesn't matter now that she's your wife."

"It does matter. You know how I felt about you then, and not much has changed."

"I would find that really hard to believe. When I was just ready to give us a try, you were already with her."

"I didn't think you wanted to be with me," he said, moving closer to me.

"I wanted you, and I thought you would have figured it out."

"I guess I was blind then; my eyes weren't open but they are wide open now." He grabbed my hand and I tried to resist. I could feel the heat from his body as he moved closer to me. I wanted to turn around and run out the door but I couldn't. I loved this man once, and I knew it had never died. I had morals and I knew that it was definitely wrong to yearn for another woman's husband.

I backed away a little when he moved his lips close to mine. "What are you doing, Daron?" I backed up even closer towards the exit.

"I miss you, Kima."

"Daron, this isn't right. Please don't," I said as I continued to weakly try and push him away.

"You know you can't resist me. You want me just as bad as I want you."

"That's not true. I . . . " His lips touched mine and he stopped me in mid sentence. I didn't want to move forward but it felt too good to back away. His lips touching mine brought back all the memories that I tried to put behind me. He held onto me tight, and I let his initiated motion finish through completely. As he began to rub his hands across my back, I felt myself getting wet down below.

He slowly hiked up my mini skirt and pulled my panties down with ease. He hadn't even touched my throbbing hot spot yet, but I was already nearing an orgasm from the way he flickered his tongue around my neck. I let out a little moan once his fingers finally made their way to my tunnel. He lifted me up onto the table, his fingers still inserted. He moved his fingers in and out slowly, causing my juices to cover his two digits completely. I nibbled on his ear as he continued using his fingers to satisfy me. I was about to burst and tried not to scream as the climax forced me to hold onto him tightly. I could hear voices outside, and as the sounds grew closer I lost my focal point.

"Daron, stop. I think Lana's coming" I said, pushing him away.

"What?"

"I hear her voice. Shit, Daron, where can I hide." I was fumbling to straighten my clothing.

"Go into the men's room; she won't come in there."

As she opened the door, he turned and greeted her. I watched from a crack in the bathroom door.

"Hey, baby, what are you doing here?" he said, trying to cover my thongs which were still lying on the floor with his foot.

"Tanya and I were going to the mall. I missed you, so I just wanted to stop by and tell you."

"You could have called me on the phone and told me that."

"Well, I wanted to tell you face to face. And anyway, I saw Kima's car outside. What is she doing here?"

"Oh, that's really why you came in; you saw her car and wanted to check on me. You ain't slick!"

"No, that's not what happened, but I would like to know what her car is doing out there."

"She came here to put down a deposit on a party."

"What party? She's having a party here?" she asked loudly.

"Yeah. She came to drop of the money and her car wouldn't start. She called some dude to come get her." He kept a straight face.

"Really?" she asked not convinced. "Well, I'm on my way to the mall. I'll see you later at home," she said before kissing him goodbye and heading toward the door. Daron followed and locked the door behind her. "You can come out now!" he yelled through the club.

"Damn, Daron, that shit was too close. This shit cannot go on. Let's just forget today ever happened!"

"I can't forget. I need you, Kima, and that's some real shit. I've fucked with plenty women but none give me the feeling that you do."

"Daron, save it. If you wanted me you would've never married her. Look, I have to go. I'm going to forget this, and I would suggest that you do the same!" I quickly walked out of the club and entered my car. I drove away with a nervous feeling in my gut. I knew how I felt about him and I also knew that it was no way I would ever forget what had just happened. It was weeks before I ran into Daron again, and I let my feelings for him take over and I gave in. I couldn't resist anymore. And though I felt guilty afterwards, I wasn't guilty enough to leave him alone. I knew he would never be mine but I imagined it each time we were together.

* * *

After my shopping outing I rushed home to get dressed and make it to Zanzibar Blue, in time for our girly dinner. It took me

three circles around the block to find a parking lot that I was willing to park my BMW in. I wasn't about to put my ride into a valet lot so some asshole could put a dent in it. Although I had an okay job, this car was a gift and I wasn't ready to pay for any damages—especially ones that I didn't cause. After comfortably parking, I began the two-block walk to the restaurant. I was greeted by the hostess and escorted to the table where my girls Cindy and Gina were waiting.

"Hey, girls, what's up?" I said before hugging them both. "Damn, I thought I was going to be the last one here. Where are Tanya and Lana?"

"I don't know. Tanya is probably trying to pry Lana away from that husband of hers." Cindy said with a chuckle.

"Yeah, they have been spending a lot of time together; I guess they've kissed and made up now" Gina spoke before taking a sip of water.

"Well, I wish they would hurry up because I'm hungry as hell," I said, rubbing my growling stomach.

"Those niggas can buy you cars but they can't feed your ass, huh?" Cindy said laughing.

"Fuck you Cindy! I can get them to buy me anything I want; don't get it twisted!" I said, snapping my fingers like the gay skit on *In Living Color*.

"I'm just playing, girl!" she said tapping, her hands on the table and laughing loudly.

"Hey, ladies, sorry I'm late. Daron was all over me and shit!" Lana said as she walked up to the table from behind.

"Where's Tanya?" Cindy asked.

"Oh, she couldn't make it, some bullshit about a babysitter. I think she lied to go see that married man she's been messing around with," Lana spoke before sitting down.

"So what's up with you and Daron?" I guess you've kissed and made up now, huh?" Gina asked, smiling.

I sat there burning inside because I was surely not interested in her reply.

"We did. He told me that he hasn't cheated on me, and I have to believe him. I know that he loves me, and I know it ain't a bitch out there that can compare to me. I dropped it and I promised him

that I wouldn't bring it up again. Then he tore my back out, if you know what I mean!" She began laughing at her insinuation of good sex.

I sat there close to vomiting. I knew that I was about to lose it, so I quickly excused myself from the table to go to the restroom.

I wanted to scream as I stood in front of the mirror. I couldn't sit and listen to stories of their happiness. As bad as it may sound, I was happy when they weren't, that's when I could spend more time with Daron. After I got myself together I returned to the table, after about ten minutes, with a blank stare on my face. I was hoping that no one would notice, since none of them even came and checked to see if I was okay after being away from the table so long.

"What's wrong with you?" Lana asked, noticing my change in appearance.

"I don't feel well all of a sudden. I think I'm going to head home and lie down," I said after grabbing my bag.

"Okay, we'll call later. Let us know how you feel," Cindy spoke.

"I will." I made my way out of the restaurant. I was so disgusted, I couldn't sit at the table with her any longer. I had been friends with Lana for over ten years, but my feelings for Daron practically changed the way I felt about her completely. There was a time when she was my only friend, and though I never told her about Daron's and my past before they dealt, I still hated the fact that she was with him. That fact made it hard for me to be the great friend that I once was. I know that most people would say that I was wrong, but I didn't give a damn.

I was getting more distressed the longer I sat and thought about it. I dialed his cell phone, and once he answered it I began to yell immediately.

"How the hell are you going to fuck me and go home to fuck her? What kind of shit is that?" I yelled into the receiver.

"Did you forget that she's my wife?" What the fuck is your problem?"

"My problem is the bullshit games that you continue to play. You told me that you were on the brink of a divorce, and then

she comes in the restaurant smiling and shit saying you tore her back out!"

"I said on the brink of divorce but we are still married."

"Fuck this, Daron! I thought things were going to change. I thought you wanted me to be happy?"

"I do want you to be happy, but it seems like the only time you are happy is when she's not, and that's the fucked-up part!"

"I'm done with this conversation Daron—*and* you. Goodbye!" I said before ending the call. He called me and left at least five messages. Once I made it home I spread out across the bed and began to cry. How did I get myself into this? I wondered what was going on with me mentally, why I continued to fall in love with him. I wanted to be in a real relationship for once in my life, but the drug dealers and other big-timers I was attracted to only did me dirty each time. I was tired of being number two. I thought I would be satisfied with the jump-off title, but I was ready to be wifey. I thought the more time I spent with Daron the more he would love me and the more likely he would be to leave Lana's ass alone.

I lay on the bed for about an hour soaking in my own misery when I heard the doorbell ring. I wasn't quick to answer it, since I figured it was the girls checking to see how I was doing. I was definitely not in the mood for a get-well session. After about five rings, I was annoyed so I got up to go answer it.

I peeked out of the peephole and noticed Daron standing there impatiently. What the hell did he want? I thought to myself. I contemplated leaving him standing there. I knew how persistent he was and I figured he wouldn't leave me alone no matter what, and it would be tough to get rid of him.

"What the hell do you want?" I asked through a small crack in the door.

"I want to talk. Open the door, Kima," Daron said, trying to push the door open.

"I don't have anything to say, and I don't feel really well. So I need to get back to bed," I said attempting to close the small space between us.

"Look, just give me five minutes. That's all I'm asking for. I need to explain some things to you."

I thought about turning him away, but my feelings for him were overriding my anger. As he stood there looking pitiful, I warmed up inside because my heart still yearned for his attention. "Five minutes, that's it!" I spoke sternly before loosening my grip on the door to allow him to enter the house.

"Look, I didn't mean to shut you out earlier, but I was a little upset that you called me yelling. I know that I was wrong to lie to you about her. It's a lot harder than I thought it was going to be to walk away from her. I know that I should have been honest with you and told you that things between me and her were going okay, but I'm sorry if I led you on."

"So what does that mean? You don't want to deal with me anymore? After I have stayed around two years, waiting for you to leave her, all you can say is *sorry*? I gave up too much."

"I didn't say that I didn't want you; I'm saying . . . I'm confused. I care for you and her; it's hard for me to make a choice."

"I can't wait around forever, Daron. I either need you to be with me or leave me alone, so that I can move on with my life."

"I can't do that." He began moving closer to me.

I pushed him away trying to avoid any physical contact. I was hurting, and I was still angry about the way he had dragged me along. "Stop it, Daron. I know what you are trying to do and it's not going to work." I backed away as I usually did when I was angry with him.

"I need you, Kima," He said, wrapping his arms around my waist and beginning to caress the small of my back. I tried to stand firm and push him away, but I needed him as much as he claimed he needed me. I felt like the biggest sucker for falling for his tricks, but he had me right where he wanted me. He softly placed a kiss on my lips that sent chills through my body. He pushed his tongue through my lips and began to massage mine with his. It was as if all of my anger was being completely drained from my body and re-filled with love.

My body was warm; my feet were tingling. I quickly forgot about Mrs. Lana. He was my man again, if only for a short time to make love to me. As his hands made their way to my panties, I became excited, anticipating him touching my wetness.

"I'll never stop wanting you," he whispered in my ear, causing me to exude an overload of lubrication.

After meeting my clit with his soft touch, I moved my hips to initiate a circular motion. This man was all I could ever ask for—minus the wife. I wanted to feel him inside of me, and his fingers caressing me were causing me to hunger for more.

"I'm going to make you mine I promise," he whispered before lifting me up to place me on the sofa. I unzipped his pants as he continued to finger-fuck me with ease. I was moaning loudly and he was growing harder with each sound I made. I pulled his manhood out and stroked it with a tight grip, not ever wanting to let it go. I rubbed his length and begged him to get inside of me.

"You want me to fuck you?" he asked in a low tone.

"Yes!" I moaned.

"I don't believe you. Tell me again." He was moving his fingers in and out a little faster.

"Yes!" I moaned, a second time.

"I still don't believe you. I need you to make me believe it," he instructed.

"Fuck me please, Daron. I need this dick inside of me!" I moaned loudly.

With that he freed his fingers from my extremely juicy tunnel and rammed his stick inside of me. I felt ecstasy as he worked in slow, steady strokes. He continued his stroke while sticking his tongue in and out of my mouth. I yelled as I climaxed, and he picked up speed when he noticed my body starting to tremble. He soon turned me over and smacked my ass a few times. I loved it. When he asked me whose pussy it was I didn't hesitate to scream his name. It did belong to him, and he knew that no matter what, I would always return to him.

He then removed his length from my wetness and quickly shoved it into my ass. I was used to this, since I had learned early on that this was one way to satisfy him. He loved a woman that could take it in the ass and that was one thing that Lana had yet to tolerate. He always called me his little soldier because, even from the first time he tried it, I always acted as if I enjoyed it. He moved in and out of my ass as I stuck two fingers inside of my tunnel to initiate another orgasm.

I was nearing another climax when the telephone started to ring. I was focused on one more nut, so I could have cared less about who was calling. Once the answering machine picked up I tried even harder to ignore it, but Daron seemed to be slowing down; he wanted to know who was calling.

"Hi. You've reached Kima. I'm sorry I'm not able to answer your call right now, but leave me a message and I'll holla back at you ASAP." *Beep . . .*

"Hey, Kima, it's Lana. I was just calling to check up on you. Hopefully you are feeling a little better than you did earlier. I would assume that I'm the only one that called, since the rest of them are tore up drunk!" She began laughing. "I hope you didn't cut out on us to go fuck some nigga. Sike, just joking. I'm on my way home now to see my baby for round two. Call me tomorrow, hooker. Bye!" *Beep.*

Daron stopped and sat down on the sofa before placing his face in his hands. "What the fuck am I doing?" He yelled. "Look, Kima, I have to go. I'll call you later," he said, fumbling to gather his clothing.

"What?" I asked, both confused and annoyed. I knew I shouldn't have let his ass in! "Where are you going?" I asked as I stood up from the sofa.

"I have to get home before she does," he said, zipping his pants.

"Why? Tell her you are working. You can't leave me hanging like that Daron," I said grabbing hold of his hand trying to get him to refocus on me.

"I'm sorry, Kima, but I have to go. I'll give you a call tomorrow, I promise."

I released my grip as he turned to walk out of the door. I wanted to beg him to stay, but I knew it would only make things worse. He couldn't live without me, but it was becoming clear that he couldn't live without her, either.

* * *

I tried to keep my distance from Daron following the incident at my house. When he walked out of the door that evening I

knew he wouldn't break his neck to call me and I definitely wasn't going to break mine to call him. I took a week off work to relax, since working a nine-to-five was something that I still hadn't gotten used to. Since I had put all the men I dealt with in the past on hold for Daron, my cash flow had slowed down, forcing me to get a job. I hated work. I was the type of chick that would go shopping and get pampered everyday with money that was given to me by various hustlers.

I went down to the salon to see if my girl, Gina, could fit me in. The shop was packed and I walked through to her station that was located in the back.

"Hey, girl. I see you're feeling better. Ain't heard from you all week; what, you got a new man or something?" she said briefly hugging me.

"No. I was just relaxing, that's all." I lied. The real reason I hadn't called was to avoid hearing about Lana and Daron.

"So what's up? What brings you down here?" she asked.

"I need my hair done; can't you tell? I wanted to know if you could hook me up. We are still going to the club tonight, right?"

"I didn't think you were going since you've been M.I.A," she said placing her hand on her hip.

"No, I'm going. So, do you think you can fit me in?"

"Yeah just come back around 3:30."

"Okay, cool," I replied before leaving the shop. I walked the block back to the parking lot and noticed Daron on the corner engrossed in a conversation with some ghetto-ass young girl trying extremely hard to stick her ass out for him to notice. I stood across the street and stared, getting angrier by the second. This nigga has the nerve to be talking to another bitch when he walked out on me for his wife. Once he realized I was standing there, he wrapped up the conversation and began crossing the street in my direction.

"Oh, you can't talk to me but you can talk to that ghetto bitch? What the fuck is all of that about Daron?" I said pointing my fingers in his direction.

"I wasn't talking to her about shit; she was asking me about the club." He said.

"Whatever Daron. She's trying to throw you the pussy, and you'll probably take it!"

"Yo, what's up with you, Kima?"

"You keep fucking around with me and I'm tired. You run out on me practically in mid-stroke after you hear Lana's voice. You felt all guilty and shit then, and now you're standing on the corner, out in the open, talking to a bitch like she won't find out about it," I yelled in frustration.

"I already told you what I was talking to her about. Besides that, I need you to stop tripping out here in the street, because someone will be quick to tell her that shit, too."

"You know what, Daron? I'm not going to stand here and tell you about how I feel about you or anything else for that matter. I'm moving the fuck on so you can kiss my black ass goodbye!" I yelled before turning to walk away.

"Kima!"

I ignored him and continued to walk to my car. Fuck this game I was through playing it. I was going to find me a man that was willing to show me the attention I needed. This bullshit with him was getting old, and all the money in the world wasn't enough to keep me hanging on any longer. I returned to the shop at three, and Gina hooked my hair up before I went home to get ready for the night.

* * *

That night the line to get into the club was ridiculous. I was planning on shining tonight and going home with a baller. I wanted Daron to see that I was over him, and this was the perfect opportunity for me to do it. I walked into the club and greeted everyone while I made my way to V.I.P. I noticed Lana and the girls at the table in the back. I walked up to them unnoticed. "What's up, bitches? Didn't expect to see me, huh?" I said, smiling as I stood at the end of the table.

"Hey, girl, I thought you had moved or something. Can't call anybody?" Lana said, smiling, before standing to hug me.

"I know I've been pretty bad with that, but about tonight: let's go get our party on!" I said before turning to go out to the dance floor.

I grabbed man after man and shook my ass all over them. I had drunk at least four apple martinis and I was feeling toasty. I could feel Daron's eyes glued to me as I made my rounds, trying to find the nigga with the most money. I wasn't about to fuck with any average Joe. After about an hour of dancing, I needed to go to the bathroom. I walked toward the restroom and felt a tap on my shoulder. I turned around annoyed; I hated for someone to approach me that way.

"What!" I yelled.

"What are you trying to do with all of the dancing and shit, make me jealous?"

"Daron, please. I already told you I was done with you. I'm trying to snag me a man, since that's a title you're obviously not trying to fill,". I yelled. "Don't forget your wife is in here, so I'm sure you wouldn't want her to walk up on us conversing."

"Fuck that! I'm not going to sit here and watch you all up on these niggas and ignore it. That's just disrespectful."

"You have some nerve to talk about someone being disrespectful. You are the one cheating on your wife!" I retorted.

"Look, let's go into the office and talk, please," he said, grabbing me by the arm.

"Daron, I came here to enjoy myself; I really don't have time for this right now."

"Please I need to talk to you." He pleaded.

"This is not the time or the place for this conversation. I told you we were through." I said as I noticed Tonya walking in the direction of the bathroom.

"What's going on? Are you okay?" she asked after noticing the looks on both of our faces. "I'm fine. This guy out on the dance floor pissed me off. I was just trying to let Daron know to keep an eye on him, because he was pretty drunk."

"Well I'll handle that for you. If he gives you any more trouble let me know," Daron said before walking in the direction of his office. I stood there for a second, contemplating on whether or not

I should follow him. But even if I wanted to, I would have to duck Tonya.

"Girl these guys are crazy when they get drunk. It should be limit on the amount of drinks they can buy," Tanya said, laughing.

"Most definitely! Well, I'll see you when you get back out to the floor," I said, cutting the conversation short. I began walking away as I waited for her to go into the restroom. Once I heard the door open and close, I turned around and quickly made my way to Daron's office. I knocked on the door, and he opened it within seconds.

"Thanks for coming to talk," he said as I entered the plush office.

"So what is it you wanted to talk about?" I asked since I knew we didn't have much time to talk.

"I'm ready to leave her." he began to speak and I began to tune him out, since I'd been hearing this same tune for the last two years. "I need someone like you in my corner; Lana can't be who I want her to be. I just need you to trust me. Do you trust me?" he asked while staring at me and stroking my hand.

"Yes, I trust you," I said excitedly, since those were the words that I'd been longing to hear.

"Kiss me," he said as he moved closer. I sucked in the smell of his cologne, and as I closed my eyes I imagined that we were somewhere else. I licked his lips. He began to fondle me. My mind was running in circles, since I wasn't sure if he was playing me again. I had fallen for his tricks over and over again. I relaxed as he backed me up against the desk that was located in the center of the office. He kneeled down and slowly raised my leg over his shoulder. He moved my panties to the side and buried his face down below. The swift movements of his tongue against my clit caused my body to shiver.

I palmed the back of his head to create more pressure before I exploded. He licked his lips as he stood up from floor. He unzipped his pants and pulled his length through his boxer shorts signaling for me to go to work. I squatted just enough so that my mouth was at an even height with it. I grabbed a hold of it and slowly licked around the head to savor the taste of the pre-cum. A sigh escaped his lips as I allowed him to shove it into my mouth. I

grabbed hold of his balls with my free hand and gently began to massage them at the same time. "You like that?" I quizzed before deep-throating him once more. "Come on and let me fuck you!" he instructed. I rose up from the squatting position and turned around facing the desk. I put one leg up on the chair and waited for him to enter from behind. He grabbed my waist and used it to aid him in pumping harder. I screamed for him to go faster, and he sped up and added more force. I heard a faint knock at the door but I didn't want to stop. I ignored it as I neared my next climax. The knock continued but we were both so wrapped up in the moment, it didn't matter what else was going on around us.

The noises we were both making were getting louder as he and I both were enjoying it. Soon the door flung open and we both stopped moving.

Tanya was standing there at the door, staring as if she'd seen a ghost.

I didn't know what to say at that moment. Daron removed his pole from my tunnel and I moved my leg from the chair. I thought for sure that Tanya was going to run out the office and tell Lana what was going on. I began to try to explain myself but then, I noticed tears streaming down from her eyes. What the hell was she crying for? I thought to myself as I paused. Daron fixed his clothing and began to walk toward Tanya, who was still sobbing at the door. "Tanya, I never meant for you to find out this way." he explained.

"Fuck you! You piece of shit, I can't believe that this entire time you've been playing me for a fool! I should have known something was up with you two," she screamed while pushing him away.

"What is going on here?" I asked, confused, since I couldn't understand what the hell she was talking about.

"He's been fucking me for a year, telling me that he was going to leave Lana and we would be together," she said as she continued to cry.

"What?" I asked.

“Yeah, you heard me right, a year!” she yelled.

"I can't believe you, Daron. How could you do this?" I said as my body filled with anger. He'd been playing me just as I suspected,

but this was so far-fetched. Screwing around with both of us and neither one of us knowing was unbelievable. A man this skillful and conniving deserved some sort of award, because he kept us going, both of us crazy in love.

"Tanya, wait!" he screamed as Tanya turned to walk out of the room. "Baby, I *am* going to be with you." He was pouring her the same lie he'd told me just minutes ago probably assuming she would run straight to Lana.

"Fuck you. Forget that you ever knew me. I hope you rot in hell!" she said as she made her way down the hall. He turned around and looked at me.

Before he could say anything, I smacked him across the face.

"I deserved that."

I decided not to say another word to him, because I was about ready to kill him for all his lies. I was going to save myself the embarrassment and walk out of here with my head held high. I would have never expected any of this by a long shot. I really thought he cared about me, but he could have cared less.

There was a time when I had men falling at my feet. I could have had any man I wanted but I chose to settle for a man that belonged to someone else. Tanya and I both learned a valuable lesson that day: leave married men alone! They are excellent liars and will tell you anything to get you in bed which, give them the excitement they are missing at home. If he'll screw around on his wife with you, nine times out of ten you're not the first or the last that he'll do it with.

I was definitely a fool for believing we would one day be together and he would be mine forever. The sex was great, but his game was even better. Tanya and I did talk following that night. She finally answered my calls after a week of me trying to get in touch with her. We both decided not to tell Lana what happened; she would find out eventually, because he would definitely not be stopping the things he did **beneath her nose** anytime soon . . .

Fantasy

Vanessa

Defoncia Herdon

A woman's walk is a prelude to who she actually is. If it is watched closely enough by a professional, he—or she for that matter—can tell everything about her in only a few moments of observation. The walk can mean one of three things. The first thing is her pace. Her pace determines the path she has chosen in life. If she has a running walk, it means she is ambitious. Now, that can be a positive or a negative aspect. Ambition itself can be good or bad; it usually depends on the individual's motives or desires. A woman who never stops to smell the roses usually drags anyone around her down on that dull and boring journey.

If it's a slow but meaningful walk, it means she handles her business and enjoys everything this thing called "Life" has to offer. The first time I saw Vanessa, her walk was the equivalent to the discovery of extra-terrestrial beings on another planet. The only men you could convince that your story of seeing her was true, had to witness the manifestation themselves to be true believers.

Her legs had the gracefulness of an ice skater in the Olympics. Her butt held her bottom half together like super glue, and I swear it must have had a subliminal light put on the inside of it, which forced your eyes to watch until she disappeared. The click of her heels on concrete was similar to the playing of the national anthem.

Some women have an ass; Vanessa had a masterpiece. Her shit swayed side to side like it had switches. And that gum she chewed ever so sweetly accented her walk like gravy on the turkey at Thanksgiving. Old men walking with their grandsons, stopped to look at her crossing the street. I swear, sometimes when she passed a church, you could hear a series of claps after she left,

which were followed by disapproving slaps women gave their spouses.

And I mean she worked it. She would walk by couples and disrupt their whole outing. She would near the couple and start off by staring the man directly in his eyes, never once blinking. Her dress normally would show off her chest to a tee. The man would be captivated by a beautiful, voluptuous woman staring at him. And after the man's eyes were transfixed on her glorious breasts, she would shift her eyes quickly to the woman's eyes. After contact is made between the two women, Vanessa, as usual, would smile an I-could-fuck-him-if-I-wanted-to-bitch-but-I-don't-want-to smirk and keep going.

In some instances, women who like women became paralyzed, just like their men had become. They were helpless victims of Vanessa's aura. The woman was bad and any man, who'd been with her once would brag about her as if she was the Taj Mahal. They didn't own it, but they'd been in it one time. Her pussy had broken up homes, turned out young boys, and even made some women leave their husbands. The pussy was as lethal as Ann Coultier becoming a part of congress. It could destroy a nation of people.

She went into the corner store on this particular hot summer night. She was greeted by low mumbles of, "Shit," from a crowd of thugs who used the front of the store, to push narcotics. She looked at one young man, smiled, and said, "Whatever, motherfucker, and kept walking. None of the men said anything else. They knew better. Vanessa had used every one of them on one occasion or another. Hell, one of the brothers got her a cell phone in conjunction with his account. Vanessa had earned pagers in the 80's, cell phones in the 90's, and cars in the millenium that soon followed. Vanessa had been a freak since high school. The boys knew she was trouble, but they felt she was worth every nut-busting second of it.

As she entered the store, the bell announced her to the clerk and the undercover police officer working security in the store. "Hello, Vanessa," both Paul and Steve said.

"Hello, boys, how you doing?" a joking Vanessa said in a She-nay-nay voice, mocking Martin Lawrence to perfection.

"Good, baby, how are you doing?" both men again said in unison. The second serenade caused Steve, the shop owner, to elbow Paul, the undercover, in hopes of permitting him to speak first. "How has life been on your side of the track?" an excited Steve said.

"Which side," Vanessa replied, moving her body in such a way that her dress seemed as if it were trying to fall off her body.

Both men's penises almost came out of their pants. As Vanessa moved down the aisle, Steve followed. Watching her ass every step of the way, he, finally decided to slow down the elusive Vanessa. "From experience, you should know I have a limp," a frustrated Steve quickly spoke.

"And from experience, you should know I have no patience, for something that is limp," a playful Vanessa said with a giggle.

"I called you last week. All I got was the voice mail," an angry and disgruntled Steve said.

"I called you last night. I was so horny, my pussy was speaking your name and requesting your tongue," Vanessa started.

As she spoke, an excited Steve almost fell as he leaned upon the bookcase, listening to Vanessa.

"And you know what happened," a flirtatious Vanessa said.

"W-W-What?" a stammering Steve finally finished.

"Your wife answered," Vanessa coldly stated.

With her response he fell off the case, he was leaning on.

Vanessa smiled proudly, her victory assured with Steve's nervous fall.

"What?" a scared Steve blurted out as he proceeded to get his six-foot and three-hundred-pound frame off the floor.

"Just kidding, stupid. The only way I would call you for dick is if I had just fucked six people and just wanted a meltdown." And with that, an already entertained Vanessa laughed. Vanessa took Steve's hand after he was up from the floor. She grabbed his middle finger, and slowly inserted it into her already soaking pussy. Vanessa kissed the shocked Steve, and began moaning

It was a scene worthy of an award, if such an award existed. The moment made the one-time self-labeled "John," sound like a fourteen-year-old with his first piece of ass. Vanessa moaned like a fresh eighteen year-old in her first porno shoot with Ron

Hightower. Vanessa's pussy created a river that Niagara Falls would've been proud of. It formed a collective pool on the man's hand, and dripped onto the floor. The man enjoyed every minute of it. Steve kissed Vanessa and treasured every lip-locking moment of it. Steve was the part-time pastor at a local church in the area. He had longed for a sexual episode that he could pour his whole heart into. Vanessa gave him this opportunity.

He often looked at every woman in the church with a lustful eye. He was a whoremonger. Both of his marriages had fell apart due to the usual adult affairs and accusations. This type of situation had no bearing on the man's compass, because at this stage in the camping trip he was no longer a Boy Scout.

Vanessa moaned and continued her tirade of selfish orgasms. Vanessa came on Steve's ever-ready hand, one orgasm after another. The amount soon became countless. As Vanessa finished her last orgasm, she decided to see how far Steve was willing to go. She slowly and gently removed his hand, and decided to make a short porno scene while she had the time and place.

Vanessa grabbed the hypnotized man's head and before Steve knew it, he was licking the snatch. With every stroke of his tongue, Vanessa moaned. The broad didn't even care who heard. The back room was far from the front, so Paul couldn't hear. If he did he would come in and try to get Vanessa to give head. Vanessa only sucked on big dicks and wet pussies. Paul didn't fall into either slot, so he could keep his lame ass on the bench.

Steve, alarmed by the noise, decided to try and comment.

Before he could get out his statement, Vanessa violently shoved his head back into the pussy. "Eat the pussy, mother-fucker, and make me cum," a demanding Vanessa furiously stated. A dominatrix was just what a man like Steve wanted. He had, on many occasions, let Vanessa beat him with a whip while he was tied up like a pig roasting at a barbeque. Steve quickly followed her command. He licked and sucked that pussy like he was a major porn star.

Finally after twenty minutes, a restless and jealous Paul decided to promote himself from undercover to lead detective. "Steve, I need the keys for the safe I got to make that deposit

you told me to make for you, before 2:00 p.m.," a concerned Paul said. Paul always deposited Steve's money for him because not too many fools wanted to rob Paul. Paul kept his gun even when he was off duty.

Steve struggled with a response.

Vanessa, by this time, was squirming and jumping like a worm in hot ashes. She moaned like hell and was stuck in heaven. Steve's tongue was going faster than a Kansas hurricane. As Steve licked Vanessa's pussy, he blew air on it. She welcomed every twist and turn of the NASCAR race, and was about to reward the mechanic in charge of the pit stop.

"I'm cuming, I'm cuming," an excited Vanessa said. She was running out of breath and felt her heart beating fast. The feeling that overcame her body was something that happened every day, but she never took it for granted. She didn't want Steve to think he wasn't appreciated. However, on a scale of one to ten, Steve's best day was a five. In Vanessa eyes, that five was about to receive a mouthful of cum.

"Steve, I need the keys," an annoying Paul said as he neared the two adults.

This statement forced a busy Steve to finally say something. Steve slowly rose to his feet; all the time during the rise, he kept his tongue on Vanessa's body. He made his way from her pussy, up her chest, and to her neck. This forced Vanessa, halfway during the rise, to moan like hell. The woman sounded like a fire alarm at eight on a Sunday morning.

After he had completely got on his feet, he angrily shouted out, "I'll be out there in five minutes. Hold your horses."

Paul jumped back and quickly returned to his original position. Steve resumed his position, too.

"Suck it," an excited Vanessa stated. Steve's re-entry into Vanessa stirred more controversy than Prince's first album cover. After what could have been mistaken for four licks, an excited Vanessa shivered and shook another mouthful of cum into Steve's mouth.

Steve wanted to please Vanessa, and he had achieved his goal. While Vanessa continued cumming, Steve kept his mouth

open and his tongue working. He almost choked on Vanessa's orgasm, but he would rather than die than fail his mission.

Vanessa finally finished her orgasm. After the last drop was deposited in Steve's mouth, she promptly and rudely pushed Steve's head away. "There you go with that shit," an upset Steve stated.

Vanessa was more than willing to admit her mistake to her sexual servant. "I'm sorry, baby, you just drive me so wild," she slyly said.

"I'm going to do more than that," Steve said while undoing his pants.

Vanessa quickly said, "Just don't spoil the moment," as she put her hands on Steve's to stop him.

"Damn, this is the tenth time I've done this," Steve said. "When do I finally get the pussy again?"

"I don't know. I'm going to have to think about it." And with that statement, both adults started to get dressed.

Both adults still felt the effects of the fantasy world. The two walked in a way in which the scene itself, lucky enough to be captured, would've been viewed as a couple in love. Although they may not have been in love, their body language said otherwise. "I would do anything in the world for you," Steve said.

"You just proved that," Vanessa said.

As the two adults re-entered the room, they both did so only to find Paul anxiously waiting.

"Damn, what the fuck ya'll been doing? About time," Paul angrily stated.

This prompted Steve to pull rank. "It's my fucking store. I come and go as I please."

Paul got the message and remembered who the boss was. Vanessa stared in Paul's eyes, hypnotizing him all the way, as she began to exit. All of a sudden Vanessa turned around to Steve. Vanessa grabbed Steve's head and gave him a passionate kiss. "Thanks for the good time," Vanessa said.

The look on Paul's face said nothing but jealousy. He wasn't jealous of Steve being with Vanessa; he was mad because she didn't invite him along. Hell, if she would have came one day

later it would have been Steve's off day. One day later and it would have been Paul's dick instead of Steve's.

As Vanessa exited the building, both men looked at her in amazement. She walked as usual, hips going from side to side. Both men observed the hot piece of ass until she eventually disappeared from sight. Both men proceeded to the safe. Steve grinned at a still angry Paul. Just the look on Steve's face prompted a short, powerful statement from Paul. "What the hell ya'll do back there, split a milkshake?" and with that he laughed and continued walking to the safe. Steve ran to look in the bathroom mirror. After he had reached his destination, he made a terrible discovery. Steve hadn't cleaned his mouth off and still had some of Vanessa's orgasm in the corners of his mouth.

As Vanessa exited the store, the crowd of thugs still stared. She walked across the street to continue on her route. The boys, just like any other men with vision, watched her like a hawk. "That's a bad broad," one thug said while watching her infamous walk.

The local vegetable salesmen were steady preparing for the days business. They were checking vegetables and stocking inventory to be sure the day's demands would be met. Vanessa stopped all that shit. I mean, all the men looked like a sheet of invisible ice had fell upon them, they all stood still. She walked and popped that gum and waved at all the grocers as she passed by. "Hi," Vanessa said.

"Hello," the men replied once again in unison. One stock boy, holding a crate of tomatoes, accidentally dropped them to the floor. He did so while trying to reply to Vanessa. He, like every other man, thought Vanessa was personally speaking to him. They watched the woman until she disappeared from sight.

Vanessa was on her way to work; this was her usual routine for the morning. The Steve episode fell into the "Right-time, Right-place category. She just happen to see him and decided to treat her pussy. In her eyes, she saw it as a hell of a way to start the day.

As she entered her office building, she approached the security desk. Vanessa was greeted by a deep, somewhat feminine, voice.

"Good morning, Ms. Vanessa."

It was Trudy, the head security officer. Trudy looked like a female wrestler with a mini mustache and a steroid diet.

Vanessa, never one to shy away from something different, greeted the guard with the same enthusiasm as always. "Hey, what's up, baby? How are you doing today?" Vanessa replied. Vanessa's response broke down the wall that Trudy usually put up to keep her image tough. For when Vanessa was in her presence, Trudy did something few people had ever seen her do: Be nice.

"Great. My girlfriend and I have got a new place uptown and we love it. It is beautiful and big, just like me. She's out of town this weekend. I'm having a get-together this Saturday; I wanted to know if you wanted to come," Trudy finished.

"I'd love to come, I see when the cat is away the mice will play," Vanessa said. "I have plans Saturday, but catch me another time, okay?"

Vanessa continued her adventure. As she walked she thought to herself about how much she loved sex. The woman loved to fuck men and women. Trudy was no different than a man. The first time she and Trudy had fucked, Trudy ended up asking her to be her girlfriend. Vanessa thought Trudy was a terrible lover. However, just like the six-inch-dick boyfriend she'd had in college, whom she pretended to enjoy only to fulfill his sexual orgasms, the broad faked it.

Vanessa was taught by her senior physical education teacher. This was the woman she'd had her first lesbian encounter with. It happened on a hot spring day after soccer practice. Vanessa was in the showers, the last piece of pussy left. It was like a setup for a bad B-rated movie. The kind of movie that involved no penetration, no dicks, just two women going at it. Yet this would be one of the few first unrecorded times that two parts of the same gender would cause a foreign one to orgasm.

Evelyn, the teacher, had a body of her own. The chick had a fat ass and breasts that spoke to you each time she passed by. She entered the showers, looking for Vanessa. To her surprise, Vanessa was waiting on Evelyn to find her. Evelyn walked up to Vanessa and got down on her knees. Vanessa grabbed Evelyn's head and shoved her into the pussy. The thrust was polite and

sensual. Her pussy gyrated on Evelyn's tongue feverishly. Vanessa started to twist and turn with every pull of Evelyn's tongue. During her latest twitch, Vanessa said, "Eva, make me feel like a woman."

Evelyn was so into it, by this point she was rubbing her own clit. Vanessa came three times. Each time, Evelyn welcomed each burst with an enthusiastic tongue. Both of the women were satisfying each other. They had longed for each other's bodies since the first time they laid eyes on each other. The meltdown started sensual and ended up being downright nasty. The two did everything under the sun that afternoon. After the episode, as Vanessa was getting dressed, she decided to show Evelyn how special the older woman made her feel.

After completely dressing, she went to Evelyn's office. Evelyn, who was cooling down by this point, was sitting at her desk. As Vanessa entered the office, she walked up and went to kiss Evelyn. Evelyn quickly turned her face away from Vanessa's. Then Eva rose from behind her desk and put her arm around the young girl. She then proceeded to tell Vanessa, "I loved what we did today, baby, I really did, but it was just a fuck."

The words cut Vanessa like a knife; she didn't deal well with rejection. Hell, any man she had been with wanted more and they always tried to get her to be their girlfriend. The hurt was all over Vanessa's face.

She politely removed Eva's arm and left the room. Vanessa was in such a rush, she left one of her favorite shirts. The two parties never spoke again. She came to find out, from one of Eva's other lovers, that Eva had faked it with Vanessa. She had said Vanessa was a selfish lover and an overrated fuck. She had thought Vanessa was cute the whole time in school, but was disappointed when she got the package. Vanessa learned all this from female classmates. This hurt Vanessa. It would make her into the sex machine she would grow to be.

As Vanessa harped on the memory, she was interrupted by a voice. The voice spoke in a low, deep baritone.

"Tell me a secret, baby."

Vanessa laughed hysterically. She turned to find out it was Chris. Chris was supervisor of the marketing department at the firm. Vanessa had fucked Chris maybe forty times the past year she had been employed with the company. "How are you today?" Vanessa said in a playful manner.

"I'm good. I'd be better if I had you to myself," a joking Chris said as he rubbed his hands on her thighs. It was like her thighs fit right into the palm of his hands. Even handling her in this way made him want to turn into a monster, right in the office. His office did provide all of his private talks with Vanessa to be just that—private.

Vanessa laughed and giggled, staring into his eyes the whole time. Chris was the one person she could settle down with. Vanessa thought Chris was fine in every sense of the word. Vanessa saw him as someone whom she had only met one other time in her lifetime—a real man. It was like he understood her and compromised with her sexuality. Chris knew Vanessa was a freak, but he never condemned her for it. It was almost as if he found it entertaining in a sense.

Chris wanted Vanessa to himself, but he knew such a feat was impossible. A freak is a freak, but Chris also knew having her to come home to would be the pleasure of a lifetime. And in a sense Vanessa wondered what it would be like to come home to Chris. She just sat and stared at Chris after she had slowly removed his hands from her hips. There was only one flaw with Chris: Chris was married with two kids. Actually Chris was unhappily married with one brat. The jury was still out on the second one. Chris's wife was a whore from hell. She had fucked owners of pro teams, professional athletes, singers, and even a few politicians. Some of the men had even used Chris's bed for a personal playground. The irony of the episodes was that they usually occurred when Chris was out on a business trip.

He took fictional trips with Vanessa, only about thirty minutes from his home. Chris usually had one of his security people ride thru his home to make sure his wife had begun her infidelities so that he could begin his own.

Vanessa was special to the man, and he was special to her. Chris knew most women had experimented with lesbianism at

one time or another. This was no shock to him. He just loved the way Vanessa was so free. Her energy transferred to his every time they were together, and the tougher it became for him to go home. Vanessa loved every fucking minute of it. "I need to get ready for the day," Vanessa said as she quickly made her exit.

This prompted Chris to say, "Let's have lunch today."

Vanessa had suspected it was coming. "Just call upstairs; you know the extension." She left quickly and briskly, leaving Chris no time for a response. Vanessa preferred it that way.

On her way to the elevator she passed the head boss's office. She took her time passing it, making sure her steps built up the excitement to the listener as she grew closer. Her skirt hiked up her legs as she continued her journey. She wanted her skirt to get as high as it could get; seduction was her game.

As she made it to the elevator, a familiar voice said, "three minutes and two seconds late."

"Mustafa, why are you even talking to me after last week?" an angry Vanessa said.

"Because I can. I got my eye on you," a staring Mustafa said as he disappeared around the corner. The two had been an item once upon a time, but it didn't work out.

Finally Vanessa had reached her office. As she passed through, she passed a guy who was patting his braids. She told the young man, "Hold all my calls except Chris's."

The young man said, "Yes, ma'am, no problem."

As Vanessa entered the office, she immediately made herself comfortable. Vanessa slid off her panties, patiently awaiting Chris's call. Most of the paperwork was finished, and it was Friday. This meant the weekend was next. Vanessa was tired of playing with the young boy. She liked that young dick and it made her feel young again. She liked that feeling. She had lost her heart somewhere along her walk in life, but he reminded her of what it felt like to love again.

She decided to listen to her messages. As she listened to each plea from men who had discovered her work number, she giggled with laughter. The men sounded like a bunch of pussy-whipped high school boys. Each man sounded more pathetic than the previous one. She enjoyed listening to the men who had

felt her once before beg for a second helping. The woman was like a human potato salad at a family picnic. She was the side dressing, and people couldn't have the main course without her.

A knock at the door interrupted Vanessa's activities. "Come in."

To her surprise, it was Chris. Chris said, "Hey, I had to come and see you." Vanessa just smiled and said, "I know. I've been waiting."

Chris locked the door behind him and proceeded toward his ultimate fantasy.

Vanessa put both of her feet on the table. As Chris made his way toward Vanessa, he unbuckled his belt and started to undo his pants. Vanessa was dripping wet just from the anticipation of the situation. She thought Chris had a big dick and she enjoyed a big dick just like an energized tongue. She eyeballed Chris's zipper with the anticipation of a shuttle launch. Chris whipped out his dick, all eleven inches was as hard as a bat. An intrigued Vanessa decided to try to put every inch of his dick in her mouth. Vanessa grabbed Chris's dick and put it to the back of her throat. She instantly choked. The spit from the ingestion caused Chris's dick to grow another inch. She told Chris to grab her hair and shove her head on it. He did it and lost control. He started to pump Vanessa's head so hard, he felt like her mouth was the pussy.

Not being able to take anymore, Chris lifted Vanessa up and decided to show her how much his daily workout kept him physically fit. He grabbed the small-framed woman and put her on his dick while he was still standing. He pumped her pussy three times real hard. The woman came instantly. Her orgasm covered his hairy legs. The cum was thick, and it left a mark as it dried on Chris. He was still banging Vanessa.

Vanessa was breathing uncontrollably and squeezing Chris. She cried a little bit and whispered sweet nothings in his ear. She told him he was the best, and it rang in his ears over and over as he pleased her.

Chris decided to switch it up and make the vixen beg for mercy. Chris laid Vanessa down on the table. As Vanessa's long hair relaxed itself onto the table slowly, Chris decided to slow

down the tempo. He slowly put his dick inside Vanessa so that she could feel every ridge of his head. She accepted the feeling with a moan that demanded a response from Chris. The response was "Aaah."

Vanessa put her hands on Chris's mouth. Everybody knew she was the slut of the office. However, she did not want to advertise. The woman knew her aura was enough. She vibrated on Chris's dick to the point of his orgasm. She felt his cum and decided to kiss him. Vanessa loved to kiss, but just like a prostitute she had learned it was bad for business. She didn't want to fall in love with Chris, but her heart wouldn't let her be convinced otherwise.

Vanessa went to move and, to her surprise, a still hard Chris started back pumping. He was ready for seconds, and who was Vanessa to deny him of that right? That was the main reason Vanessa loved Chris. Chris showed her how he felt about her, not just using words to express his feelings. Vanessa was a real emotional lover, and in order to tame her it would take someone with the same type of passion. Chris tongue-kissed Vanessa. Vanessa, unable to resist Chris's manhood, complied with his demands. Chris pumped slow. He wanted her to know he felt like a king with his queen.

"Put it in me as deep as you can get it," Vanessa whispered in Chris's ear.

"I'll try, baby girl," an eager Chris said. With that Chris tried to pump every bit of dick he had into the broad. And she accepted every inch. Chris was just what Vanessa wanted. Chris loved the fact that a sister could be so giving but at the same time so sincere. Vanessa moaned like hell as Chris plowed her over and over again. Each moan overshadowed the sound of the last one.

Vanessa's voice started to fade out during the fuck. The song *Two Occasions* by the Deele came on. Vanessa came so hard, Chris didn't know if he had already blown his load. Chris felt like he didn't, but the shivers in his body and feeling in his penis told him otherwise. "I love you."

"I love you, too," a captivated Vanessa said. Let's face it, Vanessa loved anybody and everybody. Her pussy was like public

transportation. The only thing that mattered was if you were in the right place at the right time. Vanessa moaned over and over, once again.

She meant what she'd told Chris, but she also knew herself. Vanessa knew she couldn't be faithful even if her life depended on it. If the moment presented itself she would do almost anything. Vanessa loved the fact that Chris was so easy and at the same time so gullible. Most men knew that Vanessa was a superfreak. In the immortal words of Rick James, "She was a girl you couldn't take home to mother, but she will never let your spirits down." Every inch of dick he put inside of Vanessa was a gift to her. The feel of her hair made his dick grow harder and harder. Vanessa wanted him to feel like a man.

Chris came all over Vanessa's pussy then decided to do something extremely nasty. Chris grabbed Vanessa's head while she was on the table. Chris put so much cum in Vanessa's mouth, she had to swallow and breathe at the same time. Vanessa almost choked in doing so.

Vanessa then cleaned Chris's penis slowly with her mouth. Vanessa got up and wiped her mouth with her own shirt. After wiping, she grabbed Chris and kissed him.

"Why won't you commit to me?" Chris said as he got dressed.

Vanessa looked like Janet Jacme or Jenna Jameson after a group sex session. Vanessa's pussy was still cumming as she attempted to get dressed. Vanessa had been satisfied, and the rest was history. There were not many men who'd done that, and Chris should've been awarded a gold medal, at least in Vanessa's eyes.

Chris was in another world, as he walked out. He reached the elevator and decided to do something he had been thinking about. Chris walked back to Vanessa's office. It was obvious that no one had heard them. Business in the hall went on as usual; co-workers got coffee, and the usual office gossip took place. Chris turned and headed for Vanessa's office.

As he entered unannounced, Vanessa jumped up like a Jack in the Box.

Vanessa smiled at Chris's boldness. Vanessa wanted him to be more vocal. Vanessa stood and just looked at the exasperated man.

Chris grabbed Vanessa and kissed her. "I want you to be my woman. I'm serious," a determined Chris said. Chris had every intention in the world of taking control of his destiny.

Vanessa decide to see how much ground she had. "I've got a meeting at four. I'll call you then," Vanessa coldly said.

Chris bowed his head in defeat and started back toward his office. He said nothing as he exited the room. His heart was in his stomach, and he felt like someone had just licked all the red off of his candy. As he caught the elevator, he thought about the whole situation. Why did he love a woman like Vanessa? Vanessa was candy for the body but poison for the soul. Chris knew that, but it was almost like she was heroin. Chris couldn't live with her, but he would die without her.

At the same time, Vanessa was day-dreaming of her dream lover. Vanessa thought Chris was the shit. Vanessa didn't deal well with true affairs of the heart. Vanessa just liked everybody else's merchandise; she was a serious window-shopper. Chris may have been gone, but Vanessa could still feel the effects of his handiwork.

Vanessa could have smacked that motherfucker when they were fucking. The only reason she didn't was because she didn't want to scare him off. Vanessa got rough when the sex was good, and that was evident the night she had scratched Chris's back raw. This was only after a bottle of Möet and a three-hour-long fuck. Vanessa thought and pondered about Chris. She decided to go to his office and speak with him. As she left her office, she told her male secretary, "Hold all my calls." As Vanessa caught the elevator, she felt her heart beat profusely as she waited to arrive at the tenth floor. She was sweating and nervous. What if Chris had changed his mind about her. Vanessa hated rejection; it was one of the main reasons she had been single for so long. The price of having her heart broke was not worth the time that went into it. She was like most black women in the 90's. She had met so many losers, the pain was not worth the gain. She felt like she could do bad by her damn self. And

bad is just what the woman did. Vanessa finally reached Chris's office only after sweating for what seemed like an hour waiting for the correct floor to come up. Vanessa walked into Chris's office, only to be confronted with his jealous secretary, Jillian.

Jillian had fucked Chris on four different occasions and had expected to replace his wife. There was no way in hell Chris was going to let that happen. Jillian had sucked Chris's dick so many times during her first week tenure, she got sick. Jillian ended up having to have her stomach pumped. This procedure alone caused her boyfriend to leave. Jillian pulled the Be-my-man-or-else-shit, and she received a visit from Human Resources. The man in charge asked her if she had made advances toward Chris, and she quickly recanted all the crazy shit she had said before. From that point on, the two never resumed their activities.

Vanessa was interrupted by Jillian.

Jillian said, "Excuse me, ma'am, do you have an appointment?"

Vanessa did something Florida Evans would have been proud of. Vanessa yelled out, "Damn, Damn, Damn." She jumped around while saying it. Chris heard Vanessa and hurried to hear what had brought his love goddess back to his door. Chris ran to the door and entered the hall. The man's presence completely backed up his reputation. One thing you learn is that a true man's entrance changes the whole room. Chris's entrance did just that. Both Vanessa and Jillian grinned as Chris entered the room.

Chris quickly grabbed Vanessa's hand and they left the room. Chris, only after seating Vanessa, came back to Jillian's desk and said, "Hold all my calls." Chris slammed the door behind himself. Chris knew Jillian had gotten the point. Like a high school athlete at a cut list; he was not on.

Jillian hung her head and continued with her assignment.

Vanessa sat in Chris's office and just stared into his eyes. The girl was so good at what she did. Vanessa said "I was thinking." But she was interrupted by Chris's phone ringing.

Chris said, "What the fuck?" Before he knew it, Jillian came through on the loudspeaker. She said, "Your wife said the check bounced. She needs to talk to you." Vanessa pretended to choke and said, "Haterade."

Chris busted out laughing. Chris told Jillian to patch her through.

Vanessa sat surprised and somewhat bewildered. Vanessa saw something for the first time as she sat and watched Chris speak with his wife. Vanessa discovered that Chris did love his wife. And no matter what Vanessa said or did, she could never change where the man's heart was. Chris would always go home to his wife and check on his family. That is when Vanessa discovered something that could be stronger than good pussy,—family.

Vanessa was selfish and she knew it. Vanessa couldn't share Chris with his family, not even his kids. This fact hit Vanessa like a ton of bricks. The load only increased when she heard Chris silently mumble, "I love you," as he got off the phone with his wife.

Chris started to resume his conversation with Vanessa, only to be halted in his tracks like Bo Jackson's career.

Vanessa said, "I've been thinking. We have a good time, don't we?"

"Yes, we do, baby. That is all the time," a satisfied Chris said as he rubbed his penis at her statement.

Vanessa continued, "Let's just keep it like that." And with that Vanessa got up and walked out.

Chris's mouth was wide open. He couldn't believe what just happened. He chased Vanessa to the elevator, and decided to talk to her.

The secretary must have lost thirty calls during the fiasco, as she watched from her desk.

"I love you. Why don't you understand that?" a confused Chris stated.

Vanessa said," Yea, you love me. I could have sworn I just heard you say that to someone else."

Chris dropped his head and said, "That is my family, I don't love my wife."

Vanessa said, "I could have sworn I heard different." The elevator arrived like a coaster in a Broadway play. Vanessa entered the elevator, and told Chris to call her later.

Chris told her, "I love you."

Vanessa responded with a look that Bin Laden would have considered dangerous. Vanessa was hurt by her realization but it was a long time coming. Vanessa had played with fire and finally got burnt.

As Chris watched the doors close on the elevator, his eyes watered. Chris loved that pussy.

As Chris passed by the secretary's desk, he was approached by Jillian.

Jillian decided to play the rebound role. "If there is anything, I can do for you—," she was interrupted by a door slamming in her face.

Chris was so mad, he left work early. He stormed right out of the building. Chris didn't give a fuck. Hell, he was the boss. As he left the building, he thought of Vanessa. He loved everything about the broad. As Chris left the parking deck, a million thoughts raced through his mind; Vanessa was the focus of almost every one of them.

He thought of the situation so much, he almost ran a red light. As Chris reached downtown on his way home, he saw something that was something of a message. Chris passed the mural of a woman who looked just like Vanessa, which a graffiti artist had sprayed on one of the buildings downtown. It was rumored the artist had did it in Vanessa's likeness after watching her walk to work. Just like the other men who had spied the vixen, she was permanently burned in the man's memory.

The picture looked just like Vanessa. Chris stared at the mural, slowing down to observe it more carefully. Chris saw something, at that moment, that had escaped his sight so many times before. Vanessa could never really be captured, no matter how hard the pursuer tried. She was just like sunset, meant to be seen but impossible to ever be captured completely.

Chris reached home in less than ten minutes. As he walked thru the door, he smelled the sweet smell of aromatherapy candles burning in the air. Chris made his way back to his bedroom, only to find his wife, Shakira, waiting in an extremely lovely piece of lingerie.

She lay out like the Beauty of the month in a Black Tail magazine.

"What's up baby?" Chris said as started to unbuckle his pants.

She smiled and wiggled in the bed. She loved Chris and there was no doubt of that. Shakira had decided to wait on her man this particular evening. As Chris took off his clothes, Shakira eyed every part of his body. She couldn't help herself, Chris loved every moment. Chris took off his underwear and revealed his penis.

Shakira looked at his piece of work and smiled. The dick was big. It made her giggle with anticipation. The good thing about being married to a lover is you never get bored. Shakira laid her morning glory out to be viewed by her husband.

Chris knew not to be slow and methodical with his activities. He knew he hadn't had a shower, and he was worried Shakira would smell Vanessa. To avoid all of this confusion, he decided to proceed with business as usual. Chris put his dick all the way in his wife. The one good thing about being married is you never go without pussy. Not that Chris ever did that; it's just that he loved the fact that Shakira belonged to him.

Shakira opened her legs in the air. Her skin smelled like cocoa butter, and it filled the room. Chris could smell it, and it just made him want to be rougher. Chris grabbed his wife's legs and began to pump. He hit that pussy hard, and Shakira screamed every time he did so. Shakira had a small frame and it fit like a charm. Shakira felt good on his dick, and Chris couldn't deny it. He loved his wife, and showed her with every thrust he had to offer. He knew she really cared what happen to him. Hell, he married her, so he couldn't deny that.

Shakira loved the way her husband's body felt on hers. Shakira came over and over again. Chris's dick welcomed every burst and continued pumping. Chris and his wife never really did anything wild. The fact that they were in love was enough, to cause them to cum.

Chris tongue-kissed Shakira every time he put his dick in her. Then, all of a sudden, Chris decided to treat his wife like Vanessa and blow her mind. Chris took his dick out of Shakira, slowly, causing her to cum as he exited. Chris then grabbed Sharika off of the bed. Chris turned her body so that she was facing the wall, shadowing his feet. Chris, put Shakira's ass in his face. Upon

seeing his target, Chris launched his heat-seeking missile into Shakira's pussy.

Shakira lost her breath because this was not something she was use to. Shakira said to Chris, "Baby, do the damn thang."

Chris first licked Shakira's ass and shoved his tongue into her pussy. Shakira came as soon as he did so.

Shakira grabbed her husband's dick and started sucking. Shakira started off fast, and then slacked off like a North Carolina spring shower. She slowly put the dick in her mouth, and she made sure to put a lot of spit on it. Each slurp was juicer than the last. Her ass was receiving the same treatment, why not return the favor?

Chris slurped her ass over and over again. He went from pussy to asshole, back and forth. Chris was determined to get over Vanessa. Chris decided enough was enough. He wanted some more of his wife's pussy.

Then before, Chris could go to the next phase of his plan, the freak came out of Shakira. Shakira bobbed up and down on Chris's dick while she jumped up and down on Chris's mouth. He was getting his brains sucked out. The two went at it for a while, and Shakira came in Chris's mouth.

Chris was trying not to cum to fast, and he was having a hell of a time doing so.

Shakira rose from the blowjob; the demon that had possesed her obviously was in full control. Shakira turned and faced her husband. Chris was sprawled out from head to toe, face covered with cum and dick covered with spit.

Shakira inserted her husband's dick and started to ride it. She did this only after kissing her husband in the mouth.

Chris was frozen stiff, still in shock at his wife's behavior. Chris started to rub his wife's chest and touch her nipples. Chris then grabbed her ass, as she sat on top of him, and proceeded to fuck the shit out of Shakira.

Shakira screamed with joy as Chris beat up his wife's pussy. The pussy was dripping wet and close to the grand finale.

Chris was about to come as well, and knew he couldn't hold out much longer. He loved the way she felt, it was as if Chris had forgotten why he loved his wife.

They fucked for fifteen minutes, before Shakira decided to deviate from the plan. She quickly re-assumed her 69 position and started back sucking her husband's dick. All at once both parties came on each other. Chris received a second blast of Shakira's warm hot pussy in his mouth. On the other end, Shakira choked and swallowed Chris's load. As Chris came he told his wife, "I love you."

Shakira, lost in another world, said, "Vanessa," as she released the rest of her orgasm in Chris's mouth.

Crossing the Line

Dywane D. Birch

I'm sitting here at my desk, wondering how—well, I already know how, so, when—the clear, well-defined boundaries I once held onto began to unravel and slip through my neatly, manicured fingers. I knew there'd be no turning back. I had crossed the forbidden zone. What had started out as a professional session suddenly swirled into a pool of unadulterated lust. And now, I'm caught up in a whirlwind romance—well, in my mind, that is—with a man whom I will never have a future with, a man whom I would probably risk my career for if it weren't for the fact that I was a rational woman. Or was I? Was this just a figment of my imagination, or was I going insane? I guess the only way to decide *that* is to start from the beginning.

"Damn, baby," Gerald whined, wiping the sleep from his eyes and rolling over in bed while watching me get ready for work. "You too damn sexy to be leaving up out this house."

I smiled. Gerald and I had been dating for two years, engaged for three, and now living together for the past six months. And he was slowly beginning to get on my nerves. I couldn't put my finger on why. He just was. He was handsome. Intelligent. And definitely a great catch. But I was starting to think marriage wasn't in the cards for me—well, not with him, anyway. Or maybe it was the living together that wasn't working for me. I mean, I loved him, but not in that tingly, make-your-heart-wanna-melt kind of way.

We'd set a wedding date three times, and each time I ended up pushing it back. The last time I changed the date, I gave him the lame excuse that I thought we should wait until *after* he finished graduate school. That was over a year ago. And still no wedding bells. Truth be told, I wasn't sure if he was the man for

me. But the sex was superior and he took good care of me, materially speaking. His six-figure salary as an investment banker spoke for itself. And I had the five-carat rock set in platinum, and the 2005 745i BMW, to prove it. And, for now, that's all that really mattered. I already knew *if*—and when—I did decide to marry him, it would most likely be more for security than love.

He sat up on his arms. "I wish you'd quit that damn job. I hate you going into that piece with all them knuckleheads gawking at you."

I dramatically rolled my eyes up in my head, knowing exactly where this was heading. Gerald had a serious problem with me working around a bunch of men—particularly men in prison. It didn't matter to him that it was a Youth Correctional facility for males, ranging from age sixteen to twenty-eight depending on their crimes. In his eyes, age was nothing but a number. If they were anywhere near me, they were all still men.

Gerald had no problem sharing his disapproval every chance he got. Which was practically every damn day. But I was not going to let his dismay dictate my line of work. I happened to be a thirty-four-year-old psychologist and the youngest woman in the department. Not to mention being the *only* sistah on the mental health team. Besides, the pay was great—and I was damn good at what I did. So, Gerald could kiss my dimpled ass.

"Because it pays the bills," I finally responded, easing my arms into my silk blouse and then stepping into my knee-grazing skirt. I slipped my feet into my Prada sling-backs, adjusting the straps.

"No, I pay the bills," he corrected, pulling his nude body out of bed.

I glanced down at his semi-hard dick, swaying from side-to-side. The sight of his nine-inch thickness made my pussy twitch. If I had had enough time, I would have given him some of my bomb head for the road. Dick sucking was an art that I had perfected years ago. A craft I prided myself on. There were some women who refused to take the dick in their mouths; then, there were some who only half-heartedly sucked the dick, maybe on special occasions—or because it was absolutely necessary to

keep their men from straying. And then there was me: A certified dick-sucking, ball-gargling, cum-swallowing freak. There was just something about the way his fat dick and heavy balls felt in my mouth that drove me—and him—wild. Whenever I had him in my mouth, I was in complete control. I had the power to make his head spin and his toes curls. I could bring him right to the brink of ecstasy, then leave him hanging or push him right over the edge. The choice was mine. He knew it. I knew it. And I loved it. Morning, noon, or night, I would suck him speechless. Right down to the last damn drop. Oh, well.

"Or have you forgotten?" he questioned, snapping me out of my trance.

"Forgotten, what?"

He repeated himself, "That I pay the bills."

I sucked my teeth, ignoring his remark. "Well, it keeps me looking fly," I retorted, staring into the oval wall mirror while applying a coat of cranberry-wine lipstick. I seductively licked my lips. "And you know how you like your baby to look good."

"Yeah, but not when you flossin' around a bunch of pussy-deprived convicts. I can just see them all sniffing around you like dogs in heat."

I had to chuckle to myself at the notion of a bunch of incarcerated men howling, scratching and barking just to get a sniff of my panties. Of course, I kept my visualization to myself.

I put on my matching blazer, hoping it would hide my curvaceous figure. I sighed when I realized it barely covered my butt. Nothing did. "Gerald, please. You're letting your imagination get the best of you. I don't know how many times I got to tell you that the only contact I have with any of them is when they come into my office for a session or if I have to go to one of the units for something. My contact with the majority of them is limited. And they *all* know I have boundaries. Besides, it's not the inmates you have to be concerned with." I threw that in just to agitate him more. He frowned. I broke into a wide smile. "I'm just joking. There's nothing a man with a state number in a tan uniform, or with a badge, can do for me. You know the only man in my life is you."

"And I better be," he responded, walking up behind me, then grabbing me by the waist. "I don't want to have to put a cap in nobody's ass." He kissed me on the back of my neck. "Damn, you smell good."

I smiled at the thought of Gerald going into a trigger-happy rage. Shooting up the town like he had lost his mind, missing everything in sight. We both knew he'd never held a gun in his life. And would probably end up shooting himself in his attempt. But I decided to indulge him, anyway. "Well, if you do, I'll already be at the prison waiting for you."

"Oh, you got jokes," he said, slapping me on my soft, round behind. He pressed himself against me. "Let me slide this dick up in you."

"Nope," I said, sidestepping him. "I'm gonna be late for work."

He sucked his teeth. "I don't know why you wanna work around a bunch of degenerate niggas. It's not like they're ever gonna change their ways."

"Well, someone has to believe in them," I responded, pecking him lightly on the lips before grabbing my clear-bag and keys, then heading down the stairs and out the door.

"Good morning, Doc," the CO at the entrance said, grinning from ear to ear. Every time he saw me, his eyes lit up like a Christmas tree. "How you doin' this fine Monday morning?" And every morning he greeted me with the same toothy, wide-mouth smile. With the big teeth and huge pink gums. He sort of reminded me of that talking horse, Mr. Ed. The only difference, he had a tooth trimmed in gold. *How country.* Giggling to myself, I placed my items on the table for him to inspect then walked through the metal detector.

"Good morning, Officer Jenkins. I'm fine. Thanks."

He glanced in my bag before handing it to me. "You most certainly are," he responded in a seductive tone, grazing my body with lusty eyes. He was practically drooling. He stared into my hazel eyes. "Has anyone ever told you that you have the prettiest eyes?"

"Yes," I responded. "You have. For the last three years."

"Well, when you gonna let me take you out?"

I raised my brow. "When I call *your* wife and get her permission," I responded, grabbing my things. The women in back of me snickered. That shut him up real quick. Some of these CO's wrecked my nerves trying to get their whack rap on when they had wives at home. He—like most—had me confused. I was not the one. I made a conscious decision a long time ago that I'd never play the other woman or the *jump*-off role for any one. You'll never call me Miss Lonely on Holidays.

"Well, you can't fault a brotha for tryin'."

Oh, please. The only thing you should be tryin' to do is upgrade your dental plan to get that grill fixed, I thought as I waved him on, feeling his eyes on the back of my ass. Ugh!

"You have a good day."

"And you do the same," I replied, walking toward the gates, never looking back. When the gates opened, I walked through the corridor, heading toward Correctional Waiting where my office was located.

"Good morning, Doctor Simms," several inmates said in unison. Several CO's hanging around the control center stopped talking, nodded in my direction, and spoke as well. I could feel their eyes scanning every inch of my five-foot-eight, one-hundred-and-ten-pound frame as I made my way toward them.

"Good morning," I said, smiling.

"Damn! She's fine," I overheard one of the inmates comment as I walked by.

"Yo, word is bond, she gotta fatty on her," another inmate remarked. Of course, I acted as if I didn't hear them. I kept on stepping, letting it go in one ear and out the other. Comments were typical, and I generally ignored them unless they were too graphic. Then I'd write a blue sheet—a charge—on them, and have their asses sent to lock/up. And they knew it. So, they generally were respectful. But every now and then, some clown would let his testosterone get the best of him and start talking out the side of his neck, and I'd have to have the CO's run down on him—after I cursed him out. Like the time I was walking through the hall and a line of ten inmates were heading back to

their unit, and one of them stated, "Damn, that bitch is fine. I'd suck her pussy dry."

I stopped dead in my tracks and turned around. I was livid. I'm not sure if it was being called a *bitch* that set me off, or if it was the overall statement. All I know is I was about to go off. "All of you stop," I ordered, walking up to them. "What was that I just heard?"

A few shook their heads. Some shifted their eyes. The others looked down. "You ain't hear nothing," one of them stated. He was tall and lanky with twists.

"Shut your damn mouth," I snapped, forgetting my profess-sionalism. "Don't you dare stand here and insult my intelligence. I know what I heard. And let me explain this to you: Number one, I'm not a bitch. But if you want to see a bitch, I'll show you one; number two, none of you will ever get an opportunity to suck *any*thing of mine. So don't play yourself. And number three, instead of worrying about sucking *my* pussy you should be worrying about getting the hell out of prison, and staying out. Now all of you take the wall." They sucked their teeth, knowing somebody—if not all of them—was about to catch a charge.

"What the fuck," a thick-lipped brotha snapped.

"Excuse you? You have something you want to say?"

He turned his head.

"I didn't think so." Three CO's and a Sergeant came rushing down to see what the problem was.

"Everything okay, Doc?" the Sergeant asked.

"No, it's not," I replied, nastily. "Somebody in this line decided to call me out my name and say some disrespectful stuff. And I'm not the one."

"Give me your damn ID's," he barked. They all huffed, pulling them out, and handing them over. "You assholes want to disrespect a lady, then I got something for your asses."

"Yo, this is some bullshit," one of them said. "I'm tryna get home to my family. Ain't nobody disrespect her."

"Sarge," I said, calming myself. I really didn't want to see them all get into trouble for one ignorant fool. "I just want the one who said it to be man enough to admit it."

"You pick one. And he's out of here."

"He knows who he is," I replied, catching his eyes. I folded my arms across my chest, tilting my head. "I'm waiting." He refused to open his mouth, so I pointed him out. "That's him, right there."

The CO's snatched him up, yanking him out of the line. "It wasn't me," he snapped. "I swear."

"Don't lie," I said certain of his voice pattern. I looked him up and down, frowning. "It was you. And you know it."

"If she said it was you, then it was you. The rest of you get back to your unit. Before I lock all your asses up." They scattered like roaches, except for one who just had to have the last word.

"Yo, that's fucked up," he replied. "How she know he's the one that said it."

I smiled. "Young man, come back here." He shuffled back over to me. "'Cause I have bionic ears and I know what I heard. And I know who said it. Now if *you* want to wear it, then you can. Otherwise, take your knotty-assed head back to your unit and mind your damn business."

And from that point on, they knew—CO's and inmates—not to let the title and designer wears fool them. Having a Ph. D did not keep the ghetto from coming out if—and when—necessary. If you stepped out of pocket, I'd slay you with a string of expletives that would make your head spin without ever raising my voice. I stood at the next gate, patiently waiting for the CO to finish shouting a bunch of orders to a group of inmates who apparently were out of place.

"Up against the wall, you assholes," he snapped. One of the young men tried to speak, but he cut him off. "Did I ask you to open your fucking mouth? Say one thing, and I'll lock your dumb ass up."

I cringed. I hated when they spoke to them like that. No matter what they did to get themselves here, they were still human, and didn't deserve to be treated like animals. I made a mental note to speak to the Lieutenant about his subordinatc's mouth the next time I saw him.

"Excuse me," I said, glancing down at my timepiece, then at him, trying to keep my annoyance in check. He was a tall, dark-skinned man with big red lips and a huge forehead. And he had

the nerve to be sporting cornrows. Ugh! Anyway, I almost got the sense he was ignoring me as he kept on yelling at the inmates, acting as if I weren't standing there. *I know this Flying Monkey sees me.* I repeated myself, "Um. Excuse me, Sir. Do you mind opening the gate so I can get upstairs? I'm late for my meeting." One of the things I hated most about working in the prison system was that some—not all, but definitely *some*—of these CO's barely made it out of high school, and they were walking around acting like they were hot shit. It really didn't take a rocket scientist to shuffle keys around and push buttons all day. But they acted like the world revolved around them. Go figure. And some of these female CO's were no better with their weave-wearing, mannish-looking selves, trying to give me fever. Cutting their eyes at me like I stole something from them, then talking about me behind my back. How juvenile is that? But like I always say: Don't hate me 'cause I'm small in the waist and pretty in the face. And, *yes*, the shoulder-length hair is *all* mine.

He finally acknowledged me, walking his pigeon-toed self in my direction. "For you," he replied, breaking into a smirk, "*any*thing."

He brushed by me. *Asshole!* I rolled my eyes as he stuck the key in the slot, turned it, then slid the metal door open. "Thank you," I said, ascending the stairs. When I reached the top of the landing, I noticed the waiting area was packed with brown faces—faces of brothas, waiting to be seen by Parole, Classification, and Mental Health. Several broke their necks to get a look at me as I spoke to the Officer manning the station desk. "Good morning, Jackson. How's my favorite CO doing today?" Jackson was one of the few officers I actually liked. He had been working in corrections for over twenty years, and was nearing retirement. And complained about everything.

"Better, now that you're here," he responded, parting a kind smile.

"Looks like it's going to be a busy day."

"Tell me about it. Every week it's the same shit. I keep telling Administration about calling all these damn inmates up here then taking all day to get to them. All you need is twenty-five, at the most, up here at a time. Then, when you're almost done with

them, I can call the housing units and have twenty-five more sent up." He shook his head, "Here it is nine o'clock and Classification hasn't started yet. These are some backwards sons of bitches."

I smiled. "Well, if it'd make your job any better, I'll be sure to breeze through my sessions for you. Give me five minutes to get settled then you can send down my first appointment."

"Will do."

"Can I get an appointment with you?" someone yelled out.

"Me, too," someone else chimed. "My heart aches."

"I done told ya'll 'bout yelling out of this room," Jackson scolded, standing in the doorway. "Don't make me write your ass a blue sheet."

I shook my head, heading toward my office.

Subconsciously, it started—I'm talking about my mental wandering—the minute he walked into my office. Handsomely chiseled from the sweetest graham-cracker crust, dipped in the finest milk chocolate, then gently rolled in a handful of nuts. He had that just-stepped-out-of-the shower-then-rubbed-down-in-my-best-oil smell going on. He smelled . . . delicious. His uniform was neatly pressed, and his shirt was tucked into his pants. His mustache and goatee were freshly trimmed around a set of juicy, full red lips. I had to catch myself from drooling as I continued my assessment of his physical attributes: Five-eleven. Maybe six foot. One-hundred-and-ninety-five pounds. Solid. *What in the hell is wrong with me? He's an inmate, for God's sake!* I cleared my throat and shifted into business mode.

"Mr. Watkins, please have a seat." He sat in the chair in front of me, leaning back, then resting his right ankle up on his left knee. "How old are you, sir?" I asked, picking up a pen to begin taking notes. I preferred referring to the young men who came into my office as Sir and Mr. rather than calling them inmates. It was my way of respecting them.

"Twenty-seven," he answered in a deep, baritone voice.

I smiled. "Hmm. I see here you have another eighteen months to go before your parole eligibility. Is that correct?"

He nodded, "Yes, ma'am."

"Is there any particular reason why you haven't requested to be transferred to an adult facility?" I asked, flipping through his folder. He had been at the Correctional facility for the last eight years. Apparently, he had beaten some man with a bat for trying to rape his then eighteen-year-old sister. When the man died his charges were upgraded from possession of a weapon and aggravated assault to manslaughter.

"I'm comfortable here," he responded, staring into my eyes. His gray eyes were almost cat-like. They were . . . um, hypnotizing. It was starting to get warm in my small office so I removed my jacket then reached around to turn on the air. He aimed his gaze directly at my ample breast, shifting his eyes when he noticed he'd been caught.

"Do you have any family support?" I asked, knowing all too well that many incarcerated men did not have family or friends who stuck by them during their bids.

"Yeah. My moms and sister," he answered.

"And what about your dad?" I probed. "Where is he?"

"Locked up."

I wanted to ask what for, but I could tell that he really didn't want to talk about it. So I didn't press it. It was just sad to me that many of these young brothas were following the footsteps of their fathers. Generational. That's what it was. I silently wondered when the cycle would be broken.

"Do you have any contact with him?"

He shook his head. "Nah. Not really. He writes me every now and then. But I ain't really beat for him."

"Hmm." I wanted to say more but decided against it. "Besides your mother and sister, is there anyone else in your corner?"

He smiled. "My girl."

"And how long have the two of you been together?"

"Ten years," he responded. "She's been riding this out with me."

God bless her, I thought. I didn't know how these girls did it. Coming to the prison every weekend, never missing a visit. Catching two and three buses. Accepting collect calls. Lugging babies. It couldn't be me.

"Well, I'm glad to hear you have a support system."

"Yeah, me too."

"Okay, now that we got that all out the way, let's get down to why you're here. I see you requested to be seen because you're having difficulty sleeping. Is that correct?"

"Yeah, something like that."

"Well, either you are or you aren't," I responded, tilting my head and raising my arched brow. The one thing I didn't like was my time being wasted trying to pull teeth, especially from someone who had dropped a request slip. "Which is it?"

"Yeah, I guess you can say that."

"So, tell me. What seems to be troubling you?"

"I've been having these dreams," he said, running the tip of his tongue over his top lip.

"I see," I replied, slowly squeezing my legs shut in an attempt to pinch off the stirring between my legs. I quickly made myself another mental note to fuck Gerald's brains out the minute I got home. *I knew I should have let him dick me down real quick before I left the house this morning.* "Okay. Tell me about . . . these dreams." I leaned forward, planting my elbows on my desk and clasping my hands under my chin.

He nervously shifted in his seat. "You sure you wanna know?" he asked, giving me a crooked grin filled with innuendo. "I don't know if you can handle *it*, Doc."

I smiled. "And what makes you say that?"

He shrugged, tugging at his chin. "I don't know. Just an observation."

"And what might that observation be?" I probed coyly. I was flirting with temptation, dancing with desire. And I knew it.

"If I tell you," he replied, pulling in his bottom lip, then licking it seductively, "I might end up in lockup."

My smile widened. "Is that so? Well, let me explain something to you. What you say in here can and will not be held against you. I respect confidentiality. This is a place where your secrets are safe . . . " I paused for effect. ". . . unless you intend on hurting yourself or someone else, then I have a duty to warn."

He shook his head, "Nah. It's nothing like that. I'm a lover, not a fighter, not unless I'm given a reason to." His tone was

seductive. "Then . . ." I opened the palm of my hands, twirling them in the air, " . . . what's the problem? What are you afraid of?"

"You," he responded, sitting back, fanning his legs open, then shut.

"What about *me*?"

"Doctor Simms . . . I don't know how to say this."

"Just say it," I coaxed. "Trust me. You have nothing to fear."

He shook his head. "Nah, that's ai'ight. I really don't think you're ready."

"Mr. Watkins," I replied, staring him straight in his dreamy eyes, "I am a grown woman. There's nothing you can say—or *do*—to me that will shock me."

He stared at me, fanning his legs. Open. Shut. Open. Shut. "Last night," he started, then hesitated, shifting again in his seat.

"Go ahead," I said, leaning back in my chair. He bore a striking resemblance to Boris Kodjoe. "I'm listening." As his moistened lips began to move, my mind slowly drifted to another place. A place I knew I had no business visiting. A place I knew would be dangerous. But a force greater than me was pulling me in its direction.

"I've been . . . thinking about you for a very long time. I can't get you out of my head. I lay awake at night wondering what it would be like to have you."

I looked down at his thick hands and imagined him in his cell, lying on his bunk with his hands in his boxers, stroking his dick until pre cum dripped from its tip. I tried to blink the image out of my mind. But lust had taken over.

"I'm crazy about you."

"What about your girl? How do you think she'd feel knowing this?"

He shrugged. "She probably wouldn't like it. But what she doesn't know won't hurt her. I got needs."

Before I could stop myself, the question had left my mouth.

"When's the last time you had sex?"

"Just before I got locked up," he stated, licking his sexy-ass lips. "Eight years is a long time without sex. I've been hard-ballin' it."

I nodded knowingly.

"I need some pussy, bad, Doc." His eyes bore deep into my soul. I was treading unsafe waters. I could feel myself being pulled in by its current. It was either sink or swim. Slowly, I was drowning in his gaze.

"Do you masturbate thinking about me?"

He shook his head. "All the time."

Good. I smiled, deciding I would give him just what he longed for. "Close the door," I ordered in a lascivious whisper. He twisted his body, reached over with one arm and did what he was told. I stood up, walked around my desk, then sat atop of it, slowly hiking up my skirt then spreading open my legs. I pulled my black-laced panties to the side. "Is this what you want?" I asked, revealing a soft, hairy pussy with a set of slick pink lips. I parted them with my left hand, then leaned back on my forearm.

He smiled, looking around to make sure no one would walk in. When he was certain the coast was clear, he returned his attention to the treat in front of him. "Damn, you got a pretty pussy."

"You want to taste it?"

He nodded like a kid who had just been offered a bag of candy.

"Go 'head. Stick your tongue in it."

He leaned in and obliged. I thrust my hips upward, eagerly waiting. He blew on my clit. Flicked it. Then moved his thick tongue up and down, lapping the center of my pussy. Teasing me, he flicked it again. Again. Taunting me. I arched my back, threw my head back and gasped. When his lips finally touched my soft folds of flesh, an electrical current sizzled through my body, causing my clit to swell. His lips were soft and warm as they kissed my pussy. Slowly. Tenderly. He took my breath away as his tongue found its way to my center, savoring the taste of my excitement.

"Hmmm," I moaned, licking my lips then sticking my fingers in my mouth. "That's right, lick that clit, baby. Hmmm." I was getting wetter. Hotter. I needed to feel his tongue and lips all over my pussy. "Tear my panties off," I said in a husky, lust-filled whisper. He ripped them open then slurped, and devoured

my dripping essence. His tongue traveled down to the crack of my ass then back to my pussy hole. "Uhh. Oooh. Eat that pussy. Hmmmm." I grabbed him by his bald head, pumping and grinding my pussy on his mouth. I was in full throttle, and my pussy was overheating. I wanted . . . um, scratch that, *needed* the dick. "Get up and put your dick in me." *Please, let him be circumcised, and not have a little-assed dick,* my mind whined. There was nothing more discouraging than a fine man with body for days and no damn dick. I knew I'd have a fit if he pulled out a turkey-link with a bunch of extra skin. I crossed my fingers and held my breath. Waiting. Anticipating. Hoping.

He stood up, pulled down his beige khakis, then reached down in his boxers and pulled out his dick.

Yes! I smiled, as he rubbed the length of his surprisingly long, thick circumcised dick across my blazing pussy, against my clit and then, finally, teasingly slapping my slick entrance. "Slide that big dick in me," I begged, panting and shuddering. The sight of his engorged, veined dick had me . . . had me craving, aching. Yearning for his thrust. I couldn't wait any longer. I needed him inside me—*now!*

He pushed his juicy head in my wet, willing pussy.

"Like this?"

"Oh yes."

Inch by inch, he pushed farther.

"Hmmmm."

Deeper.

"Uhhhh."

Slowly, rhythmically, he drove his dick deep in my pulsating pussy. His hand found its way to my left breast. Squeezing. Kneading. Pinching my erected nipple. A loud gasp escaped my throat as I felt myself about cum. My mind swirled into a burst of bright colors as he slid his tongue in my mouth. The scent and taste of my pussy juice on his lips and tongue had my head spinning.

"Damn, baby, this pussy's good. Oh shit!"

I matched his thrust. Clenched his dick with my pussy muscles. "That's right. Get all up in this pussy. Uhhh. Fuck. Me. Hmmm. Hmmm."

Suddenly, he reached up underneath me, cupped my ass with his big hands, then, in one swift motion, lifted my hips and mercilessly banged his dick in and out of me. I chanted, hummed. Called out to the forbidden lust Gods, wrapping my legs around his waist, squeezing his tight ass. Pulling him deeper in me. A multiple wave of orgasms rippled through my body, causing me to see stars as he fucked me with wild abandonment. "Oh. Oh. Oh. Yesss! I'm cummmmming." He was long stroking me, deep-dicking me. Hitting that spot. Making my pussy snap, crackle, and pop.

"Yeah, baby. Wet this big dick with your sweet cum. Just like that. Oh, shit! I'm getting ready to bust this nut. You want this nut?"

"Oh yes. Nut all in this pussy, baby. Oh yes! Yes! Yes!"

Thrusting.

Banging.

Moaning.

Groaning.

Grunting.

I was slipping in and out off consciousness.

Riding the wave of another orgasm.

Gliding.

Sliding.

Screaming at the top of my lungs to the Good Fuck spirits. I was at the brink of a deafening explosion. And then . . . there was knock on my door.

"Huh?" I answered, startled. Dazed.

"Doctor Simms," the voice said, standing in my doorway. "The CO told me to come down."

"Oh, yeah," I responded, cautiously trying to collect myself while motioning for him to come in. "Mr. Watkins, right?"

He nodded.

"Please have a seat."

I stared at him for a moment, hoping the scent of my wanton desires weren't lingering in the air. I let out a sigh of relief when I realized there were no traces of passion with the exception of the dampness between my legs. I shifted in my chair, gazing into his eyes.

"So, please tell me. What brings you to see me today?"

He cleared his throat and slowly began. "I'm having trouble sleeping." He paused, fidgeting in his chair.

"Take your time." I smiled, grabbed my pen, then jotted down some notes. "Everything's okay. I'm here to help you."

He finally continued . . . and I half-listened, sliding in and out of my daydream. Scribbling on my notepad until his forty-five minutes were up. At the end of our session, I told him I'd send a slip down for him to meet me again next week. He seemed relieved. I smiled, watching him leave my office. Somewhere in the dark corners of my mind I knew I had crossed the line. But I'd live on the edge . . . just a little, for now.

Fantasy

Like Father, Like Son

Autumn Knight

"Did you enjoy it?"

The voice at the other end of the phone was silent.

"I asked if you enjoyed it!"

"Yes," she said softly.

"Well, now there's nothing left to say, is there?"

"But I never intended for it to get so out of hand. I . . . " the voice on the other end sounded desperate; interrupted in mid sentence she was speechless.

"The point, my darling, is you lived out your fantasy and now the fantasy has out lived you. Nice chatting with you good; luck in the future, dear." The phone was replaced on the receiver before another word could be uttered.

"Ahh, when will they learn?" Mrs. Towson spoke to herself, exhausted, as she lay back on her velour chaise lounge, sipping her afternoon martini.

A knock on her bedroom door interrupted her train of thought.

"Enter," she replied, shifting in the lounge to see who was entering her boudoir.

"Good afternoon darling." The tall bronzed-skinned gentleman leaned over and kissed her on both cheeks.

"Good afternoon, Karl. I see you're on time for our afternoon tête-à-tête with Bryce." Mrs. Towson sighed, exasperated from the thought of dealing with yet another meeting or should she say candidate.

"Aw, come on, Sylvia. It's not that bad now, is it? You do want the best for Bryce, right?" Karl glanced over at his mother steadily sipping her martini.

"Not so bad for you, you mean; I'm sure you're enjoying the process." Mrs. Towson shook her head, downing the last of her drink.

"I must say, Bryce has kept company with some interesting characters the past several years." Karl chuckled at the expression that now graced his mother's face. "After all, mother we must be very careful of his choices. Beatrice wanted only the best for her only son." Karl walked over to his mother's window, which overlooked the garden.

"Yes, that's true, God rest her soul; but the men in this family are something to be reckoned with, I must say." Sylvia got up to check her appearance in the mirror before heading downstairs for their meeting. For a woman of a certain age she was a timeless classic. Her short gray hair was cut and styled to perfection, giving her yellow complexion a sun kissed glow. Back in her day, the old folks use to say she could pass for a white woman, with her fawn-colored hair and green eyes. She was strikingly beautiful, well-pampered, and extremely wealthy. The importance of her image dominated Sylvia's world. Well-manicured nails, her mannerism and speech displayed the epitome of a tailor-made woman.

There wasn't a social function or event that went on in West Chester County, New York she didn't know about. The Towson name was synonymous with philanthropy, finance, and wealth; they worked hard to obtain their social and economic status in society, and had to be careful who they allowed into the family circle.

After powdering her face in the mirror, Sylvia adjusted the skirt of her Chanel suit and spun around to face Karl, who already had his arm out waiting for her to accompany him.

"Shall we, my dear?" Karl motioned for her to grasp his extended arm as he led her out the room and down the lengthy hallway to the stairs.

* * *

"Relax. You're going to shake your leg loose, girl if you don't slow down."

Raven sat on the oversized couch across from Bryce, nervous as hell. She finally was getting the opportunity to meet the family, and she didn't want to fumble in any way. She knew she was getting close to Bryce's asking of her hand in marriage. They had been dating for the past year or so and were inseparable.

All the questions she had about his family, she knew, were about to be answered; Bryce never discussed her meeting the family until a month ago. The only thing she knew about them is what he allowed her to know and the secrecy was killing her inside. Raven had called her best friend Madison early in the day to discuss what she should wear and what to say to his family since they were considered the upper crust of society—hell, they were like black royalty and she was poised to be the next queen to the throne.

Bryce and she had met at a café near the financial district one evening; he was working late and stopped in to get an espresso to get him through the remainder of the night. Their eyes met while waiting for their orders; the initial attraction, she knows, was purely physical. Bryce was a handsome specimen. His caramel skin was a glow as if he received facial treatments routinely. His medium-size frame was toned with biceps that flexed through his shirt as he stirred his espresso.

Raven couldn't help but stare. Some people just reeked of sexual attraction, and he was one of them, she couldn't help herself, staring at him from head to toe, wondering how she could spark up a conversation. And, yes, wondering what his bedroom talk was like as well. She knew he'd noticed her, so she took the initiative to engage him in conversation.

"Excuse me, mister; come here often?" she smiled, looking at the twisted expression on Bryce's face. "That was corny, huh?" She laughed, extending her hand.

"Yeah, that was real corny." Bryce laughed, shaking her hand finding her humorous for offering up such a lame line.

"Well, let me start again. How are you? I'm Raven."

"Hello Raven I'm Bryce. Nice to meet you." Bryce held onto Raven's hand well after the introduction.

Raven slowly released her hand from his grip and asked if he had a few minutes to share before they left the café. Bryce

entertained her offer as they exchanged numbers before leaving their java spot.

From that meeting forward, they were constantly in touch, spending time together, and getting to know each other. It was remarkable how much they shared their aspirations in life. Everything seemed to be moving smoothly, almost seamless, as she learned what turned Bryce on and he learned what turned her on. The only difference in their two worlds was that he came from money and her family, like most, lived paycheck to paycheck. Raven knew what she wanted in life and that excited Bryce. He wanted a strong woman to share his life with, and Raven figured she fit that bill.

"Can I get you some more iced tea? Maybe that will help calm you." Bryce chuckled, seeing how nervous Raven looked sitting in his grandmother's sunroom.

"That sounds superb; I would love some more tea." Raven tried to relax.

"What? That sounds *superb*?" Bryce busted out in laughter. "Raven, relax and just be yourself, you sound like one of them stiff society types my grandmother plays bridge with." Bryce picked up her empty glass and headed to the kitchen. "Besides, my grandmother can sniff out a phony in a minute. Don't put on airs; she's like a pit bull. She can smell fear."

Raven's eyes grew huge at that statement, and she could hear Bryce laughing as he disappeared through the double French doors. Raven attempted to pull herself together as she sat back on the sofa in the beautifully decorated sunroom; white lilies were placed throughout the room, complimenting the Scandinavian wood-grain furniture. Accents of sage and cream ran throughout the upholstery giving the sunroom a whimsical feel. The sun danced off the glass solarium that overlooked the garden and the family pool. Raven took a deep breath, she could get used to this lifestyle. The sunroom was larger than her tiny, one-bedroom apartment.

It was a dream come true for her to meet someone with whom she was comfortable talking to, someone she could possibly spend the rest of her life with. Raven was determined not to let anything ruin what she found with Bryce.

"Well, well . . . who do we have here?" Sylvia's voice sang as she entered the room.

Raven stood up to face the direction of the voice. A stomach full of butterflies. It was showtime. "Hello Mrs. Towson, I'm so pleased to meet you, I'm Raven." She was graceful in her delivery, knowing Mrs. Towson had given her the once-over immediately upon entering the room.

"Oh no, dear, call me Sylvia. And this is Bryce's father, Karl. We're pleased to meet you." They both shook Raven's hand and motioned for her to take her seat back on the couch.

Raven sat back down looking at Bryce's family in front of her. She felt like they were superheroes. She was uneasy in their presence even with them trying to make her feel at ease.

"So, Raven, tell us about yourself." Karl broke the awkward silence in the room, looking her over. His son had good taste in women; she was a very attractive young lady.

Raven took her time responding. What should she tell about her family and herself and what should she leave out? Although Bryce accepted who she was, she wasn't sure if his family was going to be as accepting of her and her social status, which was challenged, to say the least. "Well, I'm in school right now, studying in the medical field."

"Oh, a doctor?" Karl chimed in.

"Ah . . . no, well . . . maybe eventually, but right now I'm attending a medical and technical institute. Raven began feeling uncomfortable.

Mrs. Towson was looking at her as if she had just cursed.

Raven could see by her expression that Mrs. Towson was not impressed with her response. "I'm very interested in cancer research, so maybe I can look into a university after my technical training is finished." Raven figured, What the hell? Put it all out there, and just try to be yourself. She looked toward the French doors wondering where Bryce was.

"Very impressive. You'll have to tell us more about that. Our family provides funding for cancer research." Sylvia was very interested in hearing more; Raven had her full attention.

Raven began to talk about her interest in the medical research field. Keeping her hands folded across her knee, she steadily kept her leg from shaking again.

Mrs. Towson seemed very amused, as did Karl.

Raven found Karl to be very charming and handsome for an older gentleman. Just as she was getting into a flow, Bryce entered the room with a tray of iced tea and a housekeeper in tow with a tray of lunch. Raven tried not to show any reaction as Bryce entered the room kissing his grandmother on the cheek. He took a seat next to her, throwing his arm behind her on the sofa. Raven couldn't believe they had a damn housekeeper, but for the size of their house, she should have known the old lady wasn't taking care of it by herself.

Mrs. Towson was well kept and it showed. She excused the housekeeper after the tray of sandwiches was set up on the miranda. Fresh fruit and pastries were later bought into the room, completing the afternoon lunch.

The meeting went very well as they all laughed and talked about mundane issues, trying to feel Raven out, and to see how serious Bryce was about his new young lady. Raven was preoccupied during the lunch as Karl kept catching her eye. She was amazed at the similarities that he and Bryce had in common. Their movements, physical attributes; his voice, although an octave deeper was mesmerizing. Even their outlook on life was incredibly mirrored as if they were twins.

Raven looked at Bryce's father, knowing this was how Bryce would look in thirty years from now, and what she saw wasn't bad at all. *Not bad at all*, she thought. Lost in thought she didn't hear the invite, from Mrs. Towson, to visit their house in the Hampton's for a weekend in three weeks. She was preoccupied with how good Karl was looking in his polo shirt and khakis that showcased a sizeable bulge in his pants.

"Dear, will you be able to join us or not?" she heard Mrs. Towson raise her voice.

Bryce nudged her leg with his knee to get her to respond to his grandmother's invite.

Raven had missed the entire conversation.

Bryce repeated his grandmother's offer before Raven finally responded.

"My apologies. I would love to join you for a weekend," Raven blurted out, smiling at Bryce. She really wanted to say *Oh hell yeah*! The closest she had been to the Hampton's was watching Diddy's party on Entertainment Tonight.

"Then it's settled. We shall have a splendid time," Mrs. Towson chimed in as she motioned for Bryce to fill her glass with some more tea.

Another hour and a half had passed before Mrs. Towson excused herself to get some rest; she had an evening function to attend and wanted to look her best. Raven was proud of how she had handled herself, and was even more relieved now that Mrs. Towson was off for an afternoon nap. Although lunch and conversation seemed to be a success, she still felt as if Mrs. Towson were sizing her up. Madison would be proud of how she had handled the Towsons filthy rich or not. Raven had used what she knew to get her through a potentially disastrous situation, and apparently it worked.

She felt self-assured as she sat and listened to Bryce and his father discussing investment options on a stock tip that Karl had just gotten wind of. Laying back into the plush pillows, crossing her legs, Raven allowed her shapely, long brown leg to swing in a steady rhythm. Raven caught Bryce glancing over in mid-sentence, licking his lips as she swung her leg he could see that she was at ease; she didn't display any of the nervous twitches from earlier.

He stood to make himself another plate, asking his father and Raven if either of them wanted anything else. They both declined his invitation.

It was then, out the corner of her eye that Raven thought she caught Karl looking at her legs in the same way that his son enjoyed looking. Raven could feel her stomach stirring with nervousness; maybe it was embarrassment, or maybe she was turned on by his glances.

The afternoon at the Towsons couldn't have ended soon enough as she told Karl good-bye, shaking his hand. His grip felt strong, and she was turned on by his touch.

Bryce drove Raven home and barely got her into her apartment door before she removed her dress and stood in front of him with a pink bra and thong. She slowly backed him into the living room. Bryce hadn't noticed the look in her eyes on the ride to her apartment. He couldn't understand what had occurred to turn her on, from the time they had left his grandmother's house to now, nor did he care.

Raven was a very sexual creature and willing to please him; straight or kinky, she loved it all.

Bryce was turned out by her sexual appetite, and that was refreshing to him. He had had his share of dead weight in his bed, or the women who wanted to save the pussy for marriage; he was sick of that shit. He wanted his share then and now. Having someone like Raven, who was willing to try anything once, was like Christmas morning over and over again. Raven was beautiful. Her long brown kinky hair sat just above her shoulders; she had the deepest brown eyes and mocha skin that smelled of sweet nectar.

Bryce stood in the middle of her living room watching her lowering his pants to his knees, she wasted no time taking his rawness into her mouth, sucking as if she were a hungry baby on a nipple. She consumed Bryce until he began stroking her mouth. She was working his erection so well, he closed his eyes tightly and swore he was inside her pussy. The heat of her mouth had to be 98.5 degrees and growing.

Unable to contain himself he held her head firmly for balance as he thrust back and forth, letting out a beastly growl. His legs began buckling from the pressure of her head game. The more he moaned, the wetter her mouth felt as he fell onto her sofa.

Raven crawled over to the couch, positioning herself back between his legs. He finally released an uncontrollable orgasm. Raven began rubbing Bryce's dick with her hand. She placed his nut sack in her mouth and rhythmically shuffled his sack between the pockets of her cheeks. Raven's tongue savored every lick until

she sucked him back to erection, sending Bryce squirming, begging her to fuck him. He was undeniably turned out.

"Tell me what time it is, like I taught you, baby," Raven's raspy voice commanded as Bryce's sack fell from her mouth.

"It's time for that nappy dugout to get some work, bitch," Bryce replied on command.

Raven cracked up at his proper ass trying to sound grimy. Laughing, she climbed on her lover and rode him until he delivered an explosion deep inside her walls.

Lying on the couch, exhausted from their escapade, Bryce listened to Raven tease him about the noises he had made during their sexcapade. He didn't mind her taunting one bit; his time with her allowed him to escape from his world and become a freak in hers. He had become more adventurous in their sessions and, from her responses, he was satisfying her well.

Raven woke up to an empty apartment. It was 11:30 p.m. Bryce had left over three hours ago, and she still felt a tingling sensation between her legs. It was amazing that she was able to bring out of him the lust and desires to explore his sexuality with her so freely. If his prim and proper family only knew how much of a freak their Bryce was, she was sure they would be appalled. "Shit, it's always the proper ones that are the closet freaks" she spoke out loud walking through her empty apartment.

Turning on the faucets she adjusted the water temperature for a warm and soothing bath for the evening.

Glancing at her nakedness in the mirror, her nipples were erect as she palmed her breast. Closing her eyes, she escaped in the moment, rivaling in the touch of her fingers kneading the plumpness of her breast. The coolness of the air on her skin bought her back to her reality of being alone and desiring something that just wouldn't allow her peace.

Picking up her clothes from the living room floor, she couldn't shake the real reason that set her off on Bryce tonight. Raven hadn't stopped thinking about his father and wondered what it would be like to have him. She had sucked Bryce's dick so well she imagined herself on her knees in the sunroom giving Karl a little taste of what his son often received.

Raven lit the candles in her bathroom. The steam filled the air as she tested the water with her toe before immersing her body into the creamy foam. Running her washcloth along her brown skin, her body was relaxed as she recalled the day's events. she had pleased her man to the utmost tonight, and now she was about to please herself as her hands made their way to the throbbing mound between her legs. The remnants of Bryce's sex game left her longing for more. Resting her head against the back of the bathtub, she positioned both legs on each side of the tub as she began working on the sensation that was calling her. Closing her eyes, she was taken in by the smell of fresh mango that permeated from her bath water. The scent reminded her of a tropical island as her fingers worked circular motions around her clitoris; the motion of her hand was concentrated as she spread her legs wider to receive her island treat. Moving her ass along the bottom of the warm tub the water created swirling waves continuously smashing against the pink opening between her legs.

Raven moaned as each stroke caused her clitoris to harden. Her body floated as she saw palm trees blowing in the island wind. The white sands under her naked body was warm and felt soft between the crack of her ass. "Welcome, Raven, I've been waiting for you," the voice called out as a man knelt between her legs, nibbling at her soaked pussy. Removing her fingers, she allowed the tanned gentleman to lick her pussy and enjoy her pink erection. He nibbled insatiably. Her body rose with every motion of his tongue; this shit was pure torture. He was controlling her every move as she thrust her clitoris against the rawness of his extended tongue. He was calling her body to release; she was in paradise as she lay back enjoying Karl tongue-fucking her on their private island. The continuous pounding against her clitoris from his tongue sent her into a violent scream, "I'm cumming, Karl, motherfucker, I'm cumming!" Raven's body convulsed several times as her bath water emptied from the tub. Lying in the shallow pool of water, she couldn't move as she closed her eyes and fell off to sleep.

The next couple of weeks only offered routine work—sleep and seeing Bryce. Yeah, she would like to say that her days were just routine, but Bryce's father had remained on her mind every single day since she'd met the man. Yes, he's attractive, successful, and smart, but he's her boyfriend's father. She was hoping that with their trip to the tropical island the other night would end the affair. "That's not the fucking case, though, is it, Raven?" she spoke to herself while having lunch.

For the past week she has fucked Bryce's father on the train, in his office, at the salad bar, and doggy style in goddamn Central Park. These torrid fantasy's were driving her crazy, not to mention making a mess of her good lingerie, it was humiliating enough that she fantasized about a man old enough to be her father, but to walk around with a wet pussy for a week was getting out of hand. She had even gone into one of the student lounges, which rarely got used at the school, so she could masturbate when the pounding of her pussy wouldn't cease. She just needed to feel his presence like on the island.

What the hell was happening? She couldn't wait to see Madison tonight so she could just put the shit out on the table, desperately hoping Madison would have some advice. Besides, she could see what's been happening with her girl's life, which never had a dull moment to spare.

* * *

"Bryce, I've never seen you so upbeat. I'm glad to see you're relaxing more and glad it's not all office and no life." Sylvia continued to eat, observing her grandson's new disposition.

"Grandmother, you worry about me too much. I work to have the life I want, and maybe one day I will have a family of my own to raise."

"Bryce, darling, don't you think I understand that? It just seemed to me you weren't really enjoying life anymore, especially after your mother passed, God rest her soul. Umph, umph, umm." Sylvia closed her eyes shaking her head from side to side. She loved Bryce's mother. Karl had found a gem in Beatrice, and she was the type of woman Sylvia was glad to

have in the family. It devastated the family when she passed away. The cancer had moved so quickly through her body, no amount of money in the world could have saved her.

Sylvia was determined that Beatrice's dreams for Bryce were fulfilled, from his education to his selection of the appropriate woman to share his life with. Bryce completed his MBA from Wharton after the death of his mother and was doing quite well working for one of the most prestigious investment firms in the country. The Towson name was well known and Sylvia had to make sure Bryce understood that whomever he chose to be his wife would be his business; however, she would not have them carrying the Towson name if they weren't up to Towson standards. Sylvia watched, smiling as her grandson shoved his dinner into his mouth; they were having chicken and dumplings, one of his favorite's, prepared by her, especially for him. Some things never change, no matter how old he became.

"Grand, now what are you smiling about?" Bryce looked up from his plate to catch his grandmother's loving gaze.

"Oh, nothing, darling. I just love you so much and want the best for you."

"I know that Grand, believe me. I'm very happy; my career is going extremely well; and I believe I have finally found my wife in Raven." He lowered his eyes, returning to his meal not waiting for a response.

"She seems like a lovely young lady; I look forward to getting to know her a little better." Sylvia wiped her mouth placing her napkin in her plate.

"Grand, you need to give her a chance. It's true she may not have our background or financial means, but what does that mean in the scheme of it all?" Bryce wiped his mouth, sitting up from his plate. He knew his grandmother wasn't going to let it end there.

"It means a lot if you're trying to build a life Bryce. Your mother was not from a wealthy background but her drive, ambition, and character was like royalty. Trust me, your grandfather and I put her through a few tests before she married your father."

"And?" Bryce lifted his left eyebrow, wanting to hear more.

"And nothing, darling. You're here aren't you? There were many women vying for your father's attention, just like the

young ladies you've paraded past us. They're no longer around, so I'm figuring they weren't worthy of your love." Sylvia rose and began clearing the table.

"Not worthy, or you and dad scared them off." He began laughing, offering to help clear the table.

"Just sit still, love; I'll handle it. Besides, I sent the housekeeper home early. This will give me a little exercise for the day." Sylvia disappeared into the kitchen.

Bryce knew his grandmother's intentions were good, but sometimes she could be so overbearing. He sat back in his chair, reminiscing on his mother's advice, which suggested that he worked smart and enjoy life. "Bryce, ain't nothing free, not even your name. We work hard to maintain our reputations in life; when it's all done, all you have to stand on is our word, dignity, and name." The room felt eerie as his mother's words whispered in his ear. She was a classy woman, just like his grandmother, and he missed her terribly.

Bryce remained at the table thinking about the memories of his mother and grandfather. Sitting quietly he began to think about Raven and how happy she makes him. It was something about her. He longed to be with her as often as he could. She was always happy to see him, and lately her sexual appetite seemed to be on overdrive. There was no opposition from him on that.

Bryce had his share of the society types. He had witnessed first hand the prudes not wanting to suck a dick or the case of "Oh no, not me. I don't do those type of things." Pure-as-the-driven-snow bullshit echoed many a night through his bedroom when he wanted his dick sucked or wanted to stroke an ass. That shit was a wrap before he could even get the head of his dick out of his boxers.

He liked to explore all sexual desires and fantasies with his partner; that was non-negotiable. He felt himself to be an experienced lover, not one who dogged women but one that was willing to satisfy them just as much as having his own desires fulfilled. Raven satisfied that part of him she provided him the ecstasy and fantasy exclusively. Although she was struggling to make ends meet financially, she had the potential and desire to

make things happen for herself if given the opportunity. He had finally found a complete package in Raven. Mind, body, and soul—she was the one. It wouldn't be long before he was going to pop the question. Bryce closed his eyes and sat quietly, listening to his grandmother hum *Amazing Grace* as pots clanged in the kitchen.

"You wanna do what with whom?" Madison lifted her head from the refrigerator, mouth full of cold pizza.

"I didn't say I wanted to do anything. I've been having these fantasies and they're driving me crazy," Raven responded to Madison, quickly trying to justify her lustful urges.

"Do you know that man is old enough to be your father fresh ass?" Madison lowered her head back into the fridge, searching for her next quick snack.

"Age doesn't have anything to do with it; the bigger issue is this man is the father of my future husband, and I've been fantasizing about fuckin' him." Lowering her head, Raven began massaging her temples. A headache was on its way.

"Yeah, you're right about age; it doesn't mean a damn thing. I had a few college men when I was a freshmen in high school." Madison gulped bottled water, flopping on the couch next to Raven. "But, hey, those were college men, not old-ass men. Besides, I heard old men had worms."

Madison looked at Raven dead serious about what had just come out of her mouth.

Raven looked over at Madison, who hadn't stopped snacking since she walked in the damn door. "You're a fool, Madison. Yeah, he's got a worm alright, and it ain't the kind you're talking about, either, fresh ass."

"And you know this because . . ." She grinned through the chunks of pizza in her mouth.

Raven shook her head, ignoring her girlfriend. She could be so off the beaten path at times. Raven needed her support, not to be entertained. She wasn't in the mood.

"Yeah, now I'm a fresh-ass grown woman." Madison grinned, still chomping away at the slice of pizza. Madison had

no problem with her sexuality; she had men the way men had women no apologies for how she lived her life. The men in Madison's life varied from hood regulars to professional men; of course; she preferred the latter; they came with more perks and conversations that were of interest. The girl always had a story to share about her soap opera life.

Madison had this hood rich persona, caramel skin, blonde weave, tight jeans, and canal street knock-offs mixed with the authentic labels—gifts from the professional men in her life who bought her attention. Along with this image came many glares from women on the block. "A straight whore," girls from the neighborhood voiced their distaste of Madison and what they perceived she stood for. Jealous-ass bitches always expected the worst but Madison could give a fuck swinging her fat ass extra hard, especially when their men accompanied them. She flowed through the neighborhood as if she owned it, and that's what Raven loved about Madison. She wasn't going to let no one shake her, shit-talkers and all. They'd been friends since grade school; she was always there for support. That's what mattered to both of them.

"So what you going to do, Rave?" Madison sat staring as if Raven had the answer tattooed across her forehead.

"Ain't shit I can do but take a cold shower and call it a goddamn day." There was no reality to Raven wanting to be with Karl; it was a silly schoolgirl crush, and she wished it would just go away. Rubbing her temples a little harder, she tried cursing away the rigid pounding that was now winning the battle.

"Well do you really love Bryce, or are you infatuated with his world?" Madison's full attention was focused on her girlfriend.

"Yeah . . . yeah, I do. I've never given a man the key to my apartment, Bryce has total access to me and what's mine." Raven stared blankly at Madison.

"Then shake this silly fantasy and make it happen. Has his family accepted you?" Madison continued on with her snacking. "I was invited to their house in the Hampton's. We leave next Friday," she responded dryly, head throbbing. The voo-doo didn't work; she had a full blown migraine.

"The Hamptons!" Madison sat straight up on the couch. "Oh, girl, so they really got a couple of dollars, huh?" she continued on nonstop in her conversation, never noticing there was no response from Raven. "I know I told you before not to stress it because, after all, they are only people with money, but you're a good girl; Rave; I wouldn't let them get away. This is war, baby, and you need to make sure you secure your future," Madison's voice faded slightly as she headed back to the kitchen.

Sitting silently, staring at the coffee table, Raven couldn't believe that she was allowing this stupid little fantasy to get the best of her. She once read somewhere that fantasizing was healthy for a relationship, maybe just not for her relationship.

"Hey, Raven," Madison was now screaming from the kitchen, "you need to take your ass right to the Hamptons and seal the deal, momma, I mean, put the thing-thing on Bryce. "He should be asking for your hand in marriage before you make it back here to the Brooklyn Bridge." Madison was smacking her lips on her next snack.

Raven couldn't part her lips to speak her head was throbbing uncontrollably and she was squinting through her right eye, trying to catch a part of Madison's conversation. The girl was talking so damn fast, she didn't care to translate any of her advice, not to mention she was back in the refrigerator grazing like a fat-ass cow.

Lying back on the sofa, Raven closed her eyes, trying to get peace from her migraine. The last thing she remembered hearing was Madison mumbling something about placing strawberries and whipped cream in the crack of Raven's ass and having Bryce eat them from the back to the front. As enticing as that sounded, that was the last thing on her mind. Besides, Madison probably would steal that little trick for her next session.

The weeks passed so quickly there was no time to catch her breath, let alone pack for the weekend. Between work and bonding with Bryce's grandmother, Raven didn't have a moment to herself. It was 1:00p.m. and Bryce would be picking her up at 2:00p.m. She hadn't finished packing. A suitcase and

two overnight bags were sitting in the middle of the living room; they'd been packed and unpacked four times. Making her mind up on what to bring for the weekend turned out to be a very challenging process she didn't want to wear anything that was too provocative, yet all her weekend gear was pretty relaxed and sexed out. The past few weeks had marked a turning point for Raven with Sylvia, and she wasn't about to screw her process up over a few provocative outfits.

Although Sylvia took up a lot of her time, she figured that to be a good thing for keeping her mind occupied and off of Bryce's father. The need to seal her relationship with Bryce was top priority, and it didn't include a threesome with his Pops. Everything was running smoothly during the week, until Karl stopped by his mother's house while Raven was there having dinner. Just the sight of him made her uncomfortable; she politely greeted him and kept her eyes focused on the plate of food in front of her.

Sylvia and Karl went on with their conversation about an upcoming charity event. The two of them continued to talk for a few minutes before Karl bent over and kissed his mother on the cheek.

"I'll check on you after my meeting this evening." Karl rubbed his mother's shoulder before leaving her side.

"Nice seeing you again as well, Raven." He winked his eye as he disappeared from the dining room.

Mrs. Towson didn't miss a beat. She continued with their discussion becoming increasingly comfortable with Raven. They sat and talked nonstop.

Raven was sure Bryce had a lot to do with his grandmother's newfound interest in her but, more than anything, she knew Sylvia wanted him to be happy. For the most part, their conversations remained lighthearted. When Sylvia quizzed Raven on her future plans, she even discussed Bryce's mother. There was no denying how much Beatrice meant to the family. Sylvia held her as some type of superwoman. Raven soon realized why Bryce spoke so often about his mother; she was the center of his universe.

In the midst of Sylvia going on and on about Beatrice, the desire for Karl that evening hadn't stopped. Raven couldn't help how she was feeling; just seeing him brought out an arousal. Her nipples were so hard she wanted to feel his salt & peppered mustache brush across them.

Sylvia excused herself and went upstairs. Raven had to act quickly on her opportunity to give Karl what he had been staring at from day one. A little sample of his son's prize pussy wouldn't hurt. After all it would be best if they kept it all in the family, anyway. She moved towards Karl, unbuttoning each button of her silk shirt,

Karl parted his lips, staring at Raven from the other end of the table, unzipping his pants. He allowed his manhood to flop from the opening. The size of it was more than she had expected.

Raven was a willing participant ready to satisfy him with all she had. Getting down on her knees she crawled towards him, taking his grown man in her mouth. Savoring his flavor, she felt the need to relieve him from his long day's work. Raven's mouth was juiced over as she worked feverishly, wanting to taste him before sharing her own juices with him. She moved her wet mouth along his shaft, making sure she was able to lick every vein in his dick.

He began to moan and pump his head deep into the back of her throat.

Raven was turned on by the challenge. She tried to swallow his entire dick, allowing his rawness to hit the side of her jaws with and exuberant force.

"Raven, did you hear what I said, sweetie?" Sylvia's voice was a harsh welcome back to reality.

"I'm sorry, Mrs. Towson. What did you say?" she responded, obviously in a delayed state from her fantasy.

"Did you want me to lower the air conditioning; you have goose bumps all over your arms, dear." Mrs. Towson motioned for her housekeeper to adjust the temperature on the central air in the house.

"No, Mrs. Towson, I'm fine. She rubbed her hands over her arms, before folding them in front of her, to conceal her erect nipples. Raven was horny as hell and soaking wet between her

legs. She was hoping her skirt was catching the sloppy wetness that was seeping from her steamy crotch and dripping onto Sylvia's fabric-covered dining room chairs.

"Well, as long as you're comfortable, dear." Mrs. Towson was watching her every move.

Raven was nervous as hell, wondering if Sylvia knew she was just giving her son a damn good head job. What the hell is she staring at? Raven's mind began to taunt her with paranoia. She lifted her glass of water and took a sip before speaking. "Mrs. Towson, I really enjoyed dinner this evening. In fact, I've enjoyed the time we've been sharing, getting to know each other." She sipped some more water. Her mouth had suddenly become awfully dry.

"So have I, Raven. I think you're a lovely young lady; I can see why my grandson is so smitten with you." Clearing her throat, Mrs. Towson continued to speak. "I may seem to be a bit stern at times, but it's important to make sure you bring the right type of people into your inner circle. Do you understand what I'm saying to you, dear?" She sat back and continued to watch Raven intently.

"Yes, I understand. I know how important your family is to you, and if I were in your shoes I would want the same thing, too." Raven sat back in her chair looking Sylvia over as well.

"Well, Raven, maybe one day you will be," Sylvia replied before asking her to join her in the solarium for after-dinner cocktails or tea. Mrs. Towson began walking to the other room.

Raven pushed her chair back from the dining room table. The wetness between her legs alerted her that her pussy was still dripping from the fantasy. She quickly snatched the cloth napkin from her dinner plate, placing it between her legs, wiping the wetness that had been festering for the past twenty-five minutes.

"There, Raven, that's better." She sighed. "Now you're ready for that cocktail."

Pushing her chair back under the table, Raven shoved the pussy-soaked napkin into her purse as she entered the solarium to join Mrs. Towson.

The day couldn't have been more perfect if she had planned it herself. Bryce had arrived thirty minutes late to pick Raven up for their trip and, little does he know, she was just closing her bags when he arrived at the door. The sun felt so warm on her legs, beating through the sunroof. A tingle ran throughout Raven's entire body giving her a satisfying peace.

Bryce couldn't keep his hands off her legs as he drove into a countryside paradise.

"You look beautiful, Raven." Bryce continued to rub his hand over her thighs.

"Thanks baby, I'm looking forward to this weekend. I've been so tense. I need a relief, and this weekend getaway is the perfect medicine." Raven shifted in her seat to stop her thighs from sticking to the leather seats. She loved Bryce's car; it was a bitch-catcher, a 745iL head-turner. Females were always leaning up to see who was driving, and Raven loved to recline the seat back and peek up when one of them called themselves hollering at her man.

"A weekend, huh? Girl, you packed enough shit for an entire month." Bryce glanced at his back seats, looking at all the bags.

"Shut up, boy. If your trunk was cleared out from all your stuff, I could've put the rest of them in there." Raven playfully smacked Bryce's hand from her leg.

"Sensitive, are we?" Bryce smiled as he placed his hand back on her thigh, squeezing for comfort. Bryce looked very nice while dressed in a pair of jeans and a simple Polo top. He smelled of her favorite cologne, Ferragamo, which he had been wearing the first day they met. Bryce began to move his fingers towards Raven's inner thighs hitting them lightly she automatically parted her legs, allowing his fingers to explore the crotch of her shorts.

The friction he was causing between her legs was so arousing he knew it didn't take much to take her there lately. Bryce was taking advantage of every moment.

There were no complaints on her behalf; she was willing to satisfy him at all cost. Raven couldn't keep still as the escape of moans soon drowned out Dwele's crooning on the radio.

There was no competition. Bryce lowered the volume so he could enjoy the music his lover was creating,

Raven reached down to unzip her shorts, kicking them to the floor, positioning her feet against the walnut grained console. She reclined her seat as far back as it could go.

Bryce implanted his middle finger between her legs. Its thickness felt like a small dick, one that Raven would be disappointed with if he possessed. Thank God that wasn't the case. Moving his finger inside her walls, he tested to see how much she could handle. He offered two more fingers into Raven's soaked pussy, taking them out every few strokes to lick them before placing them back into the moistness. The gyrating and moaning was mounting as he continued to maneuver the stretch of highway. The trip to the country seemed to go on forever as he continued to drive and she continued to be finger-fucked while watching the sky pass by through the open sunroof.

"Wake up sleepy head. We're here."

Raven awoke to Bryce tapping on the passenger side of the window. Sitting up groggy from a deep sleep, thanks to her man, she reached down to pull the zipper all the way up on her half zipped shorts. After climaxing several times on the way to the Hamptons, Raven had retrieved her shorts from the passenger side floor but had had no energy left to zip them before falling off to sleep."How long was I asleep, baby?" Raven aligned her body horizontally, zipping up the shorts.

"Let's just say I finished two CDs and stopped at the store twenty-five minutes ago and you didn't budge once." Bryce opened the car door, extending his hand for Raven to grab.

"Well, you're the one that got me started. What did…"

Bryce placed his finger over her mouth, signaling for silence.

She loved when he took control of the situation.

"If I have my way, Raven, I want to make you feel that good all weekend long." He leaned over and planted a kiss on her lips his mustache tickled her nose.

Laughing, she couldn't control the excitement that had mounted in her for the weekend. The house was half the size of their home in Westchester, NY; but with that said, it was still a huge piece of property. The circular driveway was paved with

stone and what looked to be small pieces of colored glass. It had a real art deco appeal; it reminded her of the houses that were shown in Miami Beach on MTV Cribs. There were beautiful orange flowered shrubs that covered the front of the house, and they complimented the beige and cream stone-washed façade. To the left of the house, ivy grew up the side, adding even more character to the country home estate. Bryce had begun to grab the bags from the car, lining them up on the front steps, allowing Raven to take in her surroundings.

She noticed Karl's SUV sitting in the driveway along with some sort of two-seater sports car.

"Oh, it looks like your dad and grandmother are already here." Raven tried to sound nonchalant but her heart began to race; the nervousness of being around Karl all weekend was beginning to stir deep within.

"It looks that way." Bryce looked at the cars as he entered the house, calling for his family.

"Hey we're here. Is anyone home?" Bryce walked through the downstairs with no reply from the obviously empty house.

The inside of the house was just as gorgeous as the outside, contemporary furniture sprawled throughout the house, vibrant colors dominating the walls of every room of the house, except the bedroom, where soft dreamy colors were used, promoting comfort and solace. After Bryce gave Raven the complete tour, she was more than impressed with the five-bedroom getaway with master bathrooms in three of the five rooms. The kitchen was gourmet-style, with an island and a seated nook carved right out of the bay window.

"Bryce this is beautiful. It's like having a small piece of paradise outside of the city. I don't even feel like we're anywhere near New York." Raven spun around in the kitchen like a little girl; the space was huge and felt light and airy.

"Yeah, we like it. My grandmother and I don't come up here much. My dad and mom use to spend a lot of time here." Bryce was quiet for a moment.

"All the decorating of the house was her idea. She loved this type of stuff, and we never really changed it. My dad spends

time here by himself sometimes." Bryce walked towards Raven, pulling her into him.

"Well, we're going to have a great time this weekend with everyone, so let's just relax and let things unwind." She hugged Bryce around his waist, feeling his thoughts drifting away.

"Hey, boy, did you hear what I said?"

"Yeah, baby, I heard you. That's not it. I just wish my dad would find a companion; my mother has been dead for some time, and I know she wouldn't want him to spend his years alone." Bryce looked into Raven's eyes.

"Your dad never dates at all?" She was being nosy for the sake of being nosy.

"Yeah, he does, several women, in fact; but none of them measure up to my mom, so I guess he just feels it's just something to do until the right one comes along." Bryce shook his head as he began to laugh.

Frowning, Raven wanted to know what was so funny with that comment.

Bryce hugged her tighter. "Yeah, my dad is acting like a pimp at his age. Women are going crazy trying to be with him, and he's acting like a high school boy with his hormones out of control."

"You find that funny?" Listening for Bryce's reply, the room was silent.

"No not funny, just pathetic on his and the women's behalf. It seems the older they get the more they revert back to younger years. These grown-ass women are laying up with my father, hoping to be the wife."

"Can you blame them, Bryce? You and your father are both handsome, educated, funny, and . . ." Raven stopped in mid sentence.

"Go ahead, you can say it Raven. Wealthy, right?" They sat down in the living room on the sofa.

"Yeah, wealthy. You two are a fantasy come true for many women, a knight in shining armor." That was the true reality as she watched Bryce pick at his belt buckle.

"Yeah, maybe that's why it's so important to get the right woman because, Raven, this is not a fantasy; it's real life, baby, real in living color."

Raven leaned over into Bryce and nestled in his arms. He was right, this was real life and not a fantasy. So, the fact that she had been fantasizing about fucking his father would not go over well in this conversation. She had to shake this silly shit. After all, she had a strong feeling Bryce was interested in making her the wife, and unlike those women who've been dealing with his father, lucky bitches, the odds of them landing his last name to seal the deal was damn near impossible. What she found in Bryce was someone who really cares for her; and from their hours of discussions, he is focused on handling their business together as a committed couple. What more could they want?

Several hours had passed before Karl appeared in the doorway of the living room. He was sweaty and had his tee shirt thrown over his shoulder. His physique was remarkable; he had obviously just returned from working out.

"Hey, what's up guys? I see you finally arrived?" Karl moved across the room, greeting Bryce and Raven before flopping onto the large leather ottoman that sat in the middle of the room.

"Finally arrived?" Bryce began laughing. "Pops, we arrived over two hours ago. I took Raven on a tour of the grounds, and we even ate lunch. The question is where have you been?"

Karl shook his head laughing. He was gone longer than he had anticipated. He wanted to be at the house to greet Bryce and Raven when they arrived, but his country jog allowed his mind to wander and so did he. "Alright, wise ass, I'm glad you guys are settled in. I had the grocery store deliver some food for us for the weekend, and they still forgot one of the ingredients I need for my pasta dinner."

"Oh, you cook?" Raven asked Karl, trying to keep her mind off of how good he was looking. Sweaty or not, the man was fine as hell.

"Do I cook? Young lady, you're in for a treat. I can throw together a mean Italian meal, wine and hot baked bread included." Karl smiled at Raven confident in his statement.

Raven looked over at Bryce, who was cosigning his father's declaration by nodding his head. "Well, alright then, I can't wait to taste that meal. It'll be nice to have the men cook for the ladies this weekend." Raven, of course, was referring to her and Mrs. Towson.

"Hey, speaking of ladies, where is grandmother?" Bryce asked his father.

"I forgot to tell you that your grandmother couldn't make it this weekend, but she sends her love and hopes everyone enjoys themselves. She'll see you when you get back." Karl stood up swinging his shirt back over his shoulder. He excused himself before leaving to take a shower.

Raven felt a stirring deep within. The thought of Mrs. Towson not being there was exciting but dangerous; she knew Mrs. Towson watched her like a hawk, so she would have been on her "A" game. Her fantasies about Karl had taken over for the last several months, and although Bryce prospered from her overly sexed hormones, this weekend was going to be tough. Just thinking about Karl had made her wet between her legs. She wished she could join him in the shower and assist in removing the layers of sweat from his body.

"Well, baby girl, it's just the three of us for the weekend, so just relax and let your mind run free, no stress, all pleasure and margaritas." Bryce kissed Raven on the cheek as he got up to make them margaritas.

"Mango please, with sugar on the brim!" Raven called after Bryce, placing her order.

The remainder of the evening was very enjoyable. They played games, drank, and took a walk together, sharing time and just acting silly. The country setting was spread apart; you definitely needed a car to get around, and the nearest grocery store was a good twenty minutes one way. Bryce showed Raven a couple of the other houses that were included in the private residential area; they were just as beautiful as the Towson's home, with affluent couples occupying those homes as well.

Their night ended with a candle-lit barbecue on the deck and more cocktails.

Raven felt peaceful and at ease with her decision to accompany Bryce for the weekend. After a hot shower, Raven climbed into bed with Bryce and made love to him, showing her appreciation for his choice to share his life with her. She fell off to sleep not once thinking about Karl.

Raven awoke in the middle of the night. Her mouth was dry and felt like cotton. The alcohol she had consumed earlier left her dehydrated. Bryce looked so content sleeping, she didn't want to awake him. She tip toed to the adjoining bathroom in their room to get a quick drink of water. No cups in sight, she cupped her hands, attempting to quench her thirst. "This shit isn't working." Raven was frustrated, looking around, hoping a cup would magically appear. Leaving the bathroom, she slipped into her panties and decided to sneak down to the kitchen, remembering the bottles of spring water in the refrigerator. It was 3:30a.m. according to the alarm clock in their bedroom. The house was eerie and still as Raven made her way to the kitchen. She retrieved a bottle of water from the fridge. Closing the door, the lights in the kitchen were flipped on blinding her.

"I'm sorry, I didn't mean to scare you. I thought I heard some movement in here." Karl stood in the kitchen, looking at Raven who was frozen in position, her hand shielding her eyes from the bright light.

There she stood with her bottle of water, panties, and no bra. Raven felt embarrassed and aroused. At the same time, she moved the bottle of water in front of her chest, trying to block her now erect nipples. "I'm so embarrassed." Raven began walking towards Karl to exit the kitchen. "I was thirsty and I . . ." Not able to finish her sentence, she was busy watching the erection in Karl's pajama pants. Raven's heart began to beat at an accelerated pace. She felt excited, and this was her chance to make those fantasies a reality.

As she exited the kitchen, she lowered the water bottle so Karl could get a good look at her chocolate nipples. Tracing the outline of her nipples with her finger, she placed her finger in her mouth and spoke. "I'm so sorry, Karl. I should have dressed

completely before coming to the kitchen; I just thought everyone would be asleep." Raven batted her eyes as the look of innocence now made her appear even sexier.

"It's fine, Raven. We'll keep this between us, and I'll see you in the morning." Karl licked his lips several times and didn't once try to conceal his hand grasping his erect penis. Raven lingered in the doorway a minute longer before turning around and slowly, walking back to her bedroom.

The next morning was awkward at breakfast as Karl and Bryce did much of the talking. Raven watched the both of them and knew that if Karl would have approached her last night, she would have fucked him right there on the kitchen floor. *Am I a whore*? Raven began having conversations with herself, trying to understand why one minute she was so focused on Bryce and the next minute she wanted his father.

"Does that sound like a plan to you, Raven?" Karl looked at her as she finished her Belgian waffles and eggs.

"Excuse me?" Raven stopped chewing.

"I thought I would fix my famous Italian meal for us tonight. Bryce is going to have you out all day, so tonight we'll have the dinner I promised." Karl smiled at Raven, knowing she was feeling awkward after last night.

"That sounds good to me." Raven smiled, only looking in Bryce's direction. She was glad he had an entire day planned because, after last night, she couldn't bear to be around Karl any longer than she had to be.

The Hamptons were beautiful; there were so many beautiful fields of flowers in all colors, they looked like painted pictures pulled from a magazine. The houses were beyond what she imagined she swore she recognized them from one of those entertainment shows.

Bryce drove her through several of the gated communities and introduced her to some of his acquaintances he'd known for years. He showed her a different side of his world. This is who he was, lavish houses, quaint bistros, yachts, and private beaches. This

type of shit she only dreamed of, and soon this would be her world as well. Their day was nonstop.

Raven felt exhausted as Bryce pulled the car into the driveway. She looked at her reflection in the mirror. She was a shade darker from being on the beach earlier.

When they entered the house, the smell of garlic, butter, and other seasonings met them at the front door.

"Hey, love birds. How was your day in the Hamptons?" Karl chirped from the kitchen. He was in full chef mode; soft music was playing as he maneuvered around the kitchen as if that was his chosen career.

"We had a great time, pops." Bryce moved over to one of the pots on the stove, tasting the sauce that was on simmer.

"Everything smells so delicious, Karl. So you really put it down in the kitchen, huh?" Raven sat on the stool at the kitchen counter watching her man and his father bond over a pot of sauce.

"Yeah, I do a little something. You guys have at least an hour or two before we eat, so go relax." Karl continued to sauté the Italian sausage, checking the flame before placing it in the sauce.

"Cool I need a shower. The sand from the beach is everywhere, and a little rest won't hurt, either." Raven hopped down from the stool, headed towards the bedroom.

"I can help you wash that sand away if you like?" Bryce teased Raven.

She rolled her eyes playfully, disappearing from the kitchen.

The cool jet streams of water from the showerhead relived Raven's sun-drenched skin. She lathered her body with honeysuckle body wash and let the foam run between every crack and crevasse on her body. Her sun-tanned body looked like two shades of chocolate fudge; her Brazilian-waxed pussy looked more tempting now that her skin was two different shades of brown. This was her last full night in the Hamptons, and she would make sure it was a memorable one for Bryce. Stepping out of the shower, Raven toweled herself off and began singing. She felt wonderful. She wanted to look sexy tonight for her man; she knew exactly what she would wear. Raven stopped singing as she entered their bedroom and began smiling. Laying

on the bed was a beautiful fresh-cut stem of lavender, a blindfold, handcuffs, and a note that read:

Beautiful one;

I hope you enjoyed your shower. Please relax and place the blindfold on. I'll return to you in five minutes . . . No questions . . . do as you're told and be a good girl!

Raven was excited at the thought of her man being so creative and freaky. She was more than willing to obey. She finished drying her body off, and smoothed body cream all over to soften her sun-drenched skin. Raven blindfolded herself and lay her naked body on the cool sheets. The chill from the sheets was so relaxing, she felt like she was floating on a cloud.

There was a knock on the door.

Startled, Raven began to giggle as she called for her lover to enter.

"Come in, sir." Raven laughed. "I can't believe you got me lying here blindfolded." Raven continued to ramble on.

She could hear the door open then close with the lock clicking in the air.

Her hands were separated over her head as the handcuffs were placed in position. There was no response given.

"Oh, I get it; I'm your love slave. Okay, baby, have it your way." She was really enjoying the role-play.

Raven's legs were then spread eagle, exposing her fully. She was so excited about the little game, her pussy began pulsating, waiting to be touched. Her nipples were erect. She knew her lover had to be aroused by her body, which was open for his full pleasure. Raven lay still as she felt what had to be the stem of lavender being traced down her limbs, over her arms, thighs, stomach, and breast. The flowers were brushed under her nose as she took in a whiff of their sweet floral notes. Raven began to squirm with excitement. She had never imagined her man being so erotic. His lips traced her nipples giving each one equal play.

His mustache felt coarse against her skin, making her squirm even more. He licked down to her navel as Raven raised her pussy to his mouth, begging him to fuck her. His stiff tongue plunged deep between her legs, lapping at her moistness. Raven

was out of control. As she grasped onto the headboard for balance as she moved her mound against his mouth.

"Just fuck me, baby, please; just fuck me." Raven felt sensuously tortured. Bryce had never bought this out of her before. Her pussy continued being tongued. The moistness flowed to the crack of her ass, followed by his tongue. A buzzing noise soon entered the air. Her senses were on high alert as she felt the vibration rubbing against her clitoris before entering the walls of her pussy.

Her lover continued tonguing her ass while the cold vibrator rumbled about in her hot opening.

Raven came uncontrollably as she was having both of her holes serviced. Her body convulsed shaking the bed with a force. The clang of the handcuffs rang in the air as she came over and over. As quick as she was bought to her climax, she was left alone on the bed, no handcuffs but, still blindfolded and exhausted.

The room was silent. Raven lay still five more minutes before removing the blindfold. She sat up on the bed, dazed but quietly desiring to experience the whole thing again. Left in a puddle of moistness, she pulled herself up to get dressed and saw the silver vibrator entangled in the sheets.

"This boy thought of everything." She smiled, turning on the vibrator, allowing it to massage the palm of her hand. "Who would think something this small would do such a big job?" Raven straightened up the bed and tucked the vibrator in her bag. Her and Bryce would laugh about this later. It was official: her man was a *freak*!

Raven arrived in the kitchen with a big smile on her face, looking around for Bryce.

Karl was slicing pieces of Italian bread to place in the oven. "How was your shower?" Karl asked never looking up from his work.

"It was heavenly, the best shower I've had," Raven answered, still on a high from being fucked so well. Still no signs of Bryce. She knew he was a freak but, damn, a magician, too?

"Do you know where Bryce is?" Raven peeked out on the deck, still no sign of Bryce.

"He's at the store, picking up an ingredient for my scallops. He should be back any minute." Karl answered, smiling.

"At the store?" Raven was confused.

"Yeah the store, you know how long that takes. He's been gone for over thirty minutes he should be back at anytime." Karl licked his lips, handing Raven the place settings to put on the dining room table.

Raven walked slowly towards the dining room. If Bryce was at the store, then that could only mean one thing. Raven almost dropped the place settings as she entered the dining room. Sitting in the middle of the table was a beautiful arrangement of fresh cut lavender.

"Oh god, no, this can't be real." Raven felt a mix of emotions. She was confused, scared, and angry; but the one emotion that remained was the desire to fuck him again before Bryce returned from the store. Her guilt took over as she placed the plates on the table and quickly walked out to the front driveway, awaiting Bryce's return.

It was another fifteen minutes before Bryce returned to the house with his father's missing ingredient. Raven greeted him by smacking a huge wet kiss on his lips. She pulled back slowly and stood there staring into his eyes.

"Damn, baby, if I knew I was going to get that response I would leave you alone here more often. Bryce returned her affection by kissing her on the forehead.

"No, I don't think you want to do that." Raven hugged Bryce around the waist as they entered the house.

The three of them sat down to eat. Bryce and his father were heavy in conversation about business for the first time over the weekend. Bryce barely noticed Raven not participating in the conversation; he figured her to be tired from being out earlier.

The night couldn't have ended fast enough. This was their last evening in the Hamptons, and she was planning to leave what had happened right there. Raven stuck close to Bryce for the remainder of the evening while Karl eyed her as if she were a piece of candy. She tried not to entertain the thought but she wanted him as much as he wanted her.

The next morning, Raven awoke early, anticipating her escape from the Hamptons. Not even Madison would believe the shit that took place this weekend, she thought.

Bryce and Raven arrived back in New York at dusk, enough time for her to settle in for the work week. She couldn't get what had happened off her mind. Was she going crazy or did Karl provide her with pleasure unmeasured by none?

"Okay, snap the hell out of it, Raven." She was engulfed in her thoughts; she couldn't go another day without talking to Karl about what happened.

The next day, she contacted Karl's office and asked to see him. They agreed to meet at her place. Raven had to address what had happened. The last thing she wanted was for Bryce to get wind of her torrid fantasy or his father's scheming ways.

Dressed in a skirt and tank top, Raven sat nervously on her couch, shaking her leg and sipping wine. The music of Anthony Hamilton played softly in the background. All she could think about was saving her relationship and burying what had happened in the Hamptons. She had left work early, using the excuse of an upset stomach, so she would have time to get herself together to face Karl. The knock on her apartment door startled her; Karl wasn't due for two more hours.

"Good evening." Raven looked away from Karl as if she would turn to stone if she looked him in the eyes. "You know why I asked you here, I'm sure." She was curt. "I love your son, and I do want to be his wife one day." Raven continued to babble on, shutting the door behind Karl.

"Raven, there's no doubt you love my son, but are you telling me you didn't enjoy your time in the Hamptons?" Karl moved into her space lifting her chin to see her eyes. "It's no secret you've been watching me. Baby girl, I've been watching you, too." Karl moved his hand down her shoulder and began massaging her supple breast with his hands.

"Please Mr. Towson don't . . . " Raven moved his hands.

"Don't what, Raven? We're two adults here." Karl moved in closer placing his chest against her.

"What are you worried about, Bryce finding out? My son is working late tonight; I made sure of that." Karl traced Raven's nipple with his finger.

Raven lost her breath as Karl kneaded her breast with one hand and began removing her skirt with the other. She didn't want this to happen, but she felt like the fiend in the neighborhood chasing that pipe.

Karl leaned over and kissed Raven lightly on her lips. His mustache felt just like his son's.

She was lost; there was nothing she could do as she opened her mouth to receive his tongue. Raven lifted her arms as Karl removed her shirt, and she removed her skirt and thong, standing in the middle of the living room, ready to receive a man who was damn near thirty years her junior.

Karl looked over Raven's body; it appeared even more beautiful than in the Hamptons. Her chocolate nipples were so erect as he leaned over and traced them with his tongue.

"If I give you this, there will be no more, Karl. I want to be with your son." Raven looked him dead in his eyes. There was no turning back.

He didn't hear a word she said as he inserted two fingers into her pussy and placed his tongue back in her mouth. They lay back on her sofa, lost in the moment.

Raven unzipped his pants to release his erection. His dick was a nice size. Raven pushed him back to get a full view.

Karl smiled as her eyes told the story. It was beyond what she had expected, and obviously it met her approval. Karl stood up, lowering his pants to the floor. He sat back on the sofa with Raven positioned over him.

Raven thought she was going to explode as Karl lowered her on to his erection. Palming her firm brown ass, he brought her forward so he could continue servicing her nipples.

"Oh Karl," Raven cried out, as she worked her wet pussy up and down his shaft.. He stretched her young pussy, forcing it to take all of him. They continued to fuck in all positions on her couch as she demonstrated one of the many reasons why his son was so taken with her.

"You are going to make me cum, young lady." Karl was moaning.

Raven now lay on her side as he took her from the back. Her legs were cocked open as he played with her clitoris. She teased her own nipples, about to explode as well.

Holding on to dear life, not wanting to release, Karl placed her on the floor and continued entering her from behind. His dick was so thick, Raven felt every pulse as he entered and re-entered her now-sore pussy. "I'm getting ready to cum, baby." Karl slowed his pace pulling out of Raven.

"Oh, don't stop. Just a couple more strokes." Raven begged like a crack whore for another hit.

Karl plunged his dick deep inside, pounding her walls with force.

She released, bucking wildly on her floor. Raven was wild-eyed as she pushed Karl onto the sofa and took his dick into her mouth. Her jaws pulled with great force as she sucked him off and rubbed his sack to help with the release.

"Oh shit, girl, you real good . . . " Karl grabbed a hand full of her thick hair as he fucked her mouth. She deep-throated him with such strength, he couldn't control his release. The force from his body shook him as Raven ate him entirely. He closed his eyes as his legs stiffened and released his nut into her mouth.

Raven sucked him down as the overspill from the explosion dripped onto the sides of her mouth.

It was over. Karl lay back on the sofa. Bringing his head forward he heard Raven giggling.

"Did you enjoy it?" she asked.

Karl opened his eyes, unable to speak. He sat staring past Raven.

"What's wrong, silly? Never had it that good, huh?" Raven spoke in her raspy voice.

Karl sat still without moving,

Raven turned to face the direction he was staring. Her world stopped as everything moved in slow motion. She stood to her feet, raising her hands in the direction of the door. There stood Bryce and Ms. Towson.

"Bryce, baby, please. I can explain." Tears rolled down Raven's face as a drop of cum from Karl's release dripped from her chin, splashing onto her bare foot.

"Did you enjoy it, dear?" Mrs. Towson asked.

"Oh please, you don't understand. I was doing this for Bryce and me." Raven sobbed on the other end of the phone.

"Bryce!" Mrs. Towson shouted. "Just think—he was prepared to ask you to marry him that night." Mrs. Towson smugness was felt through the phone line.

Raven sobbed loudly as the line went dead.

Ms. Towson placed the phone back on the receiver and lay back on her velour chaise, sipping her afternoon martini.

Fantasy

(N). An imagined or conjured up sequence of events, one provoked by an unfulfilled psychological need.

About the Authors

Allison Hobbs

A resident of Philadelphia, and a former singer during the era of the Philly Sound, Allison was a member of a female trio known as Brown Sugar (Allison Hobbs, Phyllis Nelson, and Karen Dempsey). The Philadelphia trio toured as background singers for Major Harris whose number one single, Love Won't Let Me Wait, allowed the group an opportunity to perform as the opening act for artists such as Marvin Gaye and Earth, Wind, & Fire. Allison is also the author of the bestselling titles Pandora's Box, The Echantress, Double Dippin', Dangerously In Love, Insatiable and the soon to be released A Bona Fide Gold Digger.

Anna J.

A writer from Philly who also walks the runway in her spare time as a full-figured model. Co-author of Stories To Excite You: Menage Quad, Anna put her writing skills to the test in this hot collaboration that was released during the fall of 2004. Her debut novel, an Essence magazine best selling novel, My Woman His Wife is high on the charts and a good read for those that enjoy a steamy love affair with a little bit of drama to boot. The continuation of the drama can be found in The Aftermath, Anna J's second novel under Q-Boro books where Monica is still off the chain, and drama is still a main factor. If your Anna J cravings still aren't satisfied you can also find other hot stories of hers in Fetish: A Compilation of Erotic Stories, Morning Noon and Night: Can't Get Enough and Fantasy: Erotic Short Stories in bookstores nationwide. Anna J. is finishing up edits on Get Money Chicks, her newest work of fiction that will be released in September of 2007.

Danielle Santiago

Author of Essence Bestseller's Little Ghetto Girl and Grindin' and founder of Mischievous Girl Foundation, which is dedicated to helping battered women and inner city girls. She resides in Harlem, New York, and Charlotte, North Carolina, with her husband and son.

Thomas Long

The author of the urban fiction smashes A Thug's Life and Cash Rules. He is also a contributing author in the best selling anthologies Around The Way Girls 2 and 3. Long's latest novel is Papa Don't Preach. The versatile and prolific author's book, A Thug's Life, has been adapted into the soon to be released DVD, 4 Life, starring Wood Harris and Elise Neal. For more info on Thomas Long or the movie, go to www.athugslife.com or www.watchmenowfilms.com

---

Keisha Ervin

Keisha Ervin is an Essence Magazine Bestselling author of Me and My Boyfriend, Chyna Black, Mina's Joint, and Hold You Down. She resides in Saint Louis, Missouri.
